New world/New words

Recent Writing from the Americas
A Bilingual Anthology

EDITED BY
Thomas Christensen

FOREWORD BY
Gregory Rabassa

TWO LINES  WORLD LIBRARY

TWO LINES world Library

The TWO LINES World Library is a new series of books featuring the best writing from around the globe. Each volume shines the spotlight on literature from a specific section of the map, or on a certain language or tradition. Guest editors, rooted and deeply schooled in their fields, edit each book.

The TWO LINES World Library continues the work of *TWO LINES: World Writing in Translation*, which has presented the best in international writing since 1994. Both the World Library and the annual anthology are dedicated to bringing the thoughts and rhythms of global literature to readers, and to celebrating the unsung work of the translator.

The TWO LINES World Library is a program of the Center for the Art of Translation, a nonprofit organization that promotes international literature and translation through programs in the arts, education, and community outreach.

Center for the Art of Translation © 2007
Introductory materials © Thomas Christensen, 2007

Editor	Thomas Christensen
Managing Editor	Sonia Valdez
Production Editor	Annie Janusch
Series Founders	Zack Rogow, Olivia E. Sears

Library of Congress Cataloging-in-Publication Data
    New world, new words, recent writing from the Americas : a bilingual anthology / edited
    and with an Introduction by Thomas Christensen; Foreword by Gregory Rabassa. — 1st ed.
        p. cm— (Two lines world library)
    Includes bibliographical references.
    ISBN 1-931883-13-0 (pbk.)
    1.Spanish American literature—20th century—Translations into English.
    I. Christensen, Thomas, 1948- II. Title. III. Series.
    PQ7087.E5N494 2006
    860.8'0980904—dc22   2006013627

Center for the Art of Translation
35 Stillman Street, Suite 201
San Francisco, CA 94107
www.catranslation.org

Book design by Adriana Pérez
Printed in Canada by Friesens Corporation
Distributed by the University of Washington Press

TWO LINES is indexed in the MLA International Bibliography.
Rights to all translations published here revert to translators unless otherwise noted.
Permissions acknowledgments appear on pages 261–263, which constitute an extension of this copyright page.
TWO LINES does not retain the right to a future reprint unless otherwise specified.

For Doña Marina, first translator of the Americas,

and for my favorite translator always, Carol Christensen

Translation is the paradigm, the exemplar of all writing.... It is translation that demonstrates most vividly the yearning for transformation that underlies every act involving speech, that supremely human gift.

—HARRY MATHEWS

contents

foreword
by Gregory Rabassa

When Ezra Pound issued his famous dictum "Make it new," he might as well have been speaking of translation. Every time we render something old into a different tongue it becomes new, some might even say original. Certainly every time Old Ez dabbled in the art of turning something Chinese into his English it was indeed something new, and there are those who say not all that Chinese.

The act of translation is nothing but a close reading, perhaps the closest possible until the day we can delve deeper into psyches. Each reader makes the text new because he or she—how inept is English in lacking a bigeneric third person—brings a unique set of references, interpretations, and expectations to the act of reading. By this token we are at two removes from the author when we read him in translation, but, again, how close to him are we really when we read him in the original?

This anthology is a tribute to the new. What really makes these writers new for me in many cases is the wise way in which they have been gathered, presented by voice, tone, rhythm, context, and the translator's own implied persona. This has led me to read them prodded along by incentives I may have lacked on first acquaintance. My baroque instincts, born of too much reading of Góngora and Mallarmé, do me the disservice, however, of starting to lump some of the stories herein collected into the categories to which they have not been assigned and to which they might well have been. This is not to criticize the arrangement. Rather, it is to show the well-nigh infinite possibilities of expression. Translation shows that a single word is really many words, the more the merrier (and I mean that literally) as we pile on languages.

The New World of the title has the possibilities of both a geographical and a temporal existence. Since the western continents were something new to Europeans, they became known as the New World, in spite of what long-

established residents such as the Maya might have thought. Today we live in a new world wrought of that encounter. The New Words are more intriguing. The authors collected here are still being discovered by readers outside their linguistic realm and in many cases they are offering something really new. The level of newness can be ascertained in the translations. The translator is often hard put to keep what is new in Spanish new in English because the act of translation itself is added newness. Originality is at stake, so we have to take the risks Pound took, for better or for worse, with his free translations.

The translations here are new in that they are not saying precisely what the author said and yet they are saying it. The violins are playing a score written for trumpets. The sound is new but the meaning is pretty much the same. This can be explained in part by that old bridal saw of "something old, something new, something borrowed, something blue." The old, the new, and the borrowed are obvious. It is the blue that grabs me. Blue has so many connotations; it could be that instinctive sense the translator must use to catch nuances that linger for a moment but flit away like dragonflies.

I find the translations of these important writers quite in tune. I would have done each one differently (including the one I did, after all this time), but that in no way demeans a single one but simply demonstrates how translation works as an art of the individual. Let the reader turn his or her mind loose on these pieces—the best and the new that have come out of Latin America—and let the reader also linger over the sensible facing versions to see how the old and the done are made new.

new world/new words

An Introduction by Thomas Christensen

The original is unfaithful
to the translation.

> — JORGE LUIS BORGES
> (1943, on Samuel Henley's 1786 translation of William Beckford's *Vathek;*
> Henley's translation was published before the original)

Broken World, Broken Words

In the *Popul Vuh,* one of the handful of Mayan texts to escape the auto-da-fé
of the Spanish missionaries of the sixteenth century, the story is told that the
first people who had speech sufficient to praise the gods were made of maize.
Their language was the language of the gods themselves. When those first
people gazed into the distance, they could see clear to the edge of the world
and the end of time. But the perfection of the people of maize alarmed the
gods, especially when they began to multiply and overrun the earth. Their
perfect speech was withdrawn, and instead each group was endowed with its
own language.

So we live in a broken world, the world of Babel. Our world is broken because
our language has been shattered into thousands of fragments. Words are no longer
the perfect, transparent embodiment of things themselves but instead are mere
pointers, signs by which we grope to know the world from multiple viewpoints.
To the translator falls the Sisyphean task of rejoining those shards and restoring
the limitless world, a seamless world again, as it once was, whole.

What is Translation?

Any time we read literature, we perform an act of interpretation. Where interpretation fades into translation is difficult to establish. If in reading Chaucer we perform an act of translation into modern English, how are we not also translating when we interpret Shakespeare? To try to draw a line where translation begins is to confront a form of Zeno's paradox. George Steiner believes that because language is constantly changing, "when we read or hear any language-statement from the past, be it Leviticus or last year's best-seller, we translate. Reader, actor, editor are translators of language out of time." But what about writing that is not distant in time but is distant in other ways, such as idiom or social milieu? Is our interpretation of such texts also an act of translation?

In a sense, language itself is a kind of translation—the transmission of messages from a speaker to a listener, just as translation, in the strictest sense, is the transmission of messages from a source language to a target language.[1] Language, and especially translation, is the fundamental expression of the recognition of the Other. "Language," Tsvetan Todorov said, "exists only by means of the other, not only because one always addresses someone but also insofar as it permits evoking the absent third person.... But the very existence of this other is measured by the space the symbolic system reserves for him." In this way, translation performs a quintessentially diplomatic function, for in the recognition of equality despite difference lies the basis of cooperation and hope for peaceful resolution of conflict. "Translation," Robert M. Adams said, "is simply a special instance of the general, but terribly fragile, power of language to cross gaps, to communicate. It leads across a somewhat wider and more precisely defined gap than everyday speech tries to cross, but attempts to connect one mind with another in much the same way."

---

1 *And if thought is a form of internalized language, as some claim—the Russian neuropsychologist Alexander Romanovich Luria, for example, who said that "apart from being a means of communicating, language is fundamental to perception and memory, thinking and behavior. It organizes our inner life"—then the labors of translators are like the synapses of collective cross-cultural cerebration, working at the planetary level to, as E. M. Forster said, "only connect."*

Yet, as the Quiche authors of the *Popul Vuh* saw, language is also a means of exclusion. In contemporary jargon, languages serve not just to communicate but also to define in-group and out-group status.[2] Extreme examples of this are esoteric and private "languages," such as those found in the Kabbalah or Tantric Buddhism. Language is a fundamental element of social cohesiveness and identity, and the other side of that coin is separation and estrangement. So the meeting of languages through the mediation of speech or writing—of *langues* through instances of *parole,* in Saussure's terms—is also a meeting of social groups. Through the act of translation, in other words, the translator draws together not just two texts, the original and the translation, but two cultures, represented by all the embodied history and intertextuality implied by those texts. Consequently, the alert translator must be sensitive to the implications of a multitude of specific choices, artfully balancing manifold references and connotations.

Cultural Transmission

Though one may imagine utilitarian origins of translation as a vehicle for trade and exchange,[3] some of the earliest written translations are of religious texts. (The extant *Popol Vuh* is a kind of translation, or bilingual edition. The Mayan text was transliterated in the Roman alphabet and accompanied by a Spanish crib.) Translations of sacred texts from Sanskrit and Pali into Chinese, for example, were instrumental in spreading Buddhism and other elements of South Asian culture into China and elsewhere. As a result, the Chinese were among the first to systematically confront some persistent issues in translation, and by the end of the fourth century a number of state-supported translation

---

2 *In a recent study, researchers at Harvard and the École des Hautes Études en Sciences Sociales concluded that young children were suspicious of foreign-language speakers even before they themselves had learned to talk. Linguistically defined identity can be clearly observed in cases where nations contain sharp language divisions, such as French and English speakers in Canada, for example. Linguistic subversion often appears in such situations—James Joyce addresses this in* A Portrait of the Artist as a Young Man. *Black English might be another example of a subversive idiom employing private signifiers.*

3 *The distinction between utilitarian and nonutilitarian exchange is evasive. The structuralist critic Jacques Ehrman has argued "that all literature constitutes an economics of language, that literature is language's economy.... Every rhetorical structure is therefore an economic system."*

bureaus were actively addressing these questions.[4] The bureaus developed in great part from the efforts of a Buddhist monk of the Eastern Jin Dynasty named Dao An (314–385), who compiled a catalogue of scriptures and directed their translation. Dao An himself, however, did not know Sanskrit, and perhaps this limitation lay behind his demand that the translations should be literal, word for word. Still, he invited the Indian monk Kumarajiva (350–410) to join him in Changan to assist in the massive translation project, even though Kumarajiva advocated a free approach to translation that disregarded the surface in an effort to reach the essence of the Sanskrit sutras.

One more Chinese translator should be mentioned before we return to the Americas. His name was Xuanzang (600–664), and his struggles to bring sacred texts from India are the subject of the popular Ming dynasty classic *A Journey to the West* (which features the marvelous character Monkey). Xuanzang insisted that translation be both "truthful" and "intelligible to the populace." In these terms we may hear echoes of the literal and the free approaches of his predecessors, Dao An and Kumarajiva. Xuanzang sought to construct a culturally equivalent text in the target language—and, incidentally, he worked both ways, not just translating into Chinese but also producing Sanskrit versions of Chinese classics such as the *Daode jing* (*Tao Te Ching*). He is therefore the model for the middle way of translation, which seeks a balance between the strict and the free.[5]

Among the American heirs of Xuanzang is Octavio Paz. Paz maintained that poetry must balance the traditional and the innovative. At either extreme, Paz said, lies failure: a poem that is too traditional offers nothing

---

4 *The translators were "usually furnished with spacious quarters within the royal precincts or in some famous temple," according to Kenneth Ch'en.*

5 *John Dryden said that translations fall into three classes: metaphrase, paraphrase, and imitation. Metaphrase is literal translation, the way of Dao An. Imitation is free translation that does not closely follow the source text; this is the way of Kumarajiva. Paraphrase is the middle way, the way of Xuanzang. This somewhat schematic discussion of Chinese translation owes a debt to Weihe Zhong's "An Overview of Translation in China,"* Translation Journal 7:2 (April 2003). For fuller and more nuanced views, see Kenneth Ch'en, Buddhism in China; Chen Fukang, A History of Translation Theory in China; and Wang Kefei and Shouyi Fan, "Translation in China: A Motivating Force," Meta: Journal des traducteurs 4:1 (1999).

new and is not worth communicating, whereas a poem that is too inventive loses its common reference and cannot be communicated.[6] So the poet must strike a balance, and, Paz added, the translator must likewise strike a balance between the literal and the interpretive. This is one way in which translation is an art form, not a mechanical process.

Here is Adams again: "There is, at one extreme, a sort of parodic parallel which maintains just the least shred of trivial equivalence in one minimal respect, so that it may violate equivalence the more outrageously in all other respects. There is, at an opposite extreme, the technique of exact literal translation, which renders the meaning of the original word for word, without respect for the violence done to the idiom of the new tongue—which is, so to speak, *abjectly* faithful. Between these two rapes—one of the From-language, the other of the To-language—all sorts of more agreeable and equable arrangements are possible. They can very well be conceived as bargains,[7] in which one sort of equivalence is accomplished at the expense of others."

The German philosopher Friedrich Schleiermacher put it this way (in 1813): "Either the translator leaves the author in peace, as much as possible, and moves the reader towards him; or he leaves the reader in peace, as much as possible, and moves the author towards him." Schleiermacher voted for the author, and he advocated a style of translation that highlighted the translated text's foreignness rather than seeking to assimilate it as a plausible target-language creation. That might be a working strategy but it is a theoretical impossibility, for to retain the text's foreignness in its totality would be to encounter Borges's paradox of a map in which one inch equals one inch.[8]

---

6 *In our post-Babel world, the limits of Paz's equation will be determined differently by each reader.*

7 *This recalls Ehrman's assertion that rhetorical structure is an economic system, as cited in note 3. It's curious that the economic model should so often emerge in discussions of translation, considering that a career in translation today is akin to a vow of poverty. Could cultural transmission be an epiphenomenon of trade and exchange?*

8 *Or perhaps his account of Pierre Menard, who happened to author a perfect duplicate of Cervante's* Quixote. *Schleiemacher is quoted in Lawrence Venuti's* The Translator's Invisibility.

Translation and Betrayal

At least by the time of Muhammad (born in Mecca around 570), translation of sacred texts came to be viewed with suspicion.[9] Muslims believe that the Koran embodies the direct word of God, presented to his prophet through the angel Gabriel. God was literally the author of the Koran—his prophet, who was illiterate, was merely his vehicle. God's language was Arabic; therefore a true Koran can only be read in that language. Copying God's work is a sacred act, with the result that many Korans are dazzling examples of book arts. But once the Word is translated, it stops being the direct word of God and becomes merely a sort of commentary, which is how translations of the Koran are usually viewed by believers. This attitude to translation reflects the recognition that all translations introduce new aspects and omit original aspects of the source text. It cannot be otherwise, for each language is a unique medium that carries an implicit corpus of intertextuality. Hence the Italian proverb *traduttore, traditore* (translator, traitor).

With the secularization of literature, it is a small step from the word of God the Author of All Things to the word of the author, writ small, of a particular text, and many authors have lamented the fallibility of translation.[10] Voltaire said that poetry couldn't be translated, demanding: "Can you translate music?" Robert Frost echoed that sentiment, calling poetry "what gets lost in translation." Samuel Johnson thought such untranslatability a good thing: "Poetry cannot be translated; and, therefore, it is the poets that preserve the languages; for we would not be at the trouble to learn a language if we could have all that is written in it just as well in a translation. But as the beauties of poetry cannot be preserved in any language except that in which it was originally written, we learn the language."

---

9 *No doubt suspicion has always clung to the translator, who, crossing borders, travels dangerous territory. Dao An's insistence on literal translation, noted above, might be seen as an expression of such suspicion.*

10 *Sometimes the failures of translation are immediately evident. Carlos Fuentes told me once about visiting Russia and being presented with an elegantly slim volume said to be the Russian version of* Cambio de piel *(A Change of Skin, which exceeds five hundred pages in the original). "We took out all the parts that wouldn't work for Russian readers," his hosts assured him. This is free translation at an extreme.*

Is poetry really what gets lost in translation? "I should say that poetry is what gets transformed," Paz argued. "Poetry is 'impossible' to translate because you have to reproduce the materiality of the signs, its physical properties. Here is where translation as an *art* begins: since you cannot use the same signs of the original you must find equivalents." Of course, the translator cannot completely reproduce the identical poetic effects of the original or we would have not a translation but a copy. Instead, new poetry must be created in the target language that is equivalent to the poetry of the original. The goal is equality in difference, which again is the ideal of the relation between the self and the other.

Perhaps the definitive example of encountering a previously unknown other is the encounter between the Old World and the New World. At the heart of this fateful encounter lies the figure of a translator. Todorov, whom I quoted earlier, has argued that Cortes's triumph in Mexico was above all a linguistic triumph. It was a triumph that could not have been easily accomplished without the assistance of the woman the Spanish called Marina, popularly known as La Malinche (or *la chingada,* "the fucked one"). She epitomizes the two sides of the translator: the facilitator and the betrayer. Paz, in *The Labyrinth of Solitude,* argues that for Mexicans La Malinche (who was Cortes's mistress)[11] represents the violated mother. Through her son with Cortes she is said to have given birth to modern Mexicans who are *hijos de la chingada*—sons of the bitch.

More recently, Chicana writers have reclaimed the figure of Malinche. After all, she was a slave (she had already been exchanged among native peoples at least twice before she was given up to the Spaniards). Moreover, some say her efforts did more to save native Mexicans than to destroy them. "Any denigrations made against her," the Chicana writer Adelaida Del

---

11 *"We touch here,"* to quote George Steiner (in After Babel) *from a somewhat different, though related, context, "on one of the most important yet least understood areas of biological and social existence. Eros and language mesh at every point. Intercourse and discourse, copula and copulation, are sub-classes of the dominant fact of communication. They arise from the life-need of the ego to reach out and comprehend, in the two vital senses of 'understanding' and 'containment,' another human being. Sex is a profoundly semantic act."*

Castillo insists, "indirectly defame the character of the Mexicana/Chicana female. If there is shame for her, there is shame for us; we suffer the effects of these implications."

Malinche—whom Bernal Díaz del Castillo called a "great lady" without whose help "we would not have understood the language of New Spain and Mexico"—is the First Translator of the Americas,[12] and I hold her to be the patron saint of American translators, those faithless and heroic slaves to the uncompromising text.

The Poetics of Equivalence

If poetry is, as Paz maintained, what gets transformed in literary translation, how is this to be achieved? The translator must create new poetic effects equivalent to those of the original—but what constitutes "equivalence"? To answer these questions requires a sophisticated understanding of the various ways in which literature signifies, a topic to which there is no end.[13] In general, texts acquire meaning through their relation to other texts, through a variety of effects, some of which are illustrated in this anthology.

The notion of "equivalence" in translation is imprecise and falls upon the translator to determine as a personal judgment. If one adheres to the relativistic anthropological view of Edward Sapir and Benjamin Whorf that each language determines a fundamentally distinct worldview, then translation might entail the explication of a succession of puzzles at the surface level. (For example, how does one translate the word *machismo*, for which English has no exact equivalent, without elaboration?)[14]

---

12 *Not chronologically first. But Cortes's first translator, Jerónimo de Aguilar, a Spaniard who had been shipwrecked and lived among the Maya before the arrival of Cortes, played a more limited and less profound role.*

13 *John Hollander says that "a theory of translation would have to be a theory of literature in general." This statement and some I have quoted from Octavio Paz are drawn from* The Poet's Other Voice *by Edwin Honig.*

14 *The practicing translator will probably choose from possible choices ranging approximately from "manliness" to "balls" (or retain a degree of foreignness and leave "machismo" untranslated) and then try to balance what is lost or gained from that with other choices—or "bargains" in Robert M. Adams's vocabulary—elsewhere.*

If, on the other hand, one subscribes to the view of transformational linguists such as Noam Chomsky and Steven Pinker that there is a universal language instinct,[15] of which each particular language is a kind of fractal manifestation, then the translator would pay less attention to surface detail, viewing translation as an alembic reduction of the original to the deep level of universal language, followed by its transmutation into the target language.

Behind the *Popul Vuh*'s account of the fragmentation of languages—and similar myths and legends from other cultures—is the notion of a universal primal language, or *Ursprache,* that has been lost. Using the transformational model, the translator is one who dives deep into the primal stream to carry the message of the text from one shore to the other. Translation then involves in effect not two but three texts, counting the invisible mediation of the implicit shared grammar that underlies both the source and the target.

New World, New Words

However translators feel about the process they are engaged in, their actual practice entails the juggling of a multitude of local choices. The translator gives up something here, then balances that loss against another opportunity, and so on in an endless series of trade-offs and reconciliations. Some of the elements the translator must be mindful of—voice, tone, rhythm, extratextual considerations, the translator's own persona—are exemplified by the following selections. These broad categories are not offered as a theory of translation, merely as a somewhat arbitrary means of highlighting the real-world concerns of working translators. Nor is any attempt made to perform critical analyses of the selections—of either the originals or the translations—which instead are presented with a minimum of comment as specimens for readers to explore on their own.

---

15 *In* The Descent of Man, *Darwin called language "an instinctive tendency to acquire an art."*

Many of the selections are drawn from the pages of *TWO LINES,* an annual anthology of international literature in English translation published by the Center for the Art of Translation. In order to make this project more focused, we have excluded Spanish-language literature from the United States and Canada, as well as Latin American literature in other languages, such as Portuguese or French. We have also emphasized literature of the past few decades rather than older works from periods that are better represented in English, although some older material could not be resisted. The one thing the selections have in common is that they have attracted the interest of some of the most interesting English-language translators. Thanks to their efforts, we hope both to illuminate the translator's art and to present a cross-section of recent American writing in Spanish.

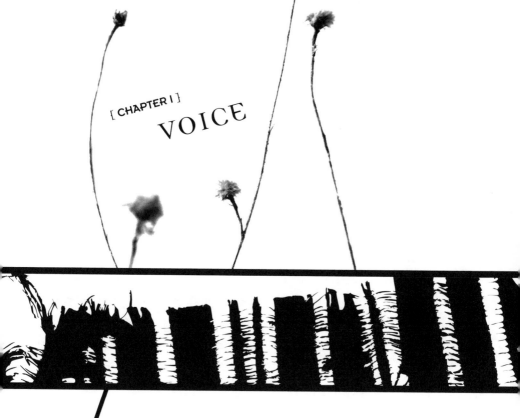

[CHAPTER 1]

VOICE

When the sands are all dry, he is gay as a lark,

And will talk in contemptuous tones of the Shark:

But, when the tide rises and sharks are around,

His voice has a timid and tremulous sound.

— LEWIS CARROLL
"The Voice of the Lobster"

Because writing exists as a means of wresting speech from the grasp of time, any text implies a voice—or voices. The Russian literary critic Mikhail Bakhtin, in an influential study, showed that characters in Dostoevsky's fiction exist as a multiplicity of distinct voices. Such multiplicity is easy to recognize in dramatic works, but to varying degrees it can be observed in other modes as well.

Writing simultaneously captures voice and erases it. The reader imagines behind the written words a voice, or multiple voices, but at the same time the orality of that voice has been stilled, embedded in the silent page through the transmigration of writing. There is a built-in tension of vocality in writing: sometimes the reader's awareness of voice comes to the foreground, at other times it recedes.

In grammar, *voice* refers to the relation between the action and the subjects and objects of that action: "The shark ate the lobster" is active voice and "The lobster was eaten by the shark" is passive voice. By analogy, voice in writing can be impersonal (for example, a Wikipedia article, which is a collaborative text produced by many contributors who mostly efface their individual voices) or strongly personal (many blogs, for instance). In creative literature a truly impersonal voice is hard to imagine. In any text we hear the voice of the author that text implies, but within that encompassing oration we can identify a further tangle of other voices. Voice in literature may be dramatic, as Bakhtin observed in Dostoevsky, or even choral, as in Joyce's *Finnegans Wake,* which can be read as the blending and blurring of several voices. And sometimes we can go still farther and speak of a collective voice—"the voice of the worker," say—which may then be incarnated in some figure—Woody Guthrie, for example, was called "the voice of the common man." All of which indicates that literary voice can be more shaded and nuanced than one might at first think.

Voice is social in essence, and it is related to character. Do we understand a literary character better through action or through voice (expressed both through spoken words and the internalized vocalizations that represent thought in literature)? The distinction may be a false one, since speaking is a kind of acting. Because voice emerges from within the body of the speaker, it is one of our main ways of glimpsing what is going on inside a person, of seeing (or seeming to see) past the persona, the mask.

How does one translate voice? In a dramatic or narrative work, should the characters speak with accents and retain their foreignness? Or should the translator render them as more familiar figures? Dorothy Parker once said of Russian novels "I do wish that as long as they are translating the thing, they would go right on ahead, while they're at it, and translate Fedor Vasilyevich Protosov and Georgei Dmitrievich Abreskov and Ivan Petrovich Alexandrov into Joe and Harry and Fred."

In translating a story by the Salvadoran writer Salarrué (Salvador Salazar Arrué), I struggled with issues of voice. Unable to think of a direct equivalent for the rural dialect of the dialogue, I ended up inventing an English patois that mixed elements from the rural South with contemporary urban slang. But perhaps the most interesting aspect of voice in this story is the way the rough voices of the characters are juxtaposed with a lyrical narrative voice that gives them resonance. For example, at the end of the story thieves kill a couple of travelers and steal their phonograph. When they crank it up, the sorrowful voice that rises out of the apparatus causes them to view themselves in a new light:

> When the phonograph stopped, the four cutthroats looked at one another. They sighed...
>
> One of them took off, sobbing into his poncho. Another bit his lip. The oldest looked down at the barren ground, where his shadow served as his seat, and, after thinking hard, he said:
>
> "We bad."
>
> And the thieves of things and of lives cried, like children from an alien world.

In her translation of Mónica Lavín's "Day and Night," C. M. Mayo deftly deals with issues such as how to let the reader know what *platillos voladores* are ("the grilled sandwiches they called flying saucers") and how to manage a succession of declarative sentences without succumbing to monotony. Perhaps most interesting, however, is her rendering of the story's narrative voice. It is a somewhat distanced voice, not attributed to a specific character, yet it is an intimate one as well. The speaker seems deeply familiar with the feelings and thoughts of the girls in the story, while the boys and the older, visiting girl, Elena, are more impenetrable. We might speculate that the narrator, who also seems knowledgeable about the world of adults, is an older version of one of the girls in the story. Her voice in effect gives birth to both the setting and the plot, as the lush narrative language mirrors both the tropical climate and the suppressed sexuality.

Francisco Hernández, in his series of Scardanelli poems, imagines the complicated voice of the German poet Friedrich Hölderlin (1770–1843), who in the madness of his final decades called himself Scardanelli. The death of Hölderlin's lover, whom he calls Diótima, aggravated his incipient insanity. "My intent," Hernández writes, "was to immerse myself in the mind of a madman and imagine the dreams, songs, letters, monologues, and hallucinations not of Hölderlin but of this other man the author of *Hyperion* imagined himself to be." Elizabeth Bell's translation convincingly captures the sense of one voice buried within another: "Your voice cowers under the shade of clouds / but winds come up and the clouds hide / in the throats of cliffs."

"Vision out of the Corner of One Eye" by Luisa Valenzuela is a monologue in which our impression of the speaker changes dramatically in a short space, as the narrator initially presents herself as a victim, only to emerge at the end as a kind of victimizer. One might view this brief story as a kind of conceit about shifting sexual dominance and submission. The sly transformation is skillfully captured by the translator, Helen Lane.

In Manlio Argueta's "Taking Over the Street," translated by Barbara Paschke, speech is internalized as a sequence of memories and impressions.

The result is a story that leaves much open to interpretation—the speaker is both guarded and revealing, and the reader forms an impression of his character from an account that is curiously fragmented yet retains a clear structure and a strong ending.

René Ariza gives us, in "The Ghost of the Pig," a comic tale that can be read as parable—the Cuban poet Alejandro Lorenzo called the story "perhaps the best metaphor of survival that I have read by a Cuban writer." Ariza, banished from Cuba for "ideological deviation" ("a charge in no small measure related to his homosexuality and flamboyant personal style," according to the translator, Michael Koch), survived in the United States as a street performer. Koch's rendition of the tale captures the child's wide-eyed comic deadpan. At the end, do we hear a hint of the grunts of the pig in the voice of the boy? "And now I talk, sing, break whatever I want and stomp on the floor, and since they are so old, they think the noise is coming from them," the narrator tells us, and we can almost see him punctuating his words with comic movements and gestures as he continues his lively rush of mostly one- and two-syllable words: "Maybe they even believe they are their own dreams and are ready to awaken from them one of these days, or that they're already on the other side, dead, and that this (my life) is their other life, the one they never lived."

el día y la noche

POR MÓNICA LAVÍN

Hubo un tiempo en que el día y la noche eran perfectamente distinguibles. Los días poseían la claridad de la alberca, la ferocidad del sol; la noche, lo impenetrable de la obsidiana. Los primos vacacionaban en la casa de Acapatzingo: un lunar entre las casas del pueblo alrededor. A la vera de la iglesia, entre los zapotales que despanzurraban sus frutos negros en el jardín, los días eran dorados como la cerveza que los padres bebían al lado de la alberca. Ellas jugaban a la escuelita con las niñas del pueblo que en la casa de enfrente habían dispuesto un chiquero vacío para hacer las veces de aula. Las niñas de la casa y las de la cuadra lo limpiaron e instalaron unas tablas para que las más chicas asistieran de alumnas, mientras las grandes daban explicaciones en el pizarrón traído de la ciudad de México. Relacionarse con las niñas que vivían en Acapatzingo les provocaba un entusiasmo que sostenía los fines de semana y esas largas vacaciones escolares. Regresaban a la casa antes de comer para darse un chapuzón. Ellos las salpicaban y se burlaban: Qué les pasaba teniendo una alberca para jugar, que si no era suficiente con ir a la escuela todos los días, qué tenían que ver ellas con las niñas pobres. A ellas les parecían bobos, insensibles. Los padres sólo advertían de cuando en cuando que no los mojaran mientras sostenían los tarros empañados y ensartaban dados de abulón con el palillo.

Ellos habían amarrado una liana al encino cuya rama se desplegaba por encima de la alberca con forma de riñón. Se subían al tronco, se colgaban de la reata y se mecían hasta tirarse justo en el centro. El más intrépido lo hacía con todo lucimiento. Tentaban a las niñas: les toca. Ellas se atrevían con torpeza. Luego se aventaban agua en la cara o jugaban a las guerritas. Las más grandes llevaban a las más chicas en hombros, lo mismo hacían ellos y forcejeaban hasta que uno de los gladiadores caía vencido sobre el agua. Se sofocaban y

Day and Night

BY MÓNICA LAVÍN

When the cousins spent their vacations in the house in Acapatzingo, the days had the clarity of a swimming pool and the ferocity of the sun; nights had the impenetrability of obsidian.

To the side of the church, among the sapodilla trees that splattered their black fruits in the garden, the mornings were golden like the beer their parents drank by the side of the pool. The girls would play "school" with the little girls from the town, as there was an empty pigsty that served as a classroom. The girls of the house and the girls of the town cleaned it and brought in some tables so that the small girls could play student while the big girls gave explanations on the chalkboard they had brought from Mexico City. Getting to know the little girls who lived in Acapatzingo was such fun; it sustained them for the weekends and these long school vacations. Before lunch, they would come back to the house to take a dip. The boys would splash them and make fun of them: What was the matter with the girls? They had a pool to play in. Wasn't it enough to go to school every day? What business did they have with the girls from the town? To the girls, the boys seemed like insensitive dopes. The parents warned, Don't get us wet, while they balanced their sweating beer mugs and speared cubes of abalone with toothpicks.

The boys had tied a rope to a branch of the oak tree that hung over the kidney-shaped pool. They would climb its trunk, hang onto the rope, and swing until they could throw themselves right into the center of the pool. The boldest one would make a somersault in the air. They dared the girls: it was their turn. The girls threw themselves in clumsily. Then they would splash water in each others' faces or play "war." The biggest girls would carry the smallest girls on their shoulders, the boys would do the same, and they would struggle until one of the gladiators fell vanquished into the water. Panting,

bebían agua de jamaica. Las mamás servían y ellas y ellos comían en la terraza aún con los trajes de baño mojados. Ellas aprovechaban para contar las cosas que ellos no podían ver por estar en la alberca azul cielo: En la casa de Marcela tienen una burra; hay un pozo para sacar el agua; la mamá hace tortillas a mano y nos convida; guardan alacranes en un frasco; hay un moño negro en la puerta que da a la casa porque se murió un hermanito cuando nació. Ellos fingían no interesarse. Acabando de comer buscaban el arco y la flecha para tirarle al plátano al fondo del jardín y disfrutar cómo se hundía la punta metálica en el fuste lechoso. Ellas querían tirar también porque el arco se tensaba muy bonito y chasqueaba en el aire cuando lo soltaban. Pero las campanas de la iglesia llamaban a llevar flores para la virgen. Ya se van las monjitas, decían ellos, porque ellas se apresuraban a vestirse, todavía con el cloro de la alberca en las pestañas y en la piel estirada por el sol y el agua. Marcela ya tocaba a la puerta: Irían a la barranca a cortar flores frescas. Salían jubilosas con sus sandalias blancas o color miel, el pelo mojado recogido con una liga de color. Ellos esperarían un rato, aburridos en la terraza, hasta que les dieran permiso de volverse a tirar al agua; sentirían más grande el espacio ahora que las niñas andaban en misa. Qué ridículas, si sus padres nunca iban.

Ellas se sentían parte de aquel enjambre de mujeres de todas edades entrando a la iglesia oscura. Se figuraban que el ramillete que sostenían en sus manos las hacía buenas. Esperaban con avidez el momento de los cantos que ellas aún no habían aprendido, para acercarse al pie de la virgen y añadir sus flores a la montaña fragante. Cada una buscaba los ojos de la virgen y guardaba un sigilo reverencial. Entre ellas ni se miraban, como si se desconocieran, como si pertenecieran al rito, a la iglesia de su casa de fin de semana desde siempre.

Por la tarde regresaban cuidando de no despertar a los mayores de la siesta y con ellos—que no mostraban el gusto por su regreso—remataban lo que quedaba de la tarde en juegos de mesa o la mímica para adivinar películas. Así llegaba la noche con sus meriendas de platillos voladores. Entonces ellos proponían cruzar el atrio de la iglesia. Ellas querían ir para comprar algo en la tiendita que estaba justo al otro lado.

they would go drink cold hibiscus tea. On the terrace, the mothers would serve the girls and boys their lunch, which they ate in their still-wet bathing suits. The girls would then tell the boys about things they could not see because they had been in the pool all day: In Marcela's house they have a she-ass; they have a well to get their water; their mother makes tortillas by hand and she gave us some; they keep scorpions in a jar; they have a black ribbon over their front door because they have a little brother who died when he was born. The boys would pretend they weren't interested. After lunch they would look for the bow and arrow so they could shoot at the banana tree at the back of the garden and enjoy how that metal tip buried itself in the milky shaft. The girls liked to shoot because of the way the bow tautened so nicely, and when they let it loose, the arrow whistled through the air. Church bells called them to bring flowers to the Virgin. There go the little nuns, the boys would say, because the girls hurried to get dressed, chlorine still in their hair and with their skin streaked by sun and water. Marcela was already at the door: they would go to the ravine to cut fresh flowers. They would go out jubilant in their white or honey-colored sandals, their wet hair pulled back with rubber bands. The boys would wait on the terrace for a while, bored, until they could get permission to once again throw themselves into the pool; the terrace felt wide now that the girls were at mass. How ridiculous: their parents never went.

Entering the dark church, the girls felt part of that multitude of women of all ages. They thought the little bouquets they held in their hands would make them good. Avidly they waited for the moment when the songs they had not yet learned would be sung, so they could come up close to the Virgin's feet and add their flowers to the fragrant mountain. In reverent silence each one searched the Virgin's eyes. They did not even glance at each other; it was as if they did not know each other, as if they belonged to the ritual, as if they had always belonged to the church of their country house.

In the afternoon, the girls would return, taking care not to disturb the grown-ups' siesta, and with the boys (who did not show any pleasure at their return) they would kill what was left of the afternoon with board games or

—Se puede rodear la iglesia por afuera—proponía una.

—Eso no tiene chiste. ¿A poco les da miedo? —se burlaban ellos.

—Para nada —decían ellas y dejaban atrás el bossa nova que oían los padres después de pedir unas monedas para comprar galletas de malvavisco rosa.

Era preciso subir los escalones que daban acceso al atrio: un lote de tierra vació donde habían visto a moros y cristianos simular una lucha y al enano Margarito—todo él pequeño como un niño—hablar con la voz tipluda. A oscuras parecía un cementerio flanqueado por la iglesia ocre iluminada de luna. Al final del atrio se distinguía el sauce, único árbol de aquel desierto. Junto a él—no se veían desde el extremo opuesto—estaban las escaleras que llevaban a la miscelánea. Ya habían cruzado el atrio de noche pero no se acostumbraban, sus corazones bombeaban con velocidad, la boca se les secaba porque en nada se parecía esa negrura que podía ser territorio de la Llorona al momento del rosario o de la liana sólo unas horas atrás. Nadie quería ser el primero o el último. Los minutos de espera para que llegara alguien, o mientras se permanecía solo para reunirse con los demás eran insoportables. Se escuchaba el aire, algunos pasos que parecían venir de la calle y sobre todo el vaivén de los pulmones como sacos a punto de explotar. Los más pequeños no podían ser ni el primero ni el último, el resto sorteaba el orden con un volado.

Una vez al otro lado, habiendo soportado un tiempo eterno de zancadillas sobre la tierra seca e indescifrable, devenía un orgullo que se soltaba en risa nerviosa. Cada uno pensaba que era la última vez que lo haría. El regreso sería en corro y por afuera de la barda. Alguien propuso juntar el dinero y comprar una cajetilla de cigarros. Y unos chicles, agregaron, para disfrazar el olor. Cerillos, insistió el de la tiendita que no tenía ningún empacho en venderles a los escuincles. No querían observadores así que dieron la vuelta a la esquina de la barda para quedar fuera de la mira del tendero y el mayor encendió el primer cigarro. Dio varias chupadas hasta que en la oscuridad resplandeció la chispa roja de la punta y lo pasó a la prima mayor. Tosió un poco. Ella intentó dar una chupada y soltó el humo esponjoso. Pasó el cigarro que provocó tos y risa entre todos y deseos de que diera la vuelta completa para arremeter otra

charades to guess movie titles. And so the night arrived with its supper of grilled sandwiches they called flying saucers. Then the boys proposed that they cross the churchyard. The girls wanted to go buy something in the little grocery store that was just on the other side.

"You can go around the church outside it," one girl said.

"That doesn't make sense. Could it be you're scared?" The boys teased.

"Not at all," the girls said and they left behind the bossa nova their parents started listening to after they gave the children coins to buy cookies with pink marshmallows.

They had to climb steps up to the churchyard, which was a vacant lot where they had seen Moors and Christians in ritual battle and heard Margarito the dwarf (who was as small as a doll, but without a big head and arms like the ones in the circus) say in a high voice that he would conquer evil. It looked like a graveyard, flanked by the moonlit ocher church. To the back of the yard they could see the willow, the only tree in that desert. Next to it, though visible from this far corner, were the stairs that went down to the little store. They were going to cross the churchyard at night, but they were not used to doing it; their hearts were pounding fast and their mouths went dry. This darkness could be the territory of La Llorona, the weeping ghost-woman. It did not look at all the way it had a few hours ago when they were saying the rosary or swinging on the rope. No one wanted to go first or be last. For unbearable minutes it seemed it was one or the other; for this reason the smallest ones did not have to participate in the coin toss to decide the order.

After an eternity of tripping over dark, dry ground, once on the other side, their fear turned to pride, which came out as nervous laughter. Each one thought it was the last time they would do that. The return would be at a full run and around the wall. Someone proposed collecting money to a buy a pack of cigarettes. And, they added, some Chiclets to hide the smell. The man in the grocery store gave them matches; it didn't bother him to be selling cigarettes to kids. Not wanting to be seen, they went around the corner of the wall, away from the man. The oldest boy lit the first cigarette. He took several

chupada. Encendieron otro cigarro pegándolo al extremo abrasivo del que se consumía, como habían visto hacerlo a sus padres. Y cuando los acabaron no sabían qué hacer con la cajetilla porque les pareció que había sido suficiente. Ya alguno estaba mareado y la boca sabía desagradable. Se repartieron los chicles de canela y caminaron despacio y callados hasta llegar a casa y terminar el día con algún programa en la televisión, todos tumbados sobre la cama del cuarto principal, entre quejas y carcajadas, hasta que el sueño los vencía.

El sábado que llegó la prima Elena con su madre a pasar el día en esas vacaciones de abril, ellos y ellas intentaron aferrarse a sus rutinas y sus horarios. Elena ya tenía trece años y se negó a jugar a la escuelita con las vecinas. Tampoco quiso tirarse de la liana en la alberca helada. Se quedó con su larga trenza rubia que le dividía la espalda en dos y su bikini azul marino, tumbada sobre los camastros. Ellas volvieron más pronto de las clases en la porqueriza y ellos dejaron de jugar a Tarzán para no salpicar su cuerpo acinturado. Comieron botana alrededor de Elena que sólo reclinó el camastro para incorporarse y estirar la mano hacia una jícama. Así tan cerca las piernas y los torsos, ellas y ellos observaron sus pantorrillas lisas. Elena se rasuraba. Las niñas quisieron quitarse la pelusa de las suyas de inmediato, los niños recostarse en aquellos muslos que comenzaban a broncearse.

Comieron haciendo menos escándalo y sin enseñarse la comida. Elena hablaba poco y se dejaba preguntar contestando con un poco de fastidio.

¿Y van a pasar aquí todas las vacaciones? —dijo de pronto.

Todos volvieron al plato de lentejas sintiendo los días por venir como una carga farragosa. Las campanas a lo lejos avivaron a las niñas. Invitaron a Elena. Ella dijo que sólo iba a misa los domingos y los chicos se quedaron contentos suponiendo que jugaría con ellos al arco y la flecha o con el rifle de diábolos, pero Elena se tumbó con una revista en la sala fresca; desde la terraza ellos la miraban de cuando en cuando sin acertar a alejarse de allí.

Ellas arrojaron las flores en el momento preciso, sintiendo cierta prisa por volver y menos devoción a los ojos santos de la figura de porcelana. Se preguntaron si Elena querría ir al atrio cuando oscurerciera. Ellos ya se lo

puffs until the tip glowed red in the dark. He passed it to the oldest girl. She coughed a bit. She took a puff and let out a plume of smoke. She passed the cigarette, which made all of them cough and laugh and want it to go around again so they could take another puff. They lit the next cigarette with the stub of the last, the way they'd seen their parents do. And when they were finished, they weren't sure what to do with the rest of the pack; it seemed to them to have been enough. Already some of them were dizzy and their mouths had a disagreeable taste. They handed around the cinnamon Chiclets and walked slowly and quietly back to the house to end the day with some TV, all of them sprawled on the mattress in the master bedroom, complaining and laughing, until sleep overcame them.

On the Saturday of their April vacation that their cousin Elena arrived with her mother to spend the day, the boys and girls tried to keep to their routines and schedules. Elena was already thirteen years old; she refused to play "school" with the neighbor girls. Neither did she want to throw herself from the rope into the freezing-cold pool. With her long blond braid that divided her back in two and wearing her navy-blue bikini, she lay down on one of the chaises.

The girls returned quickly from classes in the pigsty and the boys stopped playing Tarzan, so as to not splash their cousin's svelte body. They ate their snacks around Elena, who joined them so she could reach for a jicama. With their legs and torsos so close, the boys and the girls could see that her calves were smooth. Elena shaved them. At once, the girls wanted to get rid of the fuzz on their own legs; the boys, to lean into those bronzing thighs.

They ate with less commotion and without showing each other their food. Elena spoke little. Slightly bored, she asked if they would spend all of their vacations in this place.

The girls and boys turned back to their plates of lentils, feeling the coming days as a jumbled-up burden. Bells in the distance enlivened the girls. They invited Elena. She said she only went to mass on Sundays. This pleased the boys, as they assumed she would do archery or play with the BB gun, but Elena lay down with a magazine in the living room, where it was cooler. From the

habían propuesto. Le gustó salir de casa, parecía más simpática ahora que el sol se había metido. A ellos y a ellas les emocionó que estuviera dispuesta a aventurarse a cruzar el atrio y que no pensara que eran bobadas.

¿No salen hombres? —les preguntó cuando se distribuían el orden en la penumbra.

Habían pensado en la Llorona y otras alimañas. Los hombres no cruzaban el atrio en las noches.

¿Ni los borrachos? —preguntó.

Lanzaron la moneda. A Elena le tocó ser la primera. El primo mayor le cambió el lugar. Ella sería la segunda. Lo miraron perplejos, nunca había tenido un detalle así. Cuando todos libraron la inhóspita dimensión del atrio, ya Elena tenía la cajetilla en sus manos y repartía un cigarro a cada uno. Ni siquiera se molestaron esta vez en quedar fuera de la mira del tendero. Fumaron allí bajo el sauce, retando con bolutas de humo el negro vacío del atrio que habían dominado. Elena explicó que había que dar el golpe para fumar bien e hizo una demostración. Dio una chupada al cigarro y abrió la boca vacía para que imaginaran al humo dando vueltas en sus pulmones. Luego dibujó dos perfectas donas de humo que contemplaron asombrados. Los intentos los marearon, nadie pensó en los socorridos chicles de canela.

Regresaron a casa ligeros, con Elena caminando al centro porque ella sí sabía fumar y no había tosido y caminaba derecha como si el humo que había hecho arabescos en sus pulmones no tuviera que ver con ella. Olvidaron la televisión y se fueron al cuarto de los niños—el de las literas que daba a la terraza—a jugar botella en el estrecho espacio entre las camas donde se habían sentado. Que si los besos y las cachetadas y luego pasarse el cerillo encendido para disparar preguntas indiscretas. Y luego ya no se les ocurría nada hasta que alguien apagó la luz, y el mayor encendió la linterna y pidió que las mujeres hicieran un show para los niños. Ellos se subieron en tropel casi cayéndose a esa cama alta. Y las niñas pensaron en un baile. El mayor enfocaba como en el teatro a cada una y Elena subía la pierna como si fuera el can can. Y luego cambiaron y ellos hicieron una pirámide, uno sobre otro, que

terrace, the boys looked at her from time to time without being able to tear themselves away.

The girls tossed flowers at the appointed hour, feeling a certain haste to return and less devotion to the porcelain statue's saintly eyes. They asked if Elena wanted to go to the churchyard when it got dark. The boys had already proposed it to her. She liked the idea of getting out of the house, and while they were walking, now that the sun had gone down, she seemed more agreeable. The boys and girls were thrilled that she would venture to cross the churchyard and not think they were stupid.

Are there any men around? she asked them in the darkness when they were deciding the order. They had thought of La Llorona and other varmints. Men did not cross the churchyard at night.

"Not even drunks?" she asked.

They tossed the coin. It was Elena who had to go first. The oldest boy exchanged places with her. She would be second. The others watched this, perplexed; he had never done anything like that before. When they all reached the other side of the barren churchyard, Elena already had the pack in her hands. She gave a cigarette to each one. This time they did not bother to stay out of the shop owner's sight. They smoked there beneath the willow, with their wisps of smoke challenging the churchyard's black emptiness, which they had mastered. Elena explained that in order to smoke properly, you had to inhale, and she gave a demonstration. She took a puff on the cigarette and opened her empty mouth, so they could imagine the smoke swirling around in her lungs. Then she made two smoke rings, which they watched in amazement. They tried to do it but it made them dizzy; no one thought of those handy cinnamon Chiclets.

They returned to the house with a light step and Elena in the center because she knew how to smoke and had not coughed and walked upright as if the smoke that had made arabesques in her lungs had given her a certain pride. They forgot the TV and went into the children's room, the one with the foldout beds, which opened onto the terrace. In the narrow space between the beds they were sitting on, they played spin the bottle. Yes, kisses and slaps and then

se vino abajo cuando ellas les apuntaron con la linterna a los ojos. Entonces ellos pidieron que Elena hiciera un show sola y ellas también dijeron que sí y se subieron a la otra cama sin la linterna que se habían apropiado los niños. Elena se fue al rincón de la puerta para que ellos y ellas la miraran y entonces empezó a moverse como una mujer; las caderas para un lado y para el otro, la cintura dando vueltas. Y hacía como si se quitara los zapatos y las medias que no traía, y se volteaba de espaldas entre los silbidos de ellos y ellas que jugaban a ser los clientes de un cabaret. Y ella hizo como si se quitara un vestido y se desabotonara un brassier y lo aventó pero siguió allí con su playera de rayas rojas y sus shorts color caqui. Hasta que el más grande se atrevió y dijo: súbete la blusa. Y todos asintieron con su silencio. Y él le alumbró el talle mientras Elena tomaba el extremo de la playera y lo subía lentamente mostrando el vientre y luego los pechos redondos y erguidos. No silbaron, ni aplaudieron. El primo apagó la linterna y fue bueno que tocara a la puerta la madre de Elena para avisar que se iban.

A la mañana siguiente se asolearon en los camastros y se metieron a la alberca. Ellas no atendieron los toquidos de la puerta cuando Marcela llamó a clases, ni ellos a la liana que colgaba inútil. Dejaron pasar de largo las campanadas de la iglesia y los pasos de las mujeres hacia el barranco por la cosecha de flores. El arco y la flecha no cimbraron el aire ni hirieron la planta. Se rieron menos y jugaron poco. Sólo esperaban que llegara la noche que ya se había confundido con el día.

passing the lighted match: whoever dropped it had to answer a rude question. And then they couldn't think of anything to do until someone switched off the light, and the oldest boy turned on the lantern and asked the women to do a show for the boys. All together, almost falling over each other, the boys climbed up onto the high bed. And the girls thought of a dance. The oldest boy held the lantern like a spotlight on each girl and Elena lifted her leg as if she were dancing a cancan. Then they traded places, and the boys made a pyramid, one on top of the other, but they all fell down when one of the girls shined the lantern in their eyes. Then the boys asked Elena to do a show by herself. The girls also said yes and they climbed onto the other bed, the one without the lantern, for the boys had taken possession of it. Elena went to the corner by the door so that everybody could see her, and she began to sway like a woman, her hips one way, then the other, her waist making circles. She pretended to take off her shoes and pantyhose, though she wasn't wearing any, and she turned her back to the whistles of the boys and the girls who were pretending to be customers in a cabaret. And she pretended to be taking off her dress and unbuttoning her bra and tossing it off, though she still had on her red striped T-shirt and khaki shorts, until the oldest boy dared to say: Lift up your shirt. And with their silence, all agreed. And he shined the light on her waist as Elena held the edge of her T-shirt and slowly raised it to show her stomach and then, like a surprising landscape, her budding breasts. They did not whistle; they did not even applaud. The oldest boy shut off the lantern, and it was a good thing Elena's mother knocked on the door to say they were leaving.

The next morning they sunned themselves on the chaises and went in the pool. The girls did not answer when Marcela came to knock on the door for class, nor did the boys pay any attention to the rope that hung there, useless. The girls did not respond to the church bells or the women's footsteps as they went to the ravine to gather flowers. The arrow did not sing through the air, nor wound the plant. They laughed less and played little. They were merely waiting for the night, which they had already confused with the day.

de
Habla scardanelli

POR FRANCISCO HERNÁNDEZ

Habla Scardanelli

Hay otro y te apresa mientras duermo.
Me despiertan sus gruñidos rasposos,
los versos a ti escritos dejados en su oído
y el torrente que cae por tu garganta
buscando el corazón y su avispero.
Sin pies pero con odio me incorporo.
Recorro los brocados, las flores de tu sala.
Soplo rescoldos en la chimenea,
quiero meter las manos en las brasas,
la lengua por un anillo en llamas.
Imagino mordiscos en tu espalda,
oigo los golpes brindados por su ardor,
siento una emigración de aromas
en los sudores donde nadie te habita.
Mejor salir a caminar bajo la nieve.
Allá se quemarán los labios con el frío
y no dejaré huellas circundando la casa
porque los pies irán colgados del sombrero.
Hay otro y te ronda mientras duermo.

from
scardanelli speaks
BY FRANCISCO HERNÁNDEZ

Scardanelli Speaks

There is another and he takes you while I sleep.
I am wakened by his rasping moans,
verses written to you ringing in his ear,
the cascade gushing down your throat
to seek the wasp's nest of the heart.
Footless but hate-filled I sit up.
I gaze across your sitting-room brocades and flowers.
I blow on the embers in the hearth,
want to drive my hands into the coals,
my tongue through a ring of fire.
I picture nibblings on your shoulder,
hear the smackings of his ardor,
sense emigration of aromas
in sweatings where no one inhabits you.
Better to go out, walk in the snow.
There my lips will burn cold,
and my circlings round the house leave no track,
my feet but dangling from my hat.
There is another and he prowls you while I sleep.

Sueña Scardanelli

Tus muñecas atadas al camastro.
Un martillo golpeándote las sienes.
Ángeles protectores de escorpiones.
Un barco de leprosos por el Neckar.
Erizos a la sombra de tus pechos.
El hacha de los celos en la frente.
La maldita humedad del seminario.
El cuello del banquero tallado por un oso.

Habla Scardanelli

I

Se van, se borran, Diótima, tus rasgos,
en las aguas cenagosas del Neckar.
Tu voz se ovilla bajo la sombra de las nubes
pero soplan los vientos y las nubes se ocultan
en la garganta de los desfiladeros.
Zimmer trabaja en mi ataúd
y en la silla que ha de ocupar mi corazón lisiado.
Camino de la muerte me asaltarán visiones
que la vejez me niega.
Recordaré tus labios en la cesta de frutas del verano,
las pupilas violentas de los ángeles
y el piano donde se corrompen liebres y perdices.
Si cayeran campanas de las torres más altas,
brotarían en el huerto, ya maduras,
las letras de tu nombre verdadero.

Scardanelli Dreams

Your wrists tied to the cot.
A hammer striking your temple.
Scorpions' guardian angels.
A boatload of lepers on the Neckar.
Hedgehogs in the shadow of your breasts.
The jealousy hatchet in your forehead.
Damnable seminary dankness.
The banker's neck ripped by a bear.

Scardanelli Speaks

I

They are sinking, fading, Diótima, your features,
in the Neckar's marshy waters.
Your voice cowers under the shade of clouds
but winds come up and the clouds hide
in the throats of cliffs.
Zimmer is working on my coffin
and the chair my crippled heart will occupy.
On the road to death I will be assailed by visions
age denies me.
I will recall your lips in the summer fruit bowl,
the violent pupils of the angels,
the piano top where the hares and the partridges rot.
If bells fell from the tallest towers,
in the orchard there would spring up, fully ripe,
the letters of your true name.

II

Danzas, Diótima, y detienes al sol en su descenso.
Vas por el aire con el cabello trenzado por la luz
y en lo blanco del muro dibujas un gato de perfil.
Consciente de su prisión en la argamasa,
el gato salta en busca de tu espalda, clava las uñas
y se desliza lentamente hasta los pies girantes.
No has muerto, Diótima, no has muerto.
Me lo dicen los córvidos sin crías
y el felino que cruza, llevado por su asombro,
los llameantes peldaños del teclado.
Danzas, Diótima, y es tu cuerpo un molino
donde mueles el grano de mis huesos.

Palabras de la Griega

Las cruces en el fuego, los puños de ceniza.
La oración y la sal entre los dientes.

Los pájaros clavados en la puerta.
Las tijeras del miedo en la garganta.

El sapo enrojecido por antorchas.
La pócima en los labios, los párpados
sostenidos por alfileres.

El círculo se cierra.
Por el Río de los Nombres
va el conjuro:

Abrasaré tus huesos en invierno
morderás el verano en mis pezones.

II

You dance, Diótima, and hold back the falling sun.
Light braids your hair as you fly,
on the white of the wall you draw a cat in profile.
Sensing its plaster prison,
the cat leaps for your back, contracts its claws,
dredges them slowly down to your spinning feet.
You haven't died, Diótima, you are not dead.
The broodless crows tell me so,
and the feline dragged by its fright across
the blazing rungs of the keyboard.
You dance, Diótima, your body a mill
where you grind the grain of my bones.

The Greek Woman's Words

Crosses in the fire, fists of ash.
Prayer and salt between the teeth.

Birds nailed to the door.
Fright's scissors in the throat.

The toad red with torchlight.
The draught at the lips, eyelids
held open with pins.

The circle closes.
Down the River of Names
passes the spell:

I shall scorch thy bones in winter,
thou shalt bite summer in my nipples.

visión de reojo

POR Luisa Valenzuela

La verdá, la verdá, me plantó la mano en el culo y yo estaba ya a punto de pegarle cuatro gritos cuando el colectivo pasó frente a una iglesia y lo vi persignarse. Buen muchacho después de todo, me dije. Quizá no lo esté haciendo a propósito o quizá su mano derecha ignore lo que su izquierda hace o. Traté de correrme al interior del coche—porque una cosa es justificar y otra muy distinta es dejarse manosear—pero cada vez subían más pasajeros y no había forma. Mis esguinces sólo sirvieron para que él meta mejor la mano y hasta me acaricie. Yo me movía nerviosa. Él también. Pasamos frente a una iglesia pero ni se dio cuenta y se llevó la mano a la cara sólo para secarse el sudor. Yo lo empecé a mirar de reojo haciéndome la disimulada, no fuera a creer que me estaba gustando. Imposible correrme y eso que me sacudía. Decidí entonces tomarme la revancha y a mi vez le planté la mano en el culo a él. Pocas cuadras después una oleada de gente me sacó de su lado a empujones. Los que bajaban me arrancaron del colectivo y ahora lamento haberlo perdido así de golpe porque en su billetera sólo había 7.400 pesos de los viejos y más hubiera podido sacarle en un encuentro a solas. Parecía cariñoso. Y muy desprendido.

TRANSLATED BY Helen Lane

vision out of the corner of one eye

BY Luisa Valenzuela

It's true, he put his hand on my ass and I was about to scream bloody murder when the bus passed by a church and he crossed himself. He's a good sort after all, I said to myself. Maybe he didn't do it on purpose or maybe his right hand didn't know what his left hand was up to. I tried to move farther back in the bus—searching for explanations is one thing and letting yourself be pawed is another—but more passengers got on and there was no way I could do it. My wiggling to get out of his reach only let him get a better hold on me and even fondle me. I was nervous and finally moved over. He moved over, too. We passed by another church but he didn't notice it and when he raised his hand to his face it was to wipe the sweat off his forehead. I watched him out of the corner of one eye, pretending that nothing was happening, or at any rate not making him think I liked it. It was impossible to move a step farther and he began jiggling me. I decided to get even and put my hand on his behind. A few blocks later I got separated from him by a bunch of people. Then I was swept along by the passengers getting off the bus and now I'm sorry I lost him so suddenly because there was only 7,400 pesos in his wallet and I'd have gotten more out of him if we'd been alone. He seemed affectionate. And very generous.

ganar la calle

POR MANLIO ARGUETA

Cuando es día sábado. Cuando me ve como si no quisiera. Cuando la descubro. Cuando miro que me mira. Cuando la acribillo con una sonrisa de ay amor ya no me quieras tanto. Y la luna negra filosa de sus ojos metiéndose en mis ojos. Cuando me dice aquí le traigo; y pone el bulto encima de la mesa donde acabo de levantarme para recibirla.

Cuando la gente dice la casa solitaria del Barrio San Jacinto, sólo esos viejos que llegan en la noche cansados de trabajar de sol a sol o de estrella de la madrugada a estrella de la medianoche. Cuando la gente dice: solamente esa bichita que llega una vez por semana. Genoveva no le habla a nadie. Bueno, a veces ni a mí.

—Aquí le envían los muchachos—dice mostrándome un par de naranjas y unos nísperos de Usulután.

Cuando le digo gracias, ponelo ahí. Y me vuelvo a sentar en la mesa mientras pasa a los cuartos del del fondo, al patiecito, a la pila debajo del limonero. Cuando me dice:

—Esto se lo envía mi hermano—y me entrega un bolígrafo de siete colores.

Cuando le digo: no es para tanto, que no me hace falta el arco iris; este último no se lo digo, sólo lo pienso. Luego existo.

Cuando el compañero, el hermano, me dijo hace cuatro semanas: "Mientras, podés estar donde unos tíos abuelos, a ellos no pasan en casa". Siempre nos tratamos de hermanos, como hermanos. "Tomá este radio para que no te aburrás".

Cuando le digo que lo importante es estar de nuevo con los compañeros.

Cuando Genoveva regresa del patiecito o de la pila que hay debajo del palo de limón. Cuando entrando a la sala me dice que si no me ofrece algo. Cuando

TRANSLATED BY **Barbara Paschke**

Taking over the Street

BY MANLIO ARGUETA

When it's Saturday. When she sees me as if she didn't want to. When I notice her. When I see she's looking at me. When I riddle her with a smile of ah, my love, you don't love me like you used to. And the black moon blade of her eyes enters my eyes. When she tells me here it is and puts the bundle on the table I just got up from to greet her.

When people talk about the secluded house in the San Jacinto barrio, only those old men who get home at night tired from working from sunrise to sunset, from the morning star to the evening star. When people say: only that little creature who comes once a week. Genoveva speaks to no one. Sometimes not even to me.

"They send the young ones here," she says, taking out a couple of oranges and some medlars from Usulután.

When I tell her thanks, put them down over there. And I sit back down at the table while she goes to the back room, to the little patio, and the basin under the lemon tree. When she says to me,

"My brother sent me this," and hands me a pen of seven colors.

When I tell her: no need to make such a fuss, I don't need the rainbow; I don't tell her this last part, I just think it. Therefore, I am.

When the *compañero,* the brother, told me four weeks ago:

"In the meantime, you can stay with some great-uncles of mine, they never go into that house." Like brothers, we always called each other brothers. "Take this radio so you don't get bored."

When I tell him the important thing is to be with the *compañeros* again.

When Genoveva comes back from the patio or the basin under the lemon tree. When coming into the room she asks if she can't offer me something. When I tell her no thanks. Oh yes, hot water.

le digo que no ¡gracias! ¡ah, sí! agua caliente.

—No tenga pena—me dice. Y otra vez sus ojos descorren los vidrios oscuros para hacerme llegar al fondo de sus ojos. Pasa a la cocina. El ruido del chorro en la cafetera de aluminio. La cafetera húmeda hace ruido de fritura sobre el disco de la cocina eléctrica. Los pasos que de su cuerpo acompañado de su sombra cuentan los ladrillos de barro cocido. Los ladrillos rojos del piso. La música de la tela de su vestido turquesa con florcitas anaranjadas, como palillos de fósforos encendidos en el fondo de un cielo claro.

Cuando me dice ya me voy, con voz lenta para que nadie oiga que está hablando con alguien. Apenas veo sus labios oigo un cuento de niños en sus labios.

Cuando me digo será que me estoy poniendo viejo.

Cuando llegan los tíos abuelos en la noche. Cuando entran en la casa que es un túnel de olores encerrados. Cuando ven la luz de mi cuarto por las rendijas de la puerta vieja. Cuando los oigo murmurar al otro lado de la pared. Cuando aprieto el botón de la lamparita y ya estoy soñando.

Cuando le digo a mi compañero, a mi hermano (es lo mismo) que ya me estoy aburriendo. La noche anterior que vino a visitarme. Cuando me dice que para ganar la calle tenés que esperar un tiempo prudencial. Ese tono consolador que me fastidia. Cuando le contradigo ¿y cómo voy a ganar la calle si no salgo a la calle?

Cuando llega el otro sábado.

Cuando no recuerdo haberle dicho jamás a Genoveva una frase, pues solo nos unen monosílabos: gracias, ajá, ujum, saludos, adiós. Cuando este día le descubro en su mirada de niña con chongos de colores en su pelo que alguna edad ha de tener.

—¿Cuántos años tenés?

Cuando me responde que el próximo año va a cumplir catorce.

Cuando a su contrapregunta le respondo que más o menos treinta, pero que a esta edad no siempre se está seguro. Ganas de joder.

Adiós, hasta la próxima. Y va dejando un reguero de pólvora china en el suelo de ladrillos rojos.

No problem, she says. And again her eyes unbolt dark windows, making me fall into the abyss of her eyes. She goes out to the kitchen. The spurting noise of the aluminum coffeepot. The damp coffeepot makes a crackling sound above the hum of the electric kitchen. Her footsteps accompanied by her shadow count the baked mud bricks. The floor's red bricks. The music of her Turkish dress material with little orange flowers, like bits of phosphorus burning in the vastness of a clear sky.

When she tells me I'm going now, in a low voice so no one can hear she's talking. I scarcely see her lips, I hear a children's tale on her lips.

When I tell myself I must be getting old.

When the great-uncles arrive at night. When they enter the house which is a tunnel of trapped odors. When they see the light in my room through the cracks in the old door. When I hear them whispering on the other side of the wall. When I turn off the lamp switch and right away I'm dreaming.

When I say to my *compañero,* my brother (it's the same thing) that now I'm getting bored. Last night he came to visit me. When he tells me, in that comforting tone that gets on my nerves, that in order to take over the street you have to wait for the right time. When I answer back "And how am I going to take over the street if I never even go out in the street?"

When another Saturday arrives.

When I don't remember ever having said a sentence to Genoveva, only monosyllables unite us: thanks, aha, good, uhum, greetings, goodbye. When today I discover her in her childlike expression, in her colored curls that belong to a certain age.

How old are you?

When she answers this year she'll be fourteen.

When I answer her question, well, thirty, more or less, but at this age one is never sure. Urge to screw.

Goodbye. Until next time. And she goes leaving a trail of yellowish gunpowder on the red brick floor.

That time I saw you for the first time I was fourteen, too, and who knows

Esa vez que te ví por primera vez yo también tenía catorce años y vos a saber cuántos. A lo mejor no habías nacido. Son las cosas incomprensibles. Y pasabas frente a mi casa.

Cuando me lleva el pichelito con agua caliente y un frasco de café soluble.

Cuando me dice: ya me voy. Cuando le digo andate antes que se haga demasiado tarde. Los dos solos en la casa.

Cuando cierra la puerta. Cuando se va. Cuando siento que sus pasos llegan a la esquina. Cuando cruza la calle hacia la parada de buses, frente a la escuela de huérfanos. Cuando se sube al bus y se pierde. Cuando me despierto. Cuando la toman por los brazos y la suben violentamente a un carro-patrulla. Cuando pego un grito. Cuando los tíos abuelos se levantan y me preguntan qué pasó y yo no les respondo porque me hago el dormido. Cuando ella se niega y la arrastran hasta el carro. Cuando le preguntan que de dónde viene. Cuando tocan con fuerza la puerta de la calle. Cuando me voy por el patio del fondo y la pila debajo del limonero.

Cuando los viejos dicen nosotros no sabemos nada, no lo conocemos. Cuando Genoveva, sus ojos se han cerrado detrás de una niebla roja de sangre. Los tíos abuelos se mantienen firmes, tirados en el suelo. Cuando los puntapiés de los policías. Cuando pienso que debo irme. Cuando salto al cercado hacia el patio vecino.

Cuando gano la calle y me enfrento al vientecillo de noviembre que la hace echar a uno todas las aguas saladas, todas las victorias y esa libertad patas arriba.

how old you were. You probably hadn't even been born. Those things are incomprehensible. And you passed by in front of my house.

When she brings me a pitcher of hot water and a little jar of instant coffee.

When she tells me: I'm going now. When I tell her to get going before it gets too late. The two of us alone in the house.

When she closes the door. When she leaves. When I feel her footsteps reach the corner. When she crosses the street toward the bus stop, in front of the orphanage. When she gets on the bus and disappears. When I wake up. When they take her by the arms and violently put her in a patrol car. When I let out a cry. When the great-uncles get up and ask me what's the matter and I don't answer because I pretend I'm asleep. When she refuses and they drag her to the car. When they ask her where she's coming from. When they knock loudly on the front door. When I leave through the patio in the back by the basin under the lemon tree.

When the old men say we don't know anything, we don't know him. When Genoveva's eyes have closed behind a red cloud of blood. The great-uncles stand firm, thrown to the floor. When the police kick. When I think I've got to go. When I leap over the fence to the neighboring patio.

When I take over the street and confront a November wind that makes one shed all the salt water, all the victories, and all that backward-upside-down freedom.

el fantasma del puerco

POR René Ariza

Papá y mamá son ciegos.

Cuando yo era chiquito, salí un día gateando de la casa al traspatio. Papá tenía un cerdito que criaba para matarlo en Nochebuena. Mamá cogió al cerdito confundida y empezó a darle el pecho creyendo que era yo. (La vieja protestaba del hambre que tenía la criatura, pues al mamar, le daba dolorosos mordiscos.) A él le puso un pañal y lo metió en mi cuna, y a mí, me echó al chiquero. Esto duró algún tiempo, porque papá tampoco pudo advertir el cambio. A mí me echaban sobras de comida, mientras que a él le daban compotas, leche, jugos y puré de malanga. Sobreviví de puro milagro, pues me adapté a la sobras.

Por Navidad fue el viejo a buscarme al corral con un cuchillo enorme a la cintura. Yo gritaba y lloraba (lo que seguramente mi padre confundía con gruñidos), y tanto fue mi miedo que me hice caca encima de papá. Embarré todo al viejo, que gritaba del asco más que yo del terror. Y me soltó y corrió como un cohete a lavarse los brazos.

Mamá estaba bañando en un palanganón a lo que ellos pensaban que era el crío, y cuando oyó que el viejo llegaba, lo llamó muy asustada, ya que el niño, le dijo, "está muy extraño".

—¿Por qué?—preguntó él. Y ella le dijo: "Viejo…no es niño, es…una niña". Porque efectivamente no tenía lo que debía un machito tener, sino lo otro. (Y es que era una marrana, no un marrano, lo que estaban criando en el chiquero.)

—¿Y cómo no nos dimos cuenta antes?

—No sé, viejo, no sé. Pero, ¡qué horror!

Y mamá cogió "aquello" y le dijo a papá que tenían que ir a ver a Juliana enseguida, porque estaba segura de haber parido macho, no hembra, "qué va, m'hijo: eso debe de ser un daño que me ha echao sabe Dios qué hijo e' yegua.

The Ghost of the pig

BY RENÉ ARIZA

Mama and papa are blind.

One day, when I was very little, I crawled from the house into the backyard, where papa had a piglet he was raising to slaughter on Christmas Eve. Mama got mixed up, grabbed the pig and began breast-feeding it, thinking it was me. (The old lady exclaimed loudly about the little thing's appetite, since it was giving her painful nips as it suckled.) She diapered it and put it in my cradle, and chucked me into the pigsty. This went on for a while, since papa didn't notice anything out of the ordinary either. They threw me table scraps and gave it fruit preserves, milk, juices, and malanga mush. It was a miracle that I survived, but I got used to the scraps.

Around Christmas, the old man came looking for me in the pen with a huge knife in his waistband. I screamed and cried (which my father probably took for oinking), and my fear was so intense I went *caca* on him. I really made a mess, and he was yelling louder from nausea than I was from fright. He leaped away from me and dashed off like a rocket to wash off his arms.

Mama was bathing what they thought was their kid in a basin, and when she heard him coming back, she called out to him, startled, that something was "very strange" about their son.

"Why?" he asked. She replied, "Dear, he's not a boy, he's a girl." As a matter of fact, the piglet didn't have what a little male should have, but just the opposite. (It was really a sow and not a hog that they'd been raising in the pen.)

"And how is it we never noticed before?"

"I don't know, dear, I don't know. What a terrible mess!"

Mama grabbed hold of "him" and told papa they had to go see Juliana right away, because she was sure she'd given birth to a boy child, not a girl. "What the devil's going on? It must be a hex put on me by God-knows-what-son-of-

Después de haberle dicho a todo el mundo que era varón, ¡varón!, ¡qué pena!, ¡qué descrédito!" No sabrían ni donde meter la cara ahora.

—Vamos.

Juliana ponía algo así como una pecera llena de agua en el centro de la mesa y miraba y miraba hasta que se le alzaba el "fluío," decía ella, en forma de burbujas.

Pues mi padre y mi madre se fueron dando tumbos con el puerquito a cuestas a casa de la negra espiritista. Había un millón de gente esperando en la sala para poder consultarse, pues Juliana (decían los que decían que sabían) era buenísima.

La gente estaba loca de impaciencia. Pero mi madre, hecha una furia, dijo que ellos tenían derecho a consultarse antes por ser ciegos. Y enseñaron los ojos en blanco y empezaron a palpar la casa.

La gente no cedía: los cojos enseñaban la muleta, los mancos el muñón, los paralíticos daban gritos tocando como un tambor las sillas de ruedas de madera (que se hacían con cajones de bacalao), los enanos brincaban unos sobre los otros protestando. Pero uno se rió y empezó a murmurar, y siguió otro, riéndose bajito, hasta que fue una ola de risas que ahogó todo, porque habían visto lo que se asomaba por el bulto de trapos que mi mamá traía.

Cuando entraron al cuarto, Juliana estaba en trance, la puerquita gruñía como el diablo y el coro de la risa se oía puerta afuera.

Juliana, con los ojos como huevos hervidos, les dijo que salieran corriendo pa' la casa, que sacaran al puerco del chiquero y echaran allí al niño. Que eso les iba a traer buena suerte. Y ellos lo hicieron. Fue así que regresé al hogar de mis padres. Claro, que desde entonces, mamá y papá creyeron que yo era un puerco. Y me gritaban, por ejemplo: "Límpiate el hocico." O si no: "¡So cochino, embarraste la mesa de comida!," "Marrano, te measte otra vez en la cama!"

Me daban ¡qué palizas! por cualquier cosa, porque creían que así me iban a hacer perfecto, me volverían persona, como dicen. Y con cada paliza me daban mil consejos. Me decían que eso a mí me iba a durar bien poco, que se me iba a acabar la gozadera y el vivío de panza, porque en cuanto llegara

Eleggua. And after I've told the whole world that he was a boy, a boy! What a disaster! What an embarrassment!" They didn't know if they could show their faces now.

"Let's go."

Juliana would put something resembling a fish bowl full of water in the middle of the table and gaze and gaze until the "juices," as she put it, rose up in the form of bubbles.

So my mother and father set off, lurching along with the piglet in a basket toward the house of the black medium. There were tons of people waiting in the hall to consult her, since Juliana was excellent (or so those said who said they knew).

The people waiting were half-mad with impatience. But my mother had a fit, saying they had the right to go first since they were blind. And they showed their blank eyes and began to feel their way around the house.

The people wouldn't give way: the lame waved their crutches, the armless their stumps; the paralytics shouted as they beat the wooden wheels of their chairs (made from codfish crates) like drums; and the dwarves jumped all over each other in protest. But someone laughed and began whispering, and then another, laughing under his breath, until a wave of laughter drowned out everything, because they had seen what was peeking out from the bundle of rags that my mother was carrying.

When they entered the room, Juliana was in a trance, the little piglet was grunting like a demon, and you could hear the chorus of laughter outside the door.

Juliana, her eyes like boiled eggs, told them to dash home, get the pig out of the pigpen and throw in the child instead. That would bring them good luck. So they did. That's how I returned to my parents' home. Of course, from then on, mama and papa thought that I was a pig. For example, they would shout, "Clean your snout." Or maybe "Damned pig, you got the dinner table all muddy!" or " You little swine, you've peed your bed again!"

What a beating they'd give me for the least thing, thinking that they could

Navidad me iban a apuñalear y a servirme en la mesa con mojo y cebollitas.

Yo les decía que no, que pa' eso estaba el puerco del traspatio, y ellos me contestaban que allí el único puerco era yo mismo, que el del traspatio era el que tendría que estar en la casa con ellos porque era el verdadero niño y que, si no fuera por Juliana, yo estaría ahora en el corral comiendo sobras.

Yo les decía que yo hablaba igual que ellos y que los puercos no hablan. Y aquí empezaban a cantar bien alto haciéndose los que no me escuchaban, o si no me voceaban al oído que había aprendido todo lo que sabía por ellos, porque ellos me lo habían enseñado con cien mil sacrificios, a pesar de ser puerco. Pero que en cuanto se asomara Diciembre me fuera "apreparando" porque me iban a meter en el horno; o si no, si Diciembre se demoraba demasiado ese año, me iban a vender al tipo aquel del circo "Carparrota" para que me exhibieran como el único puerco que habla y que llora.

Entonces yo cogí un poco de miedo, ya que ellos no sabían que yo era de verdad el hijo de ellos y que el puerco era el otro. Aunque entonces pensaba también si no sería yo el equivocado y el niño fuera aquel... o aquella, yo ni sé, y yo fuera el puerquito. O que no fuera así, sino al contrario, y el niño fuera yo, efectivamente, y ellos los puercos, ciegos como dicen que son, que no quieren a nadie ni entienden nada nunca y que devoran todo lo que encuentran.

Y entonces yo cogí un poco de miedo, como ya iba diciendo, y el miedo aquel creció como si fuera un puerco enorme y jíbaro que ataca en medio de la noche. Ya todo era de miedo allí: la casa con sus muebles medio rotos e hinchados por las lluvias, y los techos de yagua temblorosos, y los pisos de tierra que se podían hundir como las tumbas en el momento menos pensando, y los espejos de los escaparates cubiertos de una lepra negra como unos mapas de países que no existen, y la mata de yagruma quejándose del miedo cuando el aire...

Entonces decidí huir de la casa, o algo mejor: hacérselos creer. Porque no me escapé, sino que me escondí hasta que me empezaron a buscar: "¡qué desgracia!"—decían—"¡qué desgracia!," quejándose seguro porque al yo irme, no iban a tener ya nada que comor cuando llegara el frío; puesto que

perfect me and turn me into a person, they said. And every beating came with plenty of advice. They told me this wouldn't last long, that the fat and rollicking times were almost over, because as soon as Christmas came they were going to carve me up and put me on the table smothered in onions and sauce.

I told them no way, that's what the pig in the backyard was for, but they responded that the only pig around here was me, and that the one in the backyard was the real child who ought to be in the house with them, and, if it weren't for Juliana, I'd be in the pen this very moment eating scraps.

I told them I spoke just like they did and pigs don't talk. Then they began singing at the top of their lungs pretending they couldn't hear me, or they would yell in my ear that they had taught me everything I know, making countless sacrifices, even though I was a pig. But that as soon as December got here, I'd better "get ready" because they were going to put me in the oven, and if not, if December came around too slowly this year, they were going to sell me to the guy from the "Tattered Big Top" Circus so they could exhibit me as the world's only talking, crying pig.

At that point I got a little scared, since they didn't know that I was really their son and the other one was the pig. Even though I was also thinking maybe I was the mixed-up one and he … or she … was really the child—who knows?—and I was the piglet. Or maybe it wasn't that but just the opposite, and the child was me after all and they were the pigs, as blind as they said they were, who cared nothing for anyone and never understood anything and devoured everything they came across.

Then I got a little scared, as I was saying, and the fear grew as if it were a gigantic wild pig running amok in the middle of the night. Now everything there smelled of fear: the house with its half-broken furniture swollen by rain, the rickety palm roofs, the dirt floors that could sink like tombs at the least expected moment, the wardrobe mirrors covered by leprous blackness like the maps of countries that don't exist, and the yagruma bush grumbling fearfully in the breeze….

Then I decided to run away from home, or, even better, just make them

no se daban cuenta de que podían matar al del corral, pero ellos se creían que aquél era su hijo: ¡Los pobres! ¡¿Cómo se iban a comer a su hijo?!

Y entonces, cuando ya me dieron por perdido para siempre, (yo me había escondido en las letrinas), volví. Pero no dije nada, sino que me asomé muy poco a poco y me quedé en la casa, pero siempre en silencio. Y de allí en adelante no volví a hablar más nunca. Gritaban mucho aquello de: ¡Ay, mi hijo! ¡Aaaay mi hijooo!, pero a mí me parece que esperaban a cuando los vecinos se metían en la casa a curiosear diciendo que iban a dar el pésame, para ver si soltaban algo: plata o comida. Muchas veces la vieja llegaba hasta mi cama, se arrodillaba allí y pasaba la mano por encima como si yo estuviera (yo creo que sospechaba que yo no me había ido). Pero como yo no era ningún bobo, en lugar de dormir sobre la cama, dormía debajo de ella: me acostumbré (y noté que era hasta mejor, pues había el calorcito de la tierra y había lo principal: que estaba a salvo del cuchillo del viejo).

Me sentaba a la mesa ellos no lo advertían. Y yo me divertía de lo lindo cogiéndoles los trozos de pan y la comida que me iban a servir. Entonces se asustaban porque pensaban que era algún fantasma y lloraban chillando: ¡Ay, mi hijito, mi hijito!

Yo creo que eso pasó porque como mataron al puerco de verdad en aquel diciembre, pensaron que se estaban comiendo su propio hijo.

Digo, eso creo yo, porque la situación era bastante cruda entonces y no podían hacer más que matarle.

Así que yo me pienso que ellos se pensaban que yo era el fantasma del puerco y que estaba vengándome por haberme comido con yuca y cebollitas.

Como ellos se creían que ya me habían asado, no podía ni chistar. Ya no había peligro porque de todo lo que hacía yo, le echaban la culpa al puerco, o a mi fantasma, o sea, al fantasma del puerco.

Lo mismo me comía la comida, que me tomaba su agua, que me ponía la ropa del viejo y lo imitaba riéndome para dentro, que cantaba y bailaba, meneándome y moviendo los labios (pues la música la hacía con el cerebro)

think I had. Because I didn't really escape, I just hid until they began to look for me. "What bad luck," they said, "What bad luck," complaining no doubt because if I were gone, they wouldn't have anything to eat when it got cold, not knowing they could kill the one in the pen, whom they still mistook for their son. Poor things! How could they eat their son?

And then, when they'd given me up as lost for good (I'd been hiding in the outhouse), I returned. But I didn't say a thing, just came out little by little and hung around the house, always keeping silent. From that point on I never spoke again. They did a lot of wailing, as in "Oh, my son! Oooooh my son!" But it seems to me they would wait until the neighbors were nosing around the house pretending to offer condolences to see if they could get some food or money out of them. The old lady would often go over to my bed, kneel down, and pass her hand over it as if I were there (I think she suspected that I hadn't left). But I was no fool, so instead of sleeping on the bed, I slept under it (which was even better, since it offered both the warmth of the earth and, most important, safety from the old man's knife).

I would sit at the table and they wouldn't notice. I had a great time grabbing pieces of bread and other food they were serving. Then they would get frightened, because they thought I was a ghost and would weep, shrieking, "My little son, oh, my little son!"

I guess this happened because they slaughtered the real pig that December and thought they were eating their own son.

I say that because I believe things were so rough around then that they couldn't do anything else but slaughter it.

So I think that they thought I was the ghost of the pig taking my revenge on them for having eaten me with yucca and little onions.

Since they believed they'd roasted me, I couldn't make a peep. There was no longer any danger because whatever I did, they blamed the pig, or my ghost, or rather, the pig's ghost.

The same way I ate their food, drank their water, and put on the old man's

mientras lloraban ellos de hambre o de sed con ojos que a cualquiera (de no saber que eran completamente ciegos) le hubiesen dado miedo.

Así pasaron meses en los que empecé, poco a poco, a hacer ruido, volviéndome más y más descuidado. Y llegaron volando los años y se fueron como auras que se dieron un banquete. Y ahora ya hablo, canto, rompo lo que quiera y taconeo en el piso, pues como están tan viejos, se piensan que ese ruido brota de ellos. Y como ya están secos, inmóviles (parecen momias), piensan que el movimiento es el de ellos, y que lo que yo hablo lo hablan ellos, son ellos. Y un día de éstos, o que ya están del otro lado, han muerto, y que es ésta (mi vida) su otra vida, la que nunca vivieron.

clothes, laughing to myself as I imitated him, singing and dancing, swaying and moving my lips (I was making the music in my mind), while they cried with hunger or thirst, their eyes enough to frighten anyone who didn't realize they were completely blind.

Thus months passed, and I began, little by little, to make noise, becoming more and more careless. The years flew in and rushed away like vultures at a banquet. And now I talk, sing, break whatever I want and stomp on the floor, and since they are so old, they think the noise is coming from them. Dry and motionless now (they look like mummies), they think any stirring is their own, that what I say is what they are saying, is what they are. Maybe they even believe they are their own dreams and are ready to awaken from them one of these days, or that they're already on the other side, dead, and that this (my life) is their other life, the one they never lived.

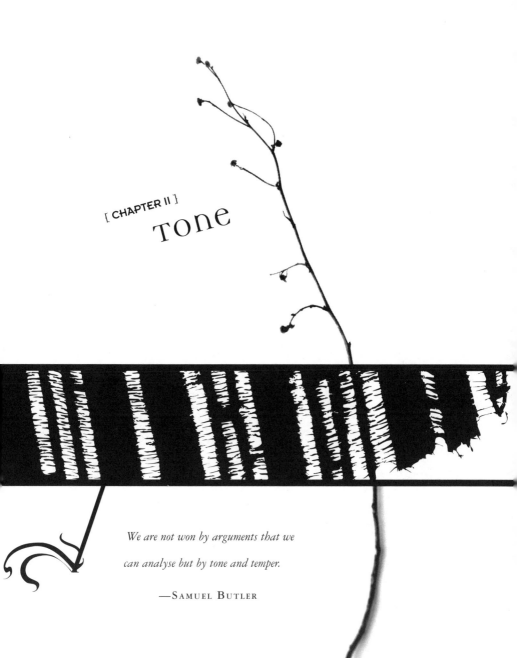

[CHAPTER II]

Tone

We are *not won by arguments that we*
can analyse but by tone and temper.

—SAMUEL BUTLER

Tone

Tone is a complicated word. It derives from a Greek word describing a tautly stretched string. Its meanings cluster around the ideas of voice and music, but we still hear echoes of the notion of stretching when we speak of "toning" our muscles.

In music, tone may refer to the particular quality of a complex sound: the same note played on a brass instrument will have a different tone when it is played on a reed instrument; but we also speak of "pure tones"—steady sounds without overtones. In the visual arts tone is most often used to describe shadings of gray in colors. In linguistics, *intonation* is one thing, *tone* another. All languages use intonation to express an attitude to the message being spoken, but some languages, such as Chinese, distinguish words themselves not merely phonetically but also by various kinds of rising, falling, or steady pitch, called tones. In most of these usages tone indicates something that is significant but nuanced, shaded. Its connotations of musicality do not so much concern the dynamism of rhythm (the subject of the next section of this book) as the complex qualities of sound itself. (In the nineteenth century, the American poet and musician Sidney Lanier asserted, in *The Science of English Verse,* that the sounds of words have qualities similar to tones in music.)

In literary discussions the concept of *tone* is also used in more than one way. We talk about a speaker's "tone of voice"—for example, a parent may demand that her restless teenager not speak to her "in that tone." The literary critic I. A. Richards used the term *tone* to describe the overall attitude of a work (or the attitude of the speaker to the listener): a piece of writing could be formal, intimate, somber, ironic, and so on. In everyday usage, the word is sometimes used to describe stylistic shadings without explicitly relating them to any overall attitude.

One factor than can affect tone is diction, which in the broadest sense is more or less equivalent to "word choice." Diction is often used to characterize

the level of formality of the vocabulary in a passage, which can range from slang to colloquial to informal to formal. But diction may also describe the extent to which language is concrete or abstract, technical or common, metaphoric or literal, and so on.

One of the most difficult tasks for the literary translator is creating tonal equivalents. The translator must first be an adept literary critic, able to identify tonalities in the original language, and then an accomplished creative writer, producing stylistic shadings and stretchings in the target language. One thing for sure—the translator must not be "tone deaf."

In "Prism," Pura López-Colomé's crisp language, with its philosophical overtones, is masterfully translated by the poet Forrest Gander. The occasional lines in prose set off the sharp, spare phrases of the other sections of the poem. López-Colomé is one of the leading translators of English language literature into Spanish, and has done Spanish versions of works by Gertrude Stein, H.D., Samuel Beckett, Seamus Heaney, and others.

John Oliver Simon, in translating Mirko Lauer's "Survival: Eight Stanzas of Commentary on the Words of Buddha," captures the poem's combination of philosophical meditation, informality, and wit. The attitude of the speaker colors every line and gives the poem its edge. The title, "Sobre Vivir," is a pun, combining *sobrevivir* ("to survive") and *sobre vivir* ("on life"). Compare the tone of that poem to Sigfredo Ariel's "The Light, Hermano, the Light," also translated by Simon, with its somber shades of isolation and dissatisfaction.

Luisa Futoransky's "Vitraux of Exile," translated by Jason Weiss, presents a voice stripped of pretense yet draped in literate diction. It seems the voice of a world-weary traveler who has acquired an international vocabulary— appropriate for a poem that questions the very nature of nationality. "Every one of the forty poems by Luisa Futoransky that I have translated," says Weiss, "has turned out to be more difficult than it seemed at first. That is because the precision of her language, her phrasing, and the informal tone of her

voice read so naturally in the original, so without pretense. Yet these same qualities do not cross over into English without posing a certain resistance, as though the honesty and closeness of her voice were hardly a 'natural' fact."

In Gabriel García Márquez's story "The Saint," the matter-of-fact voice of the narrator, a man who returns to Rome after a long absence, carries overtones of nostalgia, wonder, and, perhaps, regret. The story is a kind of inverse memento mori, in which the world fades away but the person is constant. While the narrator's life follows a normal course, both Margarito Duarte's life and his daughter's death seem to exist outside of time. Equally constant is the judgment of the translator, Edith Grossman, who captures perfectly the tone that makes the story work as well in English as it does in Spanish.

prisma

POR PURA LÓPEZ-COLOMÉ

Ansias de bienestar,
las vi recorrer el camino de costumbre,
el que va de la ciudad a alguna parte,
parte del mundo,
parte de mi adolorida humanidad,
grata aparición para quien me aguarda,
quien vive dentro de mí sin ser yo misma,
en mi sed, mis oscilantes momentos
de tribulación y paz.
Fui ellas. *Me* fui.

Suben a Chalma los peregrinos. Los que saben que la rama
seca que van cargando echará flores a lo largo del trayecto. Son
jóvenes en su mayoría. Llevan agua, un petate en que dormir y la
cotidianidad de sus vidas a la vista. Hay viejos también. Niños
sobre los hombros. El santuario avanza en busca de su sitio.

De golpe, con una pregunta
despertó su antigüedad.
¿Qué le piden al Señor
a quien veneran,
es decir,
a su cuerpo mortificado
por la fatiga de hoy
y la miseria de ayer?
Poder seguir llorando de rabia o de impotencia,
poder enfermarse más o excederse,

TRANSLATED BY Forrest Gander

prism

BY Pura López-Colomé

Those coveting health—
I saw them making their way along the worn path,
the one trailing from the city
to the far-flung parts of the world,
part of my own wounded humanity,
a sweet apparition for whomever awaits me,
living within but apart from me,
in my thirst, my shifting
moments of tribulation and peace.
I was that. They were me.

They ascend toward Chalma, the pilgrims. Knowing that, on
the way, their dry branch will break into blossom. Most are
young. They carry water, a sleeping pallet, their daily lives. A
few elders. Children on their shoulders. The sanctuary off in
search of its premises.

At once, with a single question,
their antiquity awoke.
For what do they petition
the Lord they worship,
a Lord whose body
is mortified by today's exhaustion
and yesterday's misery?
To go on crying in fury or impotence,
to sicken and sicken,
to testify to, to endure the absence of ...

poder presenciar, vivir la aterradora falta de ...
al centro del cuerno de la abundancia,
poder olvidar, sí,
al fantasma de los siete, ocho años
que arrebatado vuela sin cola o cuerda
que lo regrese a tierra,
olvidar la futura historia,
las nulas entregas amorosas.
¿Eso?
Oh, cuerpo, amo y Señor,
muéstrame un árbol creado a imagen tuya,
sinagogas, basílicas, mezquitas
cubiertas todas de ti siendo.

Se ha establecido el campamento. Es de noche. Grupos de
hombres por aquí, mixtos por allá, de mujeres con bebés y
niños más lejos. En torno a las fogatas, de pie, en cuclillas.
Comparten no el alimento ni el café, cada quien trae su itacate,
sino la razón de... y la celebran sentándose en el suelo vil,
dejando que las piedras se les entierren en los muslos, dando
de mamar al niño delante de quien sea. El calor proviene de
la cercanía de brazos, espaldas, cuellos, senos; no del fuego: de
la sangre. Hay quien cae dormido, quien cabecea, quien vela.
Ninguna necesidad de techo.

Todos estamos destinados
al compás respiratorio
con que cantan las estrellas.
Comunión de astros es ésa,
recé con terror o envidia,
una cierta rotación,
una cierta traslación,

at the very core of the horn of plenty,

to be able to forget, yes,

the seven- or eight-year-old ghost

impetuously flying without the tail or string

by which it might be tugged back to earth,

to forget the future history,

the missing relinquishments to love.

That?

O body, love and Lord,

show me a tree made in your image,

synagogues, shrines, mosques,

filled out with your being.

They've made camp. Night. Groups of men over here, mixed groups over there, women with babies and children farther off. Around the campfires, standing, squatting. They share neither food nor coffee, each bringing out their own dinner, without making excuse for ... and celebrating by sitting on the hard ground, letting rocks bruise their thighs, nursing the baby in front of strangers. The warmth whelms from the nearness of arms, backs, necks, breasts; not from fire. From blood. There are those falling asleep, those about to, and those keeping vigil. None need a roof.

We are all destined

to the measure of breath

by which the stars are singing.

A communion of luminous bodies,

I prayed in terror, in envy,

a particular rotation,

a particular translation,

the joy of the indispensable.

el gozo de lo indispensable.

Nada más.

Al día siguiente, llena de admiración y arrobo, regresé a esos lugares, deseando aspirar los últimos olores de lo que ahí se había soñado y compartido. Como quien vuelve a tocar la piedra votiva, los pies o las manos de la imagen gastada de algún santo milagroso:

No hallé sino basura.

La gran boca del Señor,

Su mal aliento.

Nothing more.

The next morning, full of admiration and rapture, I returned
to those places, hoping to breathe in the last smells of what
was dreamed and shared. Going back as though to touch the
votive stone, the feet or hands of the worn image of some
miraculous saint:

I found nothing but garbage.
The Lord's mouth agape,
stinking breath.

sobre vivir: ocho estrofas de comentario sobre las palabras del Buda

POR MIRKO LAUER

La realidad entera está en llamas, y no puedes mejorarla como frase.
En los límites de la pérdida la realidad completa se aglomera
en un hacinamiento volátil. Lo tuyo y lo del otro se consumen
reclinados contra la retina, puestos sobre la lisa palma de tu mano.
Sólo el amor es la cosa grave, la gravedad, la gravitación universal del mundo,
en que con peso igual se queman Isaac Newton y una manzana.

Nadie se baña dos veces en el mismo río, y tampoco puedes mejorarlo como frase.
El mundo carece de sombra propia, la realidad es aceite en el que flota tu corazón.
Hay puertas que se abren en el agua hirviendo: sales de un río y entras a un río;
tus huesos tiritan de ignorancia bajo todos los umbrales, mientras tu alma incauta
navega sustentada por desconocimientos y por plumas.

El silencio reúne elocuencia y peligrosidades del primer grado,
con posibilidades de palabras que son florecimientos de la epidermis,
llagas y colores varios apilados formando una torre negra. Tus hermanos
los cadáveres se calcinan en ese silencio, y las estalagmitas
atraen relámpagos babeantes que nadie osa empuñar para el sacrificio
de la realidad que se precipita sobre sí misma, con sus crepitaciones y sus llamas.

Una playa de toallas secas a la orilla de la ducha rememora crujiente
el paso de aguas en que la realidad entera se comprime y entrega
al enmugrecido inmóvil la ablución de existir en dos instantes:
en alabastro y en ónice, en la onomatopeya y en el milagro,
en la vida metafórica y en la muerte literal, en la cuna y en la cuja,
llenas sus orejas del encajado frufrú de esas combinaciones.

TRANSLATED BY **John Oliver Simon**

survival: eight stanzas of commentary on the words of Buddha

BY MIRKO LAUER

All of reality is burning, and you can't beat that as a sentence.
Complete reality accumulates in a volatile stack
at the limits of loss. What's yours and what's his are consumed
leaning against the retina, on the smooth palm of your hand.
Only love's a grave thing, grave as the world's universal gravity
which weighs equally burning Isaac Newton and an apple.

Nobody bathes twice in the same river, and you can't beat that as a sentence either.
The world lacks a shadow, reality's the oil your heart floats in.
Doors open on boiling water: you get out of one river and get in another;
your bones shiver with ignorance on all thresholds, while your reckless soul
sails on sustained by unknowns and by feathers.

Silence unites eloquence and first-degree dangers,
possibilities of words that are flowerings of the skin,
wounds and multicolors heaped to form a black tower. Your brothers
the corpses are toasting in that silence, and stalagmites
attract dribbling lightning nobody dares to grasp for the sacrifice
of reality that falls all over itself, with flames and crackling.

A rustling beach of dry towels at the shore of the shower reminds you
of the passage of water that comprises all reality and yields
the ablution of existence to the soiled unmoving in two instants:
alabaster and onyx, onomatopoeia and miracle,
metaphorical life and literal death, the cradle and the bed,
filling your ears with the boxed frou-frou of these combinations.

Las aves vuelan con las plumas encendidas, perforadas del aire combustible,
por cuyo sesgo cruzan sus demorados cuerpos hexagonales.
En los desiertos del sur la luz orada el polvo y levanta columnas frágiles
que el viento se lleva en llamaradas. Y aún lo irreal apoya la cabeza
contra la de un fósforo que estalla ante la fisión de la mirada,
presa también ella de un fuego inextinguible.

Perdonado por lo imperdonable, blasonado tu pecho con las húmedas flores,
clorofilas y cadmios de tu ramo: agua que eres y que empuñas,
fluir en que te miras y eres, impecablemente a la deriva, conculcado.
Y sales absorto de la bacanal, con las manos lavadas y un velero
rotando contra el viento de tu sueño. Esponjas que son dardos buscan tu pecho,
y encuentran tu pecho, y cruzan tu pecho, y olvidan tu pecho en sus huidas.

Nadie se ríe dos veces en el mismo baño, ni frota un cuerpo con otro
sin multiplicarlo. La conclusión banal y trágica es que la soledad
es imposible sin la ayuda de un espejo. Y sales, perplejo de la ermita, con las
    sienes heladas;
y sales del escritorio anonadado, con los fémures calados;
y sales del río y entras al río y sales del río,
por un abismo de expiación compuesto de trampolines y de pórticos.

Hay una hoguera en las doradas vísceras del cuy, la realidad entera sufre
la mancha caliente de esa incariciable mansedumbre. Tu casa arde mientras duermes,
el mundo grita mientras reflexionas, los hornos gimen con las bocas abiertas,
agobiados por una ceniza que lacera tu frente perpleja, y flota hacia el suelo verde
donde un millón de briznas se consume para hacer una pradera.

Birds fly with flaming feathers, perforated by combustible air,
their hexagonal bodies traversing, delayed along the bias.
In the southern desert light pierces the dust, lifting fragile columns
the wind carries away in flames. And even what's unreal holds your head
against that of a match which explodes in a glance's fission,
prisoner likewise of an inextinguishable flame.

Forgiven by the unforgivable, your chest boasting wet flowers,
chlorophyll and cadmium bunched: water that you are and grasp,
flow in which you see and are, impeccably adrift, molested.
And you leave the bacchanal engrossed, your hands washed and a sailboat
tacking against the wind of your dream. Sponges that are darts seek your chest,
find your chest, pass through your chest, and forget your chest in their flight.

Nobody laughs twice in the same bathtub, nor rubs their body against another
without multiplying it. Banal and tragic conclusion: it's impossible
to be alone without the aid of a mirror. And you leave your cell perplexed, your
    temples frozen;
and you leave your study wiped out, with drenched femurs;
and you get out of the river and get in the river and get in the river and get out
    of the river,
through an expiatory abyss of portals and trampolines.

There's a bonfire in the golden entrails of the guinea pig. All of reality is suffering
the burning stain of that uncaressable mildness. Your house is burning while
    you sleep,
the world screams while you contemplate, the ovens groan with jaws ajar
exhausted by the ash that lacerates your confused forehead, and floats toward
    the green ground
where a million blades of grass are consumed to make one meadow.

La luz, bróder, la luz

POR SIGFREDO ARIEL

Mirar caer la nieve en la oficina de registro
cuando uno es la señal con un pañuelo, un sauce
que huele a mar del trópico, un animal aislado.
Pudiera caer ahora mismo la nieve sobre los edificios
en copos graves
pudiera morirme si me viera en una cerrazón
que tumba la cabeza
hasta las manos de los padres
que esperan sentados en un parque
y que no saben nada.

Un hombre quitaría con una vieja pala esta ceniza.
Vagamente regresa a aquel lugar
donde llovía detrás de la cabeza
cuando tuvo otro nombre y una cicatriz en la barbilla
y era hipócrita y humano
como un pobre diablo.
Bebía en los circos de ocasión
y tenía el bolsillo repleto de llaves inservibles
y un temor absoluto de la soledad.

Seré yo mismo acaso si fuera tenedor de libros
o fuera neerlandés y conociera la magia
y si en el extremo de mi vida la nostalgia
me pasmara las manos sobre el hielo.

The Light, Hermano, the Light

BY SIGFREDO ARIEL

To see the snow falling in the copyright office
when you're a handkerchief signaling, a willow
that smells of tropical ocean, an isolated animal.
The snow could be falling right now on buildings
in solemn flakes
I could die to be seen under a closed sky
that clobbers your head down
into the hands of the fathers
who sit waiting in the park
and don't know anything.

A man could shovel away these ashes.
He wanders back to that place
where it was raining behind his head
when he had another name and a scar on his chin
and he was human and hypocritical
like any poor devil.
He drank in cheap circuses
and his pocket was full of useless keys
and he was totally scared of being alone.

I could be myself maybe if I were a bookkeeper
or a Dutchman or if I knew magic
or if in the extremity of my life
nostalgia froze my fingers to the ice.

Job no pudo reposar sin violentarse
sobre este caracol marino
y las sábanas pudieran estar llenas de asfalfas
o de termas brillantes o de casas de troncos.
Quiénes seríamos entonces / calle abajo
acaso compraríamos el periódico de la mañana
cayéndonos de sueño
y las mandarinas y el pan dulce.

Estos años románticos los querrán los hijos de los hijos
y buscarán la letra en el registro, nuestros discos,
los papeles sucios.
Voy a morir sin ver la nieve
qué hubiéramos adelantado bajo la nieve harinosa
esa pequeña aventura en nuestra luz:
el paso de un astro, la carrera de una estrella.

Estos días van a ser imaginados
por los dioses y los adolescentes que pedirán estos días
para ellos
y se borrarán los nombres y las fechas
y nuestros desatinos
y quedará la luz, bróder, la luz
y no otra cosa.

Job could lie down without effort
on one of these seashells
and his sheets would be full of thorny flowers,
log cabins, geysers shining.
Who'd we be then / down the street
maybe buying the morning paper
falling into a snooze
with mandarin oranges and sweet rolls.

My children's children will love these romantic years
looking for my handwriting in the registry, on diskettes,
on dirty toilet paper.
I will die without ever seeing snow
under the floury snow how we might have furthered
our little adventure in the light:
a meteor's passage, the track of a star.

Gods and teenagers will imagine these days
and will want these days for themselves
and the names and the dates will be erased
and all our discords
and the light will remain, hermano, the light
and nothing else.

vitraux de exilio

POR LUISA FUTORANSKY

Toda la eficacia de los nombres
que trabajosamente la imaginería construyó para fascinarte
se derrumban silenciosos:
un rico cementerio de cenizas
eso es hoy, tu geografía.

Aprendiste a costa de tu juventud
y de gran parte de tu inocencia
que estar sólo en un despojado suburbio de las pampas
o en la fastuosa Samarkanda
tiene la misma dimensión de olvido o de tragedia;
que el viento nunca tuvo piedad para esparcir
las piedras y los muertos, que sólo los turistas de solemnidad
se fotografían ante los vidrios de colores

porque decir país es musitar apenas cuatro letras
y tras ellas la densidad de secretas combinaciones
lápidas de extraños que llevan nuestro nombre
y pálidas fotos que conservan el eco de tu paso
hacia el amor o la desesperanza.
Es también la memoria de trabajos fatigosos
o quizá alguna vieja melodía
que retiene los primeros riesgos de tu juventud.

Un país es tu nombre
y la ácida violencia con que acude una palabra
a tu indefensa boca de viajero.

vitraux of exile

BY LUISA FUTORANSKY

All the efficacy of the names
that the imagery laboriously built up to fascinate you
falls silent:
a rich cemetery of ashes,
that, now, is your geography.

You learned at the cost of your youth
and most of your innocence
that to be alone in a forsaken suburb of the pampas
or in splendid Samarkand
holds the same dimension of oblivion or tragedy;
that the wind never took pity scattering
stones and the dead, that only the doomed tourists
take each other's photos before the stained-glass windows

because to say country is to whisper barely seven letters
and through them the density of secret combinations
gravestones of strangers bearing our name
and pale photos that preserve the echo of your passage
toward love or despair.
It's also the memory of tiring labors
or maybe some old tune
that retains the first risks of your youth.

A country is your name
and the acid violence with which a word comes
to your defenseless traveler's mouth.

Es un mapa con un río cuya desembocadura y nacimiento
se unen, curiosamente, en el punto exacto de la tierra
que desea abonar tu osario.

Son amaneceres, insomnios, saludos, cólera
un brazo, un hombro, diminutivos, insultos
despedidas, jardines, encuentros, temblores
promesas, otoños, rieles, desafíos
sustantivos absolutos que no admiten
otra explicación a su peso de fantasmas:
éstos y no otros.

It's a map with a river whose source and outlet
curiously unite at the exact spot on earth
that your bones wish to fertilize.

It's daybreaks, insomnias, salutations, anger
an arm, a shoulder, diminutives, insults
farewells, gardens, meetings, tremors
promises, autumns, rails, challenges
absolute nouns that allow
no other explanation for its weight in ghosts:
these and not others.

TONE

La santa

POR GABRIEL GARCÍA MÁRQUEZ

Veintidós años después volví a ver a Margarito Duarte. Apareció de pronto en una de las callecitas secretas del Trastévere, y me costó trabajo reconocerlo a primera vista por su castellano difícil y su buen talante de romano antiguo. Tenía el cabello blanco y escaso, y no le quedaban rastros de la conducta lúgubre y las ropas funerarias de letrado andino con que había venido a Roma por primera vez, pero en el curso de la conversación fui rescatándolo poco a poco de las perfidias de sus años y volví a verlo como era: sigiloso, imprevisible, y de una tenacidad de picapedrero. Antes de la segunda taza de café en uno de nuestros bares de otros tiempos, me atreví a hacerle la pregunta que me carcomía por dentro.

—¿Qué pasó con la santa?

—Ahí está la santa—me contestó—. Esperando.

Sólo el tenor Rafael Ribero Silva y yo podíamos entender la tremenda carga humana de su respuesta. Conocíamos tanto su drama, que durante años pensé que Margarito Duarte era el personaje en busca de autor que los novelistas esperamos durante toda una vida, y si nunca dejé que me encontrara fue porque el final de su historia me parecía inimaginable.

Había venido a Roma en aquella primavera radiante en que Pío XII padecía una crisis de hipo que ni las buenas ni las malas artes de médicos y hechiceros habían logrado remediar. Salía por primera vez de su escarpada aldea de Tolima, en los Andes colombianos, y se le notaba hasta en el modo de dormir. Se presentó una mañana en nuestro consulado con la maleta de pino lustrado que por la forma y el tamaño parecía el estuche de un violonchelo, y le planteó al cónsul el motivo sorprendente de su viaje. El cónsul llamó entonces por teléfono al tenor Rafael Ribero Silva, su compatriota, para que le consiguiera un cuarto en la pensión donde ambos vivíamos. Así lo conocí.

The Saint

BY GABRIEL GARCÍA MARQUÉZ

I saw Margarito Duarte after twenty-two years on one of the narrow secret streets in Trastevere, and at first I had trouble recognizing him, because he spoke halting Spanish and had the appearance of an old Roman. His hair was white and thin, and there was nothing left of the Andean intellectual's solemn manner and funeral clothes with which he had first come to Rome, but in the course of our conversation I began, little by little, to recover him from the treachery of his years and see him again as he had been: secretive, unpredictable, and as tenacious as a stonecutter. Before the second cup of coffee in one of our bars from the old days, I dared to ask him the question that was gnawing inside me.

"What happened with the Saint?"

"The Saint is there," he answered. "Waiting."

Only the tenor Rafael Ribero Silva and I could understand the enormous human weight of his reply. We know his drama so well that for years I thought Margarito Duarte was the character in search of an author that we novelists wait for all our lives, and if I never allowed him to find me it was because the end of his story seemed unimaginable.

He had come to Rome during that radiant spring when Pius XII suffered from an attack of hiccups that neither the good nor the evil arts of physicians and wizards could cure. It was his first time away from Tolima, his village high in the Colombian Andes—a fact that was obvious even in the way he slept. He presented himself one morning at our consulate carrying the polished pine box the shape and size of a cello case, and he explained the surprising reason for his trip to the consul, who then telephoned his countryman, the tenor Rafael Riberto Silva, asking that he find him a room at the *pensione* where we both lived. That is how I met him.

Margarito Duarte no había pasado de la escuela primaria, pero su vocación por las bellas letras le había permitido una formación más amplia con la lectura apasionada de cuanto material impreso encontraba a su alcance. A los dieciocho años, siendo el escribano del municipio, se casó con una bella muchacha que murió poco después en el parto de la primera hija. Ésta, más bella aún que la madre, murió de una fiebre esencial a los siete años. Pero la verdadera historia de Margarito Duarte había empezado seis meses antes de su llegada a Roma, cuando hubo que mudar el cementerio de su pueblo para construir una represa. Como todos los habitantes de la región, Margarito desenterró los huesos de sus muertos para llevarlos al cementerio nuevo. La esposa era polvo. En la tumba contigua, por el contrario, la niña seguía intacta después de once años. Tanto, que cuando destaparon la caja se sintió el vaho de las rosas frescas con que la habían enterrado. Lo más asombroso, sin embargo, era que el cuerpo carecía de peso.

Centenares de curiosos atraídos por el clamor del milagro desbordaron la aldea. No había duda. La incorruptibilidad del cuerpo era un síntoma inequívoco de la santidad, y hasta el obispo de la diócesis estuvo de acuerdo en que semejante prodigio debía someterse al veredicto del Vaticano. De modo que se hizo una colecta pública para que Margarito Duarte viajara a Roma, a batallar por una causa que ya no era sólo suya ni del ámbito estrecho de su aldea, sino un asunto de la nación.

Mientras nos contaba su historia en la pensión del apacible barrio de Parioli, Margarito Duarte quitó el candado y abrió la tapa del baúl primoroso. Fue así como el tenor Ribero Silva y yo participamos del milagro. No parecía una momia marchita como las que se ven en tantos museos del mundo, sino una niña vestida de novia que siguiera dormida al cabo de una larga estancia bajo la tierra. La piel era tersa y tibia, y los ojos abiertos eran diáfanos, y causaban la impresión insoportable de que nos veían desde la muerte. El raso y los azahares falsos de la corona no habían resistido al rigor del tiempo con tan buena salud como la piel, pero las rosas que le habían puesto en las manos permanecían vivas. El peso del estuche de pino, en efecto, siguió siendo igual cuando sacamos el cuerpo.

Margarito Duarte had not gone beyond primary school, but his vocation for letters had permitted him a broader education through the impassioned reading of everything in print he could lay his hands on. At the age of eighteen, when he was village clerk, he married a beautiful girl who died not long afterward when she gave birth to their first child, a daughter. Even more beautiful than her mother, she died of an essential fever at the age of seven. But the real story of Margarito Duarte began six months before his arrival in Rome, when the construction of a dam required that the cemetery in his village be moved. Margarito, like all the other residents of the region, disinterred the bones of his dead to carry them to the new cemetery. His wife was dust. But in the grave next to hers, the girl was still intact after eleven years. In fact, when they pried the lid off the coffin they could smell the scent of the fresh-cut roses with which she had been buried. Most astonishing of all, however, was that her body had no weight.

Hundreds of curiosity-seekers, attracted by the resounding news of the miracle, poured into the village. There was no doubt about it: The incorruptibility of the body was an unequivocal sign of sainthood, and even the bishop of the diocese agreed that such a prodigy should be submitted to the judgment of the Vatican. And therefore they took up a public collection so that Margarito Duarte could travel to Rome to do battle for the cause that no longer was his alone or limited to the narrow confines of his village, but had become a national issue.

As he told us his story in the *pensione* in the quiet Parioli district, Margarito Duarte removed the padlock and raised the lid of the beautiful trunk. That was how the tenor Ribero Silva and I participated in the miracle. She did not resemble the kind of withered mummy seen in so many museums of the world, but the little girl dressed as a bride who was still sleeping after a long stay underground. Her skin was smooth and warm, and her open eyes were clear and created the unbearable impression that they were looking at us from death. The satin and artificial orange blossoms of her crown had not withstood the rigors of time as well as her skin, but the roses that had been placed in her hands were still alive. And it was in fact true that the weight of the pine case did not change when we removed the body.

Margarito Duarte empezó sus gestiones al día siguiente de la llegada. Al principio con una ayuda diplomática más compasiva que eficaz, y luego con cuantas artimañas se le ocurrieron para sortear los incontables obstáculos del Vaticano. Fue siempre muy reservado sobre sus diligencias, pero se sabía que eran numerosas e inútiles. Hacía contacto con cuantas congregaciones religiosas y fundaciones humanitarias encontraba a su paso, donde lo escuchaban con atención pero sin asombro, y le prometían gestiones inmediatas que nunca culminaron. La verdad es que la época no era la más propicia. Todo lo que tuviera que ver con la Santa Sede había sido postergado hasta que el Papa superara la crisis de hipo, resistente no sólo a los más refinados recursos de la medicina académica, sino a toda clase de remedios mágicos que le mandaban del mundo entero.

Por fin, en el mes de julio, Pío XII se repuso y fue a sus vacaciones de verano en Castelgandolfo. Margarito llevó la santa a la primera audiencia semanal con la esperanza de mostrársela. El Papa apareció en el patio interior, en un balcón tan bajo que Margarito pudo ver sus uñas bien pulidas y alcanzó a percibir su hálito de lavanda. Pero no circuló por entre los turistas que llegaban de todo el mundo para verlo, como Margarito esperaba, sino que pronunció el mismo discurso en seis idiomas y terminó con la bendición general.

Al cabo de tantos aplazamientos, Margarito decidió afrontar las cosas en persona, y llevó a la Secretaría de Estado una carta manuscrita de casi sesenta folios, de la cual no obtuvo respuesta. Él lo había previsto, pues el funcionario que la recibió con los formalismos de rigor apenas si se dignó darle una mirada oficial a la niña muerta, y los empleados que pasaban cerca la miraban sin ningún interés. Uno de ellos le contó que el año anterior había recibido más de ochocientas cartas que solicitaban la santificación de cadáveres intactos en distintos lugares del mundo. Margarito pidió por último que se comprobara la ingravidez del cuerpo. El funcionario la comprobó, pero se negó a admitirla.

—Debe ser un caso de sugestión colectiva—dijo.

En sus escasas horas libres y en los áridos domingos de verano, Margarito permanecía en su cuarto, encarnizado en la lectura de cualquier libro que le

Margarito Duarte began his negotiations the day following his arrival, at first with diplomatic assistance that was more compassionate than efficient, and then with every strategy he could think of to circumvent the countless barriers set up by the Vatican. He was always very reserved about the measures he was taking, but we knew they were numerous and to no avail. He communicated with all the religious congregations and humanitarian foundations he could find, and they listened to him with attention but no surprise and promised immediate steps that were never taken. The truth is that it was not the most propitious time. Everything having to do with the Holy See had been postponed until the Pope overcame the attack of hiccupping that proved resistant not only to the most refined techniques of academic medicine, but to every kind of magic remedy sent to him from all over the world.

At last, in the month of July, Pius XII recovered and left for his summer vacation in Castel Gandolfo. Margarito took the Saint to the first weekly audience, hoping he could show her to the Pope, who appeared in the inner courtyard on a balcony so low that Margarito could see his burnished fingernails and smell his lavender scent. He did not circulate among the tourists who came from every nation so see him, as Margarito had anticipated, but repeated the same statement in six languages and concluded with a general blessing.

After so many delays, Margarito decided to take matters into his own hands, and he delivered a letter almost sixty pages long to the Secretariat of State but received no reply. He had foreseen this, for the functionary who accepted the handwritten letter with all due formality did not deign to give more than an official glance at the dead girl, and the clerks passing looked at her with no interest at all. One of them told him that in the previous year they had received more than eight hundred letters requesting sainthood for intact corpses in various places around the globe. At last Margarito requested that the weightlessness of the body be verified. The functionary verified it but refused to admit it.

"It must be a case of collective suggestion," he said.

In his few free hours, and on the dry Sundays of summer, Margarito

pareciera de interés para su causa. A fines de cada mes, por iniciativa propia, escribía en un cuaderno escolar una relación minuciosa de sus gastos con su caligrafía preciosista de amanuense mayor, para rendir cuentas estrictas y oportunas a los contribuyentes de su pueblo. Antes de terminar el año conocía los dédalos de Roma como si hubiera nacido en ellos, hablaba un italiano fácil y de tan pocas palabras como su castellano andino, y sabía tanto como el que más sobre procesos de canonización. Pero pasó mucho más tiempo antes de que cambiara su vestido fúnebre, y el chaleco y el sombrero de magistrado que en la Roma de la época eran propios de algunas sociedades secretas con fines inconfesables. Salía desde muy temprano con el estuche de la santa, y a veces regresaba tarde en la noche, exhausto y triste, pero siempre con un rescoldo de luz que le infundía alientos nuevos para el día siguiente.

—Los santos viven en su tiempo propio—decía.

Yo estaba en Roma por primera vez, estudiando en el Centro Experimental de Cine, y viví su calvario con una intensidad inolvidable. La pensión donde vivíamos era en realidad un apartamento moderno a pocos pasos de la Villa Borghese, cuya dueña ocupaba dos alcobas y alquilaba cuartos a estudiantes extranjeros. La llamábamos María Bella, y era guapa y temperamental en la plenitud de su otoño, y siempre fiel a la norma sagrada de que cada quien es rey absoluto dentro de su cuarto. En realidad, la que llevaba el peso de la vida cotidiana era su hermana mayor, la tía Antonieta, un ángel sin alas que le trabajaba por horas durante el día, y andaba por todos lados con su balde y su escoba de jerga lustrando más allá de lo posible los mármoles del piso. Fue ella quien nos enseñó a comer los pajaritos cantores que cazaba Bartolino, su esposo, por el mal hábito que le quedó de la guerra, y quien terminaría por llevarse a Margarito a vivir en su casa cuando los recursos no le alcanzaron para los precios de María Bella.

Nada menos adecuado para el modo de ser de Margarito que aquella casa sin ley. Cada hora nos reservaba una novedad, hasta en la madrugada, cuando nos despertaba el rugido pavoroso del león en el zoológico de la Villa Borghese. El tenor Ribero Silva se había ganado el privilegio de que los

remained in his room, devouring any book that seemed relevant to his cause. At the end of each month, on his own initiative, he wrote a detailed calculation of his expenses in a composition book, using the exquisite calligraphy of a senior clerk to provide the contributors from his village with strict and up-to-date accounts. Before the year was out he knew the labyrinths of Rome as if he had been born there, spoke a fluent Italian as laconic as his Andean Spanish, and knew as much as anyone about the process of canonization. But much more time passed before he changed his funeral dress, the vest and magistrate's hat which in the Rome of that time were typical of secret societies with unconfessable aims. He went out very early with the case that held the Saint, and sometimes he returned late at night, exhausted and sad but always with a spark of light that filled him with new courage for the next day.

"Saints live in their own time," he would say.

It was my first visit to Rome, where I was studying at the Experimental Film Center, and I lived his calvary with unforgettable intensity. Our *pensione* was in reality a modern apartment a few steps from the Villa Borghese. The owner occupied two rooms and rented the other four to foreign students. We called her Bella Maria, and in the ripeness of her autumn she was good-looking and temperamental and always faithful to the sacred rule that each man is absolute king of his own room. The one who really bore the burden of daily life was her older sister, Aunt Antonietta, an angel without wings who worked for her hour after hour during the day, moving through the apartment with her pail and brush, polishing the marble floor beyond the realm of the possible. It was she who taught us to eat the little songbirds that her husband, Bartonino, caught— a bad habit left over from the war—and who, in the end, took Margarito to live in her house when he could no longer afford Bella Maria's prices.

Nothing was less suited to Margarito's nature than that house without law. Each hour had some surprise in store for us, even the dawn, when we were awakened by the fearsome roar of the lion in the Villa Borghese zoo. The tenor Ribero Silva had earned this privilege: the Romans did not resent his early morning practice sessions. He would get up at six, take his medicinal bath of

romanos no se resintieran con sus ensayos tempraneros. Se levantaba a las seis, se daba su baño medicinal de agua helada y se arreglaba la barba y las cejas de Mefistófeles, y sólo cuando ya estaba listo con la bata de cuadros escoceses, la bufanda de seda china y su agua de colonia personal, se entregaba en cuerpo y alma a sus ejercicios de canto. Abría de par en par la ventana del cuarto, aún con las estrellas del invierno, y empezaba por calentar la voz con fraseos progresivos de grandes arias de amor, hasta que se soltaba a cantarla a plena voz. La expectativa diaria era que cuando daba el *do* de pecho le contestaba el león de la villa Borghese con un rugido de temblor de tierra.

—Eres San Marcos reencarnado, *figlio mio*—exclamaba la tía Antonieta asombrada de veras—. Sólo él podía hablar con los leones.

Una mañana no fue el león el que dio la réplica. El tenor inició el dueto de amor del *Otello: Già nella notte densa s'estingue ogni clamor.* De pronto, desde el fondo del patio, nos llegó la respuesta en una hermosa voz de soprano. El tenor prosiguió, y las dos voces cantaron el trozo completo, para solaz del vecindario que abrió las ventanas para santificar sus casas con el torrente de aquel amor irresistible. El tenor estuvo a punto de desmayarse cuando supo que su Desdémona invisible era nada menos que la gran María Caniglia.

Tengo la impresión de que fue aquel episodio el que le dio un motivo válido a Margarito Duarte para integrarse a la vida de la casa. A partir de entonces se sentó con todos en la mesa común y no en la cocina, como al principio, donde la tía Antonieta lo complacía casi a diario con su guiso maestro de pajaritos cantores. María Bella nos leía de sobremesa los periódicos del día para acostumbrarnos a la fonética italiana, y completaba las noticias con una arbitrariedad y una gracia que nos alegraban la vida. Uno de esos días contó, a propósito de la santa, que en la ciudad de Palermo había un enorme museo con los cadáveres incorruptos de hombres, mujeres y niños, e inclusive varios obispos, desenterrados de un mismo cementerio de padres capuchinos. La noticia inquietó tanto a Margarito, que no tuvo un instante de paz hasta que fuimos a Palermo. Pero le bastó una mirada de paso por las abrumadoras galerías de momias sin gloria para formularse un juicio de consolación.

icy water, arrange his Mephistophelean beard and eyebrows, and only when he was ready, and wearing his tartan bathrobe, Chinese silk scarf, and personal cologne, give himself over, body and soul, to his vocal exercises. He would throw open the window in his room, even when the wintry stars were still in the sky, and warm up with progressive phrasings of great love arias until he was singing at full voice. The daily expectation was that when he sang his *do* at top volume, the Villa Borghese lion would answer him with an earth-shaking roar.

"You are the reincarnation of Saint Mark, *figlio mio*," Aunt Antoinetta would exclaim in true amazement. "Only he could talk to lions."

One morning it was not the lion who replied. The tenor began the love duet from Othello—*"Già nella notte densa s'estingue ogni clamor"*—and from the bottom of the courtyard we heard the answer, in a beautiful soprano voice. The tenor continued, and the two voices sang the complete selection to the delight of all the neighbors, who opened the windows to sanctify their houses with the torrent of that irresistible love. The tenor almost fainted when he learned that his invisible Desdemona was no less a personage than the great Maria Caniglia.

I have the impression that this episode gave Margarito Duarte a valid reason for joining in the life of the house. From that time on he sat with the rest of us at the common table and not, as he had done at first, in the kitchen, where Aunt Antonietta indulged him almost every day with her masterly songbird stew. When the meal was over, Bella Maria would read the daily papers aloud to teach us Italian phonetics, and comment on the news with an arbitrariness and wit that brought joy to our lives. One day, with regard to the Saint, she told us that in the city of Palermo there was an enormous museum that held the incorruptible corpses of men, women, and children, and even several bishops, who had all been disinterred from the same Capuchin cemetery. The news so disturbed Margarito that he did not have a moment's peace until we went to Palermo. But a passing glance at the oppressive galleries of inglorious mummies was all he needed to make a consolatory judgment.

"These are not the same," he said. "You can tell right away they're dead."

After lunch Rome would succumb to its August stupor. The afternoon sun

—No son el mismo caso—dijo—. A estos se les nota enseguida que están muertos.

Después del almuerzo Roma sucumbía en el sopor de agosto. El sol de medio día se quedaba inmóvil en el centro del cielo, y en el silencio de las dos de la tarde sólo se oía el rumor del agua, que es la voz natural de Roma. Pero hacia las siete de la noche las ventanas se abrían de golpe para convocar el aire fresco que empezaba a moverse, y una muchedumbre jubilosa se echaba a las calles sin ningún propósito distinto que el de vivir, en medio de los petardos de las motocicletas, los gritos de los vendedores de sandía y las canciones de amor entre las flores de las terrazas.

El tenor y yo no hacíamos la siesta. Íbamos en su vespa, él conduciendo y yo en la parrilla, y les llevábamos helados y chocolates a las putitas de verano que mariposeaban bajo los laureles centenarios de la Villa Borghese, en busca de turistas desvelados a pleno sol. Eran bellas, pobres y cariñosas, como la mayoría de las italianas de aquel tiempo, vestidas de organza azul, de popelina rosada, de lino verde, y se protegían del sol con las sombrillas apolilladas por las lluvias de la guerra reciente. Era un placer humano estar con ellas, porque saltaban por encima de las leyes del oficio y se daban el lujo de perder un buen cliente para irse con nosotros a tomar un café bien conversado en el bar de la esquina, o a pasear en las carrozas de alquiler por los senderos del parque, o a dolernos de los reyes destronados y sus amantes trágicas que cabalgaban al atardecer en el *galoppatoio*. Más de una vez les servíamos de intérpretes con algún gringo descarriado.

No fue por ellas que llevamos a Margarito Duarte a la Villa Borghese, sino para que conociera el león. Vivía en libertad en un islote desértico circundado por un foso profundo, y tan pronto como nos divisó en la otra orilla empezó a rugir con un desasosiego que sorprendió a su guardián. Los visitantes del parque acudieron sorprendidos. El tenor trató de identificarse con su do de pecho matinal, pero el león no le prestó atención. Parecía rugir hacia todos nosotros sin distinción, pero el vigilante se dio cuenta al instante de que sólo rugía por Margarito. Así fue: para donde él se moviera se movía el león, y

remained immobile in the middle of the sky, and in the two-o'clock silence one heard nothing but water, which is the natural voice of Rome. But at about seven the windows were thrown open to summon the cool air that began to circulate, and a jubilant crowd took to the streets with no other purpose than to live, in the midst of backfiring motorcycles, the shouts of melon vendors, and the love songs among the flowers on the terraces.

The tenor and I did not take a siesta. We would ride on his Vespa, he driving and I sitting behind, and bring ices and chocolates to the little summer whores who fluttered under the centuries-old laurels in the Villa Borghese and watched for sleepless tourists in the bright sun. They were beautiful, poor, and affectionate, like most Italian women in those days, and they dressed in blue organdy, pink poplin, green linen, and protected themselves from the sun with parasols damaged by storms of bullets during the recent war. It was a human pleasure to be with them, because they ignored the rules of their trade and allowed themselves the luxury of losing a client in order to have coffee and conversation with us in the bar on the corner, or take carriage rides around the paths in the park, or fill us with pity for the deposed monarchs and their tragic mistresses who rode horseback at dusk along the *galoppatoio*. More than once we served as their interpreters with some foreigner gone astray.

They were not the reason we took Margarito Duarte to the Villa Borghese: We wanted him to see the lion. He lived uncaged on a small desert island in the middle of a deep moat, and as soon as he caught sight of us on the far shore he began to roar with an agitation that astonished his keeper. The visitors to the park gathered around in surprise. The tenor tried to identify himself with his full-voice morning *do,* but the lion paid him no attention. He seemed to roar at all of us without distinction, yet the keeper knew right away that he roared only for Margarito. It was true: Wherever he moved the lion moved, and as soon as he was out of sight the lion stopped roaring. The keeper, who held a doctorate in classical literature from the University of Siena, thought that Margarito had been with other lions that day and was carrying their scent. Aside from that reasoning, which was invalid, he could think of no other explanation.

tan pronto como se escondía dejaba de rugir. El vigilante, que era doctor en letras clásicas de la universidad de Siena, pensó que Margarito debió estar ese día con otros leones que lo habían contaminado de su olor. Aparte de esa explicación, que era inválida, no se le ocurrió otra.

—En todo caso—dijo—no son rugidos de guerra sino de compasión.

Sin embargo, lo que impresionó al tenor Ribera Silva no fue aquel episodio sobrenatural, sino la conmoción de Margarito cuando se detuvieron a conversar con las muchachas del parque. Lo comentó en la mesa, y unos por picardía, y otros por comprensión, estuvimos de acuerdo en que sería una buena obra ayudar a Margarito a resolver su soledad. Conmovida por la debilidad de nuestros corazones, María Bella se apretó la pechuga de madraza bíblica con sus manos empedradas de anillos de fantasía.

—Yo lo haría por caridad—dijo—si no fuera porque nunca he podido con los hombres que usan chaleco.

Fue así como el tenor pasó por la Villa Borghese a las dos de la tarde, y se llevó en ancas de su vespa a la mariposita que le pareció más propicia para darle una hora de buena compañía a Margarito Duarte. La hizo desnudarse en su alcoba, la bañó con jabón de olor, la secó, la perfumó con su agua de colonia personal, y la empolvó de cuerpo entero con su talco alcanforado para después de afeitarse. Por último le pagó el tiempo que ya llevaban y una hora más, y le indicó letra por letra lo que debía hacer.

La bella desnuda atravesó en puntillas la casa en penumbras, como un sueño de la siesta, y dio dos golpecitos tiernos en la alcoba del fondo. Margarito Duarte, descalzo y sin camisa, abrió la puerta.

—*Buona sera giovanotto*—le dijo ella, con voz y modos de colegiala—. *Mi manda il tenore.*

Margarito asimiló el golpe con una gran dignidad. Acabó de abrir la puerta para darle paso, y ella se tendió en la cama mientras él se ponía a toda prisa la camisa y los zapatos para atenderla con el debido respeto. Luego se sentó a su lado en una silla, e inició la conversación. Sorprendida, la muchacha le dijo que se diera prisa, pues sólo disponían de una hora. Él no se dio por enterado.

"In any event," he said, "they are roars of compassion, not battle."

And yet what most affected the tenor Ribero Silva was not this supernatural episode, but Margarito's confusion when they stopped to talk with the girls in the park. He remarked on it at the table, and we all agreed—some in order to make mischief and others because they were sympathetic—that it would be a good idea to help Margarito resolve his loneliness. Moved by our tender hearts, Bella Maria pressed her hands, covered by rings with imitation stones, against her bosom worthy of a doting biblical matriarch.

"I would do it for charity's sake," she said, "except that I never could abide men who wear vests."

That was how the tenor rode his Vespa to the Villa Borghese at two in the afternoon and returned with the little butterfly he thought best able to give Margarito Duarte an hour of good company. He had her undress in his bedroom, bathed her with scented soap, dried her, perfumed her with his personal cologne, and dusted her entire body with his camphorated aftershave talc. And then he paid her for the time they had already spent, plus another hour, and told her step by step what she had to do.

The naked beauty tiptoed through the shadowy house, like a siesta dream, gave two gentle taps at the rear bedroom door, and Margarito Duarte appeared, barefoot and shirtless.

"Buona sera, giovanotto," she said, with the voice and manners of the schoolgirl. *"Mi manda il tenore."*

Margarito absorbed the shock with great dignity. He opened the door wide to let her in, and she lay down on the bed while he rushed to put on his shirt and shoes to receive her with all due respect. Then he sat beside her on a chair and began the conversation. The bewildered girl told him to hurry because they only had an hour. He did not seem to understand.

The girl said later that in any event she would have spent all the time he wanted and not charged him a cent, because there could not be a better behaved man anywhere in the world. Not knowing what to do in the meantime, she glanced around the room and saw the wooden case near the fireplace. She

La muchacha dijo después que de todos modos habría estado el tiempo que él hubiera querido sin cobrarle ni un céntimo, porque no podía haber en el mundo un hombre mejor comportado. Sin saber qué hacer mientras tanto, escudriñó el cuarto con la mirada, y descubrió el estuche de madera sobre la chimenea. Preguntó si era un saxofón. Margarito no le contestó, sino que entreabrió la persiana para que entrara un poco de luz, llevó el estuche a la cama y levantó la tapa. La muchacha trató de decir algo, pero se le desencajó la mandíbula. O como nos dijo después: *Mi si gelò il culo*. Escapó despavorida, pero se equivocó de sentido en el corredor, y se encontró con la tía Antonieta que iba a poner una bombilla nueva en la lámpara de mi cuarto. Fue tal el susto de ambas, que la muchacha no se atrevió a salir del cuarto del tenor hasta muy entrada la noche.

La tía Antonieta no supo nunca qué pasó. Entró en mi cuarto tan asustada, que no conseguía atornillar la bombilla en la lámpara por el temblor de las manos. Le pregunté qué le sucedía. "Es que en esta casa espantan," me dijo. "Y ahora a pleno día". Me contó con una gran convicción que, durante la guerra, un oficial alemán degolló a su amante en el cuarto que ocupaba el tenor. Muchas veces, mientras andaba en sus oficios, la tía Antonieta había visto la aparición de la bella asesinada recogiendo sus pasos por los corredores.

—Acabo de verla caminando en pelota por el corredor—dijo—. Era idéntica.

La ciudad recobró su rutina de otoño. Las terrazas floridas del verano se cerraron con los primeros vientos, y el tenor y yo volvimos a la tractoría del Trastévere donde solíamos cenar con los alumnos de canto del conde Carlo Calcagni, y algunos compañeros míos de la escuela de cine. Entre estos últimos, el más asiduo era Lakis, un griego inteligente y simpático, cuyo único tropiezo eran sus discursos adormecedores sobre la injusticia social. Por fortuna, los tenores y las sopranos lograban casi siempre derrotarlo con trozos de ópera cantados a toda voz, que sin embargo no molestaban a nadie aun después de la media noche. Al contrario, algunos trasnochadores de paso se sumaban al coro, y en el vecindario se abrían ventanas para aplaudir.

Una noche, mientras cantábamos, Margarito entró en puntillas para no interrumpirnos. Llevaba el estuche de pino que no había tenido tiempo de dejar

asked if it was a saxophone, Margarito did not answer, but opened the blind to let in a little light, carried the case to the bed, and raised the lid. The girl tried to say something, but her jaw was hanging open. Or as she told us later: *"Mi si gelò il culo."* She fled in terror, but lost her way in the hall and ran into Aunt Antonietta, who was going to my room to replace a light bulb. They were both so frightened that the girl did not dare leave the tenor's room until very late that night.

Aunt Antonietta never learned what happened. She came into my room in such fear that she could not turn the bulb in the lamp because her hands were shaking. I asked her what was wrong. "There are ghosts in this house," she said. "And now in broad daylight." She told me with great conviction that during the war a German officer had cut the throat of his mistress in the room occupied by the tenor. As Aunt Antonietta went about her work, she often saw the ghost of the beautiful victim making her way along the corridors.

"I've just seen her walking naked down the hall," she said. "She was identical."

The city resumed its autumn routine. The flowering terraces of summer closed down with the first winds, and the tenor and I returned to our old haunts in Trastevere, where we ate supper with the vocal students of Count Carlo Calcagni, and with some of my classmates from the film school, among whom the most faithful was Lakis, an intelligent, amiable Greek whose soporific discourses on social injustice were his only fault. It was our good fortune that the tenors and sopranos almost always drowned him out with operatic selections that they sang at full volume, but which did not bother anyone, even after midnight. On the contrary, some late-night passersby would join in the chorus, and neighbors opened their windows to applaud.

One night, while we were singing, Margarito tiptoed in so as not to interrupt us. He was carrying the pine case that he had not had time to leave at the *pensione* after showing the Saint to the parish priest at San Giovanni in Laterano, whose influence with the Holy Congregation of the Rite was common knowledge. From the corner of my eye I caught a glimpse of him putting it

en la pensión después de mostrarle la santa al párroco de San Juan de Letrán, cuya influencia ante la Sagrada Congregación del Rito era de dominio público. Alcancé a ver de soslayo que lo puso debajo de una mesa apartada, y se sentó mientras terminábamos de cantar. Como siempre ocurría al filo de la media noche, reunimos varias mesas cuando la tractoría empezó a desocuparse, y quedamos juntos los que cantaban, los que hablábamos de cine, y los amigos de todos. Y entre ellos, Margarito Duarte, que ya era conocido allí como el colombiano silencioso y triste del cual nadie sabía nada. Lakis, intrigado, le preguntó si tocaba el violonchelo. Yo me sobrecogí con lo que me pareció una indiscreción difícil de sortear. El tenor, tan incómodo como yo, no logró remendar la situación. Margarito fue el único que tomó la pregunta con toda naturalidad.

—No es un violonchelo—dijo—. Es la santa.

Puso la caja sobre la mesa, abrió el candado y levantó la tapa. Una ráfaga de estupor estremeció el restaurante. Los otros clientes, los meseros, y por último la gente de la cocina con sus delantales ensangrentados, se congregaron atónitos a contemplar el prodigio. Algunos se persignaron. Una de las cocineras se arrodilló con las manos juntas, presa de un temblor de fiebre, y rezó en silencio.

Sin embargo, pasada la conmoción inicial, nos enredamos en una discusión a gritos sobre la insuficiencia de la santidad en nuestros tiempos. Lakis, por supuesto, fue el más radical. Lo único que quedó claro al final fue su idea de hacer una película crítica con el tema de la santa.

—Estoy seguro—dijo—que el viejo Cesare no dejaría escapar este tema.

Se refería a Cesare Zavattini, nuestro maestro de argumento y guión, uno de los grandes de la historia del cine y el único que mantenía con nosotros una relación personal al margen de la escuela. Trataba de enseñarnos no sólo el oficio, sino una manera distinta de ver la vida. Era una máquina de pensar argumentos. Le salían a borbotones, casi contra su voluntad. Y con tanta prisa, que siempre le hacía falta la ayuda de alguien para pensarlos en voz alta y atraparlos al vuelo. Sólo que al terminarlos se le caían los ánimos. "Lástima que haya que filmarlo," decía. Pues pensaba que en la pantalla perdería mucho de su magia original.

under the isolated table where he sat until we finished singing. As always, just after midnight, when the trattoria began to empty, we would push several tables together and sit in one group—those who sang, those of us who talked about movies, and all of our friends. And among them Margarito Duarte, who was already known there as the silent, melancholy Colombian whose life was a mystery. Lakis was intrigued and asked him if he played the cello. I was caught off guard by what seemed to me an indiscretion too difficult to handle. The tenor was just as uncomfortable and could not save the situation. Margarito was the only one who responded to the question with absolute naturalness.

"It's not a cello," he said. "It's the Saint."

He placed the case on the table, opened the padlock, and raised the lid. A gust of stupefaction shook the restaurant. The other customers, the waiters, even the people in the kitchen with their bloodstained aprons, gathered in astonishment to see the miracle. Some crossed themselves. One of the cooks, overcome by a feverish trembling, fell to her knees with clasped hands and prayed in silence.

And yet when the initial commotion was over, we became involved in a shouting argument about the lack of saintliness in our day. Lakis, of course, was the most radical. The only clear idea at the end of it was that he wanted to make a critical movie about the saint.

"I'm sure," he said, "that old Cesare would never let this subject get away."

He was referring to Cesare Zavattini, who taught us plot development and screenwriting. He was one of the great figures in the history of film, and the only one who maintained a personal relationship with us outside class. He tried to teach us not only the craft but a different way of looking at life. He was a machine for inventing plots. They poured out of him, almost against his will, and with such speed that he always needed someone to help catch them mid-flight as he thought them up aloud. His enthusiasm would flag only when he had completed them. "Too bad they have to be filmed," he would say. For he thought that on the screen they would lose much of their original magic. He kept his ideas on cards arranged by subject and pinned to the walls, and he had so many they filled an entire room in his house.

Conservaba las ideas en tarjetas ordenadas por temas y prendidas con alfileres en los muros, y tenía tantas que ocupaban una alcoba de su casa.

El sábado siguiente fuimos a verlo con Margarito Duarte. Era tan goloso de la vida, que lo encontramos en la puerta de su casa de la calle Angela Merici, ardiendo de ansiedad por la idea que le habíamos anunciado por teléfono. Ni siquiera nos saludó con la amabilidad de costumbre, sino que llevó a Margarito a una mesa preparada, y él mismo abrió el estuche. Entonces ocurrió lo que menos imaginábamos. En vez de enloquecerse, como era previsible, sufrió una especie de parálisis mental.

—*Ammazza!*—murmuró espantado.

Miró a la santa en silencio por dos o tres minutos, cerró la caja él mismo, y sin decir nada condujo a Margarito hacia la puerta, como a un niño que diera sus primeros pasos. Lo despidió con unas palmaditas en la espalda. "Gracias, hijo, muchas gracias," le dijo. "Y que Dios te acompañe en tu lucha". Cuando cerró la puerta se volvió hacia nosotros, y nos dio su veredicto.

—No sirve para el cine—dijo—. Nadie lo creería.

Esa lección sorprendente nos acompañó en el tranvía de regreso. Si él lo decía, no había ni que pensarlo: la historia no servía. Sin embargo, María Bella nos recibió con el recado urgente de que Zavattini nos esperaba esa misma noche, pero sin Margarito.

Lo encontramos en uno de sus momentos estelares. Lakis había llevado a dos o tres condiscípulos, pero él ni siquiera pareció verlos cuando abrió la puerta.

—Ya lo tengo—gritó—. La película será un cañonazo si Margarito hace el milagro de resucitar a la niña.

—¿En la película o en la vida? —le pregunté.

Él reprimió la contrariedad. "No seas tonto," me dijo. Pero enseguida le vimos en los ojos el destello de una idea irresistible. "A no ser que sea capaz de resucitarla en la vida real," dijo, y reflexionó en serio:

—Debería probar.

Fue sólo una tentación instantánea, antes de retomar el hilo. Empezó a pasearse por la casa, como un loco feliz, gesticulando a manotadas y recitando

The following Saturday we took Margarito Duarte to see him. Zavattini was so greedy for life that we found him at the door of his house on the Via di Sant'Angela Merici, burning with interest in the idea we had described to him on the telephone. He did not even greet us with his customary amiability, but led Margarito to a table he had prepared, and opened the case himself. Then something happened that we never could have imagined. Instead of going wild, as we expected, he suffered a kind of mental paralysis.

"*Ammazza!*" he whispered in fear.

He looked at the Saint in silence for two or three minutes, closed the case himself, and without saying a word led Margarito to the door as if he were a child taking his first steps. He said good-bye with a few pats on his shoulder. "Thank you, my son, thank you very much," he said. "And may God be with you in your struggle." When he closed the door he turned toward us and gave his verdict.

"It's no good for the movies," he said. "Nobody would believe it."

That surprising lesson rode with us on the streetcar we took home. If he said it, it had to be true: The story was no good. Yet Bella Maria met us at the *pensione* with the urgent message that Zavattini was expecting us that same night, but without Margarito.

We found the maestro in one of his stellar moments. Lakis had brought along two or three classmates, but he did not even seem to see them when he opened the door.

"I have it," he shouted. "The picture will be a sensation if Margarito performs a miracle and resurrects the girl."

"In the picture or in life?" I asked.

He suppressed his annoyance. "Don't be stupid," he said. But then we saw in his eyes the flash of an irresistible idea. "What if he could resurrect her in real life?" he mused, and added in all seriousness:

"He ought to try."

It was no more than a passing temptation, and then he took up the thread again. He began to pace every room, like a happy lunatic, waving his hands and

la película a grandes voces. Lo escuchábamos deslumbrados, con la impresión de estar viendo las imágenes como pájaros fosforescentes que se le escapaban en tropel y volaban enloquecidos por toda la casa.

—Una noche—dijo— cuando ya han muerto como veinte Papas que no lo recibieron, Margarito entra en su casa, cansado y viejo, abre la caja, le acaricia la cara a la muertita, y le dice con toda la ternura del mundo: "Por el amor de tu padre, hijita: levántate y anda".

Nos miró a todos, y remató con un gesto triunfal:

—¡Y la niña se levanta!

Algo esperaba de nosotros. Pero estábamos tan perplejos, que no encontrábamos qué decir. Salvo Lakis, el griego, que levantó el dedo, como en la escuela, para pedir la palabra.

—Mi problema es que no lo creo—dijo, y ante nuestra sorpresa, se dirigió directo a Zavattini—: Perdóneme, maestro, pero no lo creo.

Entonces fue Zavattini el que se quedó atónito.

—¿Y por qué no?

—Qué sé yo—dijo Lakis, angustiado—. Es que no puede ser.

—*Ammazza!*—gritó entonces el maestro, con un estruendo que debió oírse en el barrio entero—. Eso es lo que más me jode de los estalinistas: que no creen en la realidad.

En los quince años siguientes, según él mismo me contó, Margarito llevó la santa a Castelgandolfo por si se daba la ocasión de mostrarla. En una audiencia de unos doscientos peregrinos de América Latina alcanzó a contar la historia, entre empujones y codazos, al benévolo Juan XXIII. Pero no pudo mostrarle la niña porque debió dejarla a la entrada, junto con los morrales de otros peregrinos, en previsión de un atentado. El Papa lo escuchó con tanta atención como le fue posible entre la muchedumbre, y le dio en la mejilla una palmadita de aliento.

—*Bravo, figlio mio*—le dijo—. Dios premiará tu perseverancia.

Sin embargo, cuando de veras se sintió en vísperas de realizar su sueño fue durante el reinado fugaz del sonriente Albino Luciani. Un pariente de éste,

reciting the film in great shouts. We listened to him, dazzled, and it seemed we could see the images, like flocks of phosphorescent birds that he set loose for their mad flight through the house.

"One night," he said, "after something like twenty popes who refused to receive him have died, Margarito grown old and tired goes into his house, opens the case, caresses the face of the little dead girl, and says with all the tenderness in the world: 'For love of your father, my child, arise and walk.' "

He looked at all of us and finished with a triumphant gesture:

"And she does!"

He was waiting for something from us. But we were so befuddled we could not think of a thing to say. Except Lakis the Greek, who raised his hand, as if we were in school, to ask permission to speak.

"My problem is that I don't believe it," he said, and to our surprise he was speaking to Zavattini: "Excuse me, Maestro, but I don't believe it."

Then it was Zavattini's turn to be astonished.

"And why not?"

"How do I know?" said Lakis in anguish. "But it's impossible."

"Ammazza!" the maestro thundered in a voice that must have been heard throughout the entire neighborhood. "That's why I can't stand Stalinists: They don't believe in reality."

For the next fifteen years, as he himself told me, Margarito carried the Saint to Castel Gandolfo in the event an opportunity arose for displaying her. At an audience for some two hundred pilgrims from Latin America, he managed to tell his story, amid shoves and pokes, to the benevolent John XXIII. But he could not show him the girl because, as a precaution against assassination attempts, he had been obliged to leave her at the entrance along with the knapsacks of the other pilgrims. The Pope listened with as much attention as he could in the crowd, and gave him an encouraging pat on the cheek.

"Bravo, figlio mio," he said, "God will reward your perseverance."

But it was during the fleeting reign of the smiling Albino Luciani that Margarito really felt on the verge of fulfilling his dream. One of the Pope's

impresionado por la historia de Margarito, le prometió su mediación. Nadie le hizo caso. Pero dos días después, mientras almorzaban, alguien llamó a la pensión con un mensaje rápido y simple para Margarito: no debía moverse de Roma, pues antes del jueves sería llamado del Vaticano para una audiencia privada.

Nunca se supo si fue una broma. Margarito creía que no, y se mantuvo alerta. Nadie salió de la casa. Si tenía que ir al baño lo anunciaba en voz alta: "Voy al baño". María Bella, siempre graciosa en los primeros albores de la vejez, soltaba su carcajada de mujer libre.

—Ya lo sabemos, Margarito—gritaba—, por si te llama el Papa.

La semana siguiente, dos días antes del telefonema anunciado, Margarito se derrumbó ante el titular del periódico que deslizaron por debajo de la puerta: *Morto il Papa*. Por un instante lo sostuvo en vilo la ilusión de que era un periódico atrasado que habían llevado por equivocación, pues no era fácil creer que muriera un Papa cada mes. Pero así fue: el sonriente Albino Luciani, elegido treinta y tres días antes, había amanecido muerto en su cama.

Volví a Roma veintidós años después de conocer a Margarito Duarte, y tal vez no hubiera pensado en él si no lo hubiera encontrado por casualidad. Yo estaba demasiado oprimido por los estragos del tiempo para pensar en nadie. Caía sin cesar una llovizna boba como el caldo tibio, la luz de diamante de otros tiempos se había vuelto turbia, y los lugares que habían sido míos y sustentaban mis nostalgias eran otros y ajenos. La casa donde estuvo la pensión seguía siendo la misma, pero nadie dio razón de María Bella. Nadie contestaba en seis números de teléfono que el tenor Ribero Silva me había mandado a través de los años. En un almuerzo con la nueva gente de cine evoqué la memoria de mi maestro, y un silencio súbito aleteó sobre la mesa por un instante, hasta que alguien se atrevió a decir:

—*Zavattini? Mai sentito.*

Así era: nadie había oído hablar de él. Los árboles de la Villa Borghese estaban desgreñados bajo la lluvia, el *galoppatoio* de las princesas tristes había sido devorado por una maleza sin flores, y las bellas de antaño habían sido sustituidas por atletas andróginos travestidos de manolas. El único sobreviviente de una

relatives, impressed by Margarito's story, promised to intervene. No one paid him much attention. But two days later, as they were having lunch at the *pensione*, someone telephoned with a simple, rapid message for Margarito: He should not leave Rome, because sometime before Thursday he would be summoned to the Vatican for a private audience.

No one ever found out whether it was a joke. Margarito did not think so and stayed on the alert. He did not leave the house. If he had to go to the bathroom he announced: "I'm going to the bathroom." Bella Maria, still witty in the dawn of her old age, laughed her free woman's laugh.

"We know, Margarito," she shouted, "just in case the Pope calls."

Early one morning the following week Margarito almost collapsed when he saw the headline in the newspaper slipped under the door: *"Morto il Papa."* For a moment he was sustained by the illusion that it was an old paper delivered by mistake, since it was not easy to believe that a pope would die every month. But it was true: The smiling Albino Luciani, elected thirty-three days earlier, had died in his sleep.

I returned to Rome twenty-two years after I first met Margarito Duarte, and perhaps I would not have thought about him at all if we had not run into each other by accident. I was too depressed by the ruinous weather to think about anybody. An imbecilic drizzle like warm soup never stopped falling, the diamond light of another time had turned muddy, and the places that had once been mine and sustained my memories were strange to me now. The building where the *pensione* was located had not changed, but nobody knew anything about Bella Maria. No one answered at the six different telephone numbers that tenor Ribero Silva had sent me over the years. At lunch with new movie people, I evoked the memory of my teacher, and a sudden silence fluttered over the table for a moment until someone dared to say:

"Zavattini? Mai sentito."

That was true: No one had heard of him. The trees at the Villa Borghese were disheveled in the rain, the *galoppatoio* of the sorrowful princesses had been devoured by weeds without flowers, and the beautiful girls of long ago had

fauna extinguida era el viejo león, sarnoso y acatarrado, en su isla de aguas marchitas. Nadie cantaba ni se moría de amor en las tractorías plastificadas de la Plaza de España. Pues la Roma de nuestras nostalgias era ya otra Roma antigua dentro de la antigua Roma de los Césares. De pronto, una voz que podía venir del más allá me paró en seco en una callecita del Trastévere:

—Hola, poeta.

Era él, viejo y cansado. Habían muerto cinco Papas, la Roma eterna mostraba los primeros síntomas de la decrepitud, y él seguía esperando. "He esperado tanto que ya no puede faltar mucho más," me dijo al despedirse, después de casi cuatro horas de añoranzas. "Puede ser cosa de meses". Se fue arrastrando los pies por el medio de la calle, con sus botas de guerra y su gorra descolorida de romano viejo, sin preocuparse de los charcos de lluvia donde la luz empezaba a pudrirse. Entonces no tuve ya ninguna duda, si es que alguna vez la tuve, de que el santo era él. Sin darse cuenta, a través del cuerpo incorrupto de su hija, llevaba ya veintidós años luchando en vida por la causa legítima de su propia canonización.

been replaced by athletic androgynes cross-dressed in flashy clothes. Among all the extinct fauna, the only survivor was the old lion, who suffered from mange and a head cold on his island surrounded by dried waters. No one sang or died of love in the plastic trattorias on the Piazza di Spagna. For the Rome of our memory was by now another ancient Rome within the ancient Rome of the Caesars. Then a voice that might have come from the beyond stopped me cold on a narrow street in Trastevere:

"Hello, Poet."

It was he, old and tired. Four popes had died, eternal Rome was showing signs of decrepitude, and still he waited. "I've waited so long it can't be much longer now," he told me as he said good-bye after almost four hours of nostalgia. "It may be a matter of months." He shuffled down the middle of the street, wearing the combat boots and faded cap of an old Roman, ignoring the puddles of rain where the light was beginning to decay. Then I had no doubt, if I ever had any at all, that the Saint was Margarito. Without realizing it, by means of his daughter's incorruptible body and while he was still alive, he had spent twenty-two years fighting for the legitimate cause of his own canonization.

[CHAPTER III]

Rhythm

Everything in the universe has rhythm.

Everything dances.

—MAYA ANGELOU

Rhythm

Spoken language bobs on the stream of time. We remember how the speaker began, we anticipate how she will conclude. A book, on the other hand, is a dead thing that was once a log; it sits inert and unchanging on a table or a shelf. Only a reader can breathe life into it. And reading, like breathing, is by its nature rhythmic: spaces between words, the pauses of punctuation, the breaks at the end of lines and pages all mark the reader's passage through the work.

The essence of rhythm is repetition, the recurrence of recognizable elements at intervals. Consequently, rhythm "imposes unanimity upon the divergent," in the words of Yehudi Menuhin; that is, it is a unifying element. Behind the rhythm of the written medium is the rhythm of speech that we hear in our mind's ear or manifest in recitation. Rhythms of breath and gesture may be sensed behind the words on the page. Rhythm is life, a beating heart. Speech marks the passage of time and underscores our mortality; at the same time, writing freezes speech and gives it a postmortem existence.

In the English tradition, when we think about rhythm, we face the long tradition of analysis of meter in poetry, which looks for patterns of stress in versification. But stress is only one element of rhythm. Traditional emphasis on meter may yield simplified results and encourage sing-song readings. Moreover, the units of meter vary among languages and can seldom be translated directly to produce a culturally equivalent text. The foundation of English prosody (the metrical study of poetic lines) has traditionally been the foot, which is a unit of stressed and unstressed syllables (most common are the iambs—da-DUM—and the anapests—da-da-DUM), whereas Spanish meter is based not on the foot but on the syllable—a line is defined as septenary, octosyllabic, or hendecasyllabic, for example, depending on whether the final stress falls on the sixth, seventh, or tenth syllable. (Somewhat analogously, the American poet Kenneth Rexroth wrote poems based on seven-syllable lines, without much regard for patterns of stress.) Spanish has no problem

with the alexandrine line of twelve syllables (or paired six-syllable phrases), but comparable works in English are likely to use a five-foot line. Alexander Pope alluded to, and demonstrated, this in a couplet

> A needless alexandrine ends the song
> that like a wounded snake, drags its slow length along.

in which the first line is iambic pentameter (five feet in ten syllables) and the second is alexandrine (six feet in twelve syllables).

In linguistic theory, however, *prosody* has a broader meaning than it does in traditional English literary criticism, encompassing not just meter or stress but also intonation, pitch, loudness, duration, tone, timing, and other elements of speech. Creative writers certainly work with the full range of these elements and translators need to take them all into account.

In prose fiction, one of the most emphatically rhythmic writers I know is Louis-Ferdinand Céline, especially in the comic rhythms of his classical phrasing, developed in *Death on the Installment Plan* and refined in later novels. (The contemporary Colombian writer Fernando Vallejo captures something of this quality.) Céline was fascinated with dancers and dancing, and his prose has the rhythmic quality of dance. He even wrote ballets, which contain overtly rhythmic passages like this one:

> There is an enormous puff of smoke!... fantastic!... from the
> wings on the right ... The sound of a locomotive ... pistons
> ... steam ... bells ... trumpeting ... chains ... old metal ...
> all in a horrible blend.... The engineers start pushing back
> the crowd ... they clear a path ... a little boy is in front ...
> carrying a red flag and ringing a bell.... Make way ... make way!

Céline called his style an "emotive metro," alluding to the rush of his language that carries the reader rapidly along. How different Céline's emotive metro is from the imagistic metro of a famous poem by his contemporary Ezra Pound. In Pound's "In a Station of the Metro"—

> The apparition of these faces in the crowd;
> Petals on a wet, black bough.

—the images are essentially visual. Though we associate metros with motion (excepting Raymond Queneau's *Zazie in the Metro,* in which the metro never moves), this poem stops motion, like a Cartier-Bresson photograph, freezing a moment out of time. Its images function through juxtaposition, rather like a collage. But even this seemingly static poem contains rhythmic elements—which a translator would have to take note of—most obviously the near rhyme of the lines' final words. A preliminary version of the poem further emphasized its rhythmic structure, dividing each of the lines into three separate units.

The rhythms of Pound's poem are, however, certainly less regular than those of the verse that serves as an epigraph to Laura Esquivel's *Like Water for Chocolate*—

> A la mesa y a la cama
> Una sola vez se llama

—in which the singsong quality conveys a folk flavor. The verse's assertion that a person is only called once to the table or to bed establishes the connection between food and sexuality that the author develops in the novel. The epigraph is a *dicho,* a proverbial saying typically characterized by wordplay and witty observations. This *dicho* uses simple language, is remarkably concise, and is strongly rhythmic—compared to Pound's verse, it absolutely rushes to its emphatic conclusion, marked by the rhyme *llama.* My co-translator, Carol Christensen, and I rendered the epigraph as a couplet with a consonant rhyme in place of the full rhyme of the original—

> To the table or to bed
> You must come when you are bid

—hoping in this way to capture some of the quality of the original *dicho.*

In Donald Yates's astonishing translation of Edgar Brau's "The Journey,"

the author's sentences seem full of life, surging rhythmically forward in lengthy, graceful swoops. The reader might compare this story's description of a locomotive—"There, straddling the rusty rails, dark and shining, a locomotive trembles impatiently, trying to communicate with snorts and whistles and vibrating connecting rods its eagerness to depart"—to the passage from Céline cited above.

Sean Higgins's rendering of Cristina Peri Rossi's "The Uprooted" captures the nebulous, floating quality of its subjects, the rootless urban wanderers whose glances, "blue and watery," are "evasive, like that of someone who …floats in space vague and undefined." Compare the gentle rhythm of this piece with other examples in this section.

Of "A Ship's Passing," an excerpt from her translation of "Atardecer en la playa" by Bárbara Jacobs, Susan Ouriou writes, "I enjoyed trying to capture the rhythm and feeling of the original. To me, the whole rhythm of the piece is one of succeeding waves."

I expect that the other English translators of the Argentine writer Julio Cortázar—a sizeable group that includes Claribel Alegría and Darwin Flakoll, Paul Blackburn, Nick Caister, Margaret Jull Costa, Jean Franco, Elaine Kerrigan, Stephen Kessler, Suzanne Jill Levine, Alfred MacAdam, Alberto Manguel, Anne McLean, Gregory and Clementine Rabassa, and Kathleen Weaver—must have felt as I did in translating him that a great deal depends on the rhythm of his prose. Cortázar has compared his writing process to that of a jazz "take"—it must proceed seamlessly from beginning to end, propelled by an irresistible momentum: if the momentum is broken, the effectiveness of the passage is destroyed. The selection "To Dress a Shadow" here is from his "collage book" *Around the Day in Eighty Worlds*.

Another translator's take on Cortázar's jazz-like rhythm appears in Gregory Rabassa's translation of section 73 of the novel *Hopscotch*. Rabassa stays closer to the Spanish than many translators are able to do, and we can clearly sense the original text through his rendering. Only a great translator can retain

as much of the original syntax as Rabassa does and still produce a perfectly convincing English text.

A third Cortázar sample, the story "Continuity of Parks," translated by the poet Paul Blackburn, provides yet another English version of the Argentinian master. Blackburn was Cortázar's first translator, and his work has been both praised (by Lawrence Venuti, for example) and damned (by Anne McLean, for one). Both Cortázar and Blackburn were jazz enthusiasts, and, despite the translation's occasional liberty, their compatible sensibilities resulted in a highly readable English debut for the author.

El viaje

POR EDGAR BRAU

Etonnants voyageurs!

—BAUDELAIRE, LE VOYAGE, III

I

A la hora en que la noche parece recoger sus colgaduras con un tintineo de cristal helado, y las más débiles de las estrellas se arrojan a la tierra aún oscura, espantadas ante la inminente hecatombe del día, a esa hora, propicia para la urdimbre de lo inaudito y para las burbujas de lo fantástico, precisamente a esa hora, un breve tañido de campana, seco y como velado por telarañas, estremeció al pueblo dormido. A punto de retornar el silencio de los ruidos familiares, un nuevo tañido, igualmente breve, vuelve a sacudir a los durmientes, cuya soñolienta atención es seguidamente solicitada por dos o tres tañidos más, todos ellos leves y como para probar el metal de la campana. Pero después de un golpe de badajo particularmente intenso, al que de inmediato siguen otros en apremiante sucesión, extrae de la campana un retumbar agudo e interminable que, anudando sus ondas de sonido en un alargamiento de serpiente, comienza primero por recorrer las calles del pueblo con implacable sinuosidad, para luego, a través de sus imprescindibles y recién brotadas bifurcaciones, atropellar las puertas, sacudir las ventanas y, filtrándose por las hendijas, arrastrar a la calle, con el fragor de una leva guerrera, a los extrañados vecinos que aún no comprenden, pero que sin embargo tampoco pueden sustraerse al irresistible mandato de la campana que allá, en la estación abandonada, continúa repicando.

Por ello basta sólo un momento para que la calle principal, que se ha

The Journey

BY EDGAR BRAU

Etonnants voyageurs!

—BAUDELAIRE, LE VOYAGE, III

I

At the hour when night seems to gather in its tapestries to the tinkling of frozen crystal, and the weakest of the stars throw themselves toward the still-darkened earth, terrified by the imminent catastrophe of daybreak, at that hour, propitious for the plotting of outrageous things and for the bubbling up of fantasy, precisely at that moment, the brief tolling of a bell, sterile and seemingly veiled in cobwebs, shook the sleeping town. Just when the familiar silence of the ordinary is about to return, another peal, equally brief, rouses the sleepers, whose drowsy attention is immediately solicited by two or three additional tollings that seem to be testing the metal integrity of the bell. But after another especially intense stroke of the clapper, followed by others in hurried succession, the bell emits a high-pitched and continuous boom that, turning its sound waves into a lengthened serpent, begins first to course through the town's streets with implacable sinuosity, and then, by means of its necessary and repeated forkings, assaults the doors, rattles the windows and, slipping through cracks, draws out into the streets with the furor of a wartime levy the amazed occupants who do not yet understand but nonetheless cannot ignore the irresistible command of the bell that back at the station continues to toll.

It takes only a moment for the main street, which has slightly tilted so as to facilitate the procession, to overflow with the growing hubbub of the

inclinado levemente para facilitar la marcha, rebose con el rumor creciente de quienes avanzan, a paso diverso, hacia la estación. Sí, el avance es desordenado. Los niños se adelantan entre chillidos y atraviesan continuamente la calle; algunas mujeres llevan a sus mascotas en brazos; otros arrastran maletas y esquivan fastidiados a quienes se rezagan entre conjeturas. A veces alguien se vuelve como para cerciorarse de que no es el único que responde al llamado; desaparece al instante, envuelto por el clamor del gentío que avanza, frenético, entre remolinos de polvo.

Finalmente la multitud se detiene, con un gemido de asombro, frente a la estación. Allí, sobre las vías cubiertas de moho, oscura y reluciente, una locomotora tiembla de impaciencia, y con resoplidos, silbatos y sacudimientos de bielas trata de comunicar sus urgencias de partida. Los vagones, que cubren todo el andén, también se balancean y sus herrajes destellan hacia la todavía adormilada gente, que no hace más que recorrerlos con la vista.

Después de un momento, los más audaces se trepan a las escalerillas para echar un vistazo al interior de los coches, que según sus gritos están vacíos. Enseguida una voz de asombro celebra la aparición, en lo alto de la locomotora, del maquinista, un hombre de semblante rubicundo y grandes bigotes, cuyas manos regordetas alisan continuamente su uniforme azul. Desde su sitio saluda al gentío con unos ademanes ampulosos, y después, risueño y juguetón, acciona una palanca que hace surgir de la chimenea una espesa columna de humo, la cual se eleva varios metros y luego, repentinamente, a punto de precisarse en la figura de un genio o algo así, se desploma sobre la gente, que grita y se desbanda, aterrorizada. Pero es solamente una broma, un terror hecho de humo que pronto se disipa entre las risas del maquinista y de los recuperados vecinos, quienes vuelven sin embargo de inmediato a retroceder, ya que junto al maquinista y entre retazos de humo ha empezado a surgir, lenta, interminable, como brotando de un pantano, la figura colosal del fogonero, ante cuya presencia, una vez elevado en toda su magnitud, el gentío no puede reprimir un grito de espanto. Y en verdad que su aspecto es espeluznante: muy alto, un verdadero titán, su cuerpo musculoso asoma pujante por entre las aberturas

crowd advancing, at different paces, toward the station. To be sure, the procession is disorderly. The children run ahead screeching and swerving from one side of the street to the other; some women carry their dogs in their arms; others drag suitcases behind them, sidestepping the perplexed people who, falling back, are muttering curses. Occasionally, someone turns around, as if to determine if he is the only person responding to the call; he disappears immediately, swallowed up by the multitude that is frantically pushing ahead amid clouds of dust.

Finally, the mob, gasping with astonishment, stops in front of the station. There, straddling the rusty rails, dark and shining, a locomotive trembles impatiently, trying to communicate with snorts and whistles and vibrating connecting rods its eagerness to depart. The coaches, that stretch along the entire length of the platform, are also straining and their bright metal surfaces dazzle the sleepy crowd that can do nothing but stare.

After a moment, the most intrepid of the group climb up the boarding stairs to take a look at the inside of the coaches, which, to judge from their shouts, are empty. Suddenly, a cry of surprise greets the appearance, on top of the locomotive, of the engineer, a man of rosy complexion with a long mustache, whose chubby hands are stroking constantly at his blue uniform. From his vantage point he greets the crowd with broad gestures and then, with a playful smile, pulls a lever releasing a thick cloud of smoke that rises several feet in the air and then suddenly, just as it is about to assume the shape of a genie or some such creature, drops onto the people below, who run off in terror in all directions. But it is merely a joke, a frightening specter made of smoke that promptly dissipates to the amusement of the engineer as well as the relieved townspeople, who nonetheless immediately back off again, since next to the engineer, amid traces of smoke, as if emerging from a swamp, has begun to appear the figure of the fireman, whose presence, once he has risen to his full height, draws an exclamation of fright from the crowd. And in fact his appearance is frightening: extraordinarily tall, a true titan, his muscular body strains at his tight-fitting clothes, which are completely covered with soot, as is

de la estrecha indumentaria, que lleva completamente tiznada, lo mismo que la enorme cabeza donde los hirsutos cabellos punteados de renegridas motas parecen albergar una nidada de arañas. El rostro, oscuro y grasiento, aparece animado por una mueca siniestra, hecha de cálculo y suficiencia y ante la que cada vecino cree reencontrarse con un antiguo e impreciso terror. Tras apoyar sus manos como garras en el borde de la máquina, se pone a contemplar a la multitud, que continúa retrocediendo. De improviso le susurra algo al maquinista, que asiente y se vuelve. Una nueva nube de humo surge entonces de la chimenea, pero la gente, ya advertida, esta vez no le hace caso, sino que se limita a observar al fogonero, que molesto por lo fallido de la broma, desaparece en el interior de la locomotora con un gesto de fastidio.

Entretanto, el humo se ha ido transformando en una especie de niebla, la cual, al tiempo que le da al lugar un aspecto fantasmagórico, le comunica también un algo de importancia, al asemejarlo de algún modo a las estaciones de las grandes capitales, donde prestigiosos señores de impermeable se despiden de un gran amor o, recortados en un neblinoso contraluz, aguardan la contraseña de un fugitivo. Claro es que esta sensación dura solamente un instante, ya que el ir y venir de los futuros viajeros, los reclamos incipientes, las corridas infantiles y los olvidos de último momento impiden que en el lugar se instale el rumor sordo e impersonal de una estación capitalina, tan propicio para los incidentes sofisticados. Un guarda que nadie había visto hasta ese momento aparece de pronto en el andén, dando palmadas y anunciando la partida; al llegar junto a la locomotora le hace una seña al maquinista. De inmediato se oye un silbido cuya progresiva estridencia consigue no sólo que la niebla, encofrada en un remolino, se reintegre a la chimenea de la locomotora, sino también que a su término todos los pasajeros se encuentren ya ubicados en sus asientos. En efecto: cuando el silbido se acalla, en los vagones no falta nadie, e incluso aquellos que un rato antes se despedían en el andén, ahora descubren que son compañeros de viaje. Después de acomodar las maletas en las redes, los viajeros se dedican a palpar los tapizados de los asientos y la madera de las paredes con asombro y unción; todo ello es íntimo,

his enormous head, crowned with kinky hair that looks like a spider's nest. His face, dark and shiny, is fixed in an evil grin, calculated and self-sure, in whose presence each person feels himself confronted with an old, uncertain fear.

Placing his claw-like hands on the side of the engine, the fireman looks down at the crowd, which continues to move back. Suddenly, he whispers something to the engineer, who nods and turns away. Another cloud of smoke billows out from the smokestack, but the crowd, alerted to the trick, pays no attention and simply continues observing the stoker, who, annoyed at the failure of his joke, disappears inside the locomotive.

In the meantime, the smoke has begun to change into a kind of fog that, while it lends a fantastic aura to the place, also gives it an air of importance, making it appear somehow like the train stations of great cities, where imposing men in trench coats bid farewell to their lovers or, silhouetted against a curtain of mist, await the secret password of a fugitive. Of course, this impression lasts only a moment, since the milling about of the future travelers, their jockeying for position, the darting about of little children and the last-minute concerns about things left behind all prevent the creation of the low, impersonal murmur of a large city's train station, which is so appropriate to more sophisticated settings. A guard, whom no one has seen until that moment, suddenly appears on the platform, clapping his hands and announcing the train's departure; arriving alongside the locomotive, he signals to the engineer. Immediately, a whistle sounds, whose increasing shrillness not only causes the fog, whipped into a whirling cloud, to be pulled back into the smokestack, but also as it disappears has drawn all of the passengers into their seats. So it is that when it ceases, everyone is aboard, and even the people who a short time before were seeing their friends onto the train now find that they themselves are among the passengers. After having accommodated their baggage in the overhead racks, the travelers spend time delightedly examining their seats, the walls, the ceiling, decorated with an eye for warmth and intimacy, and no matter where one sits, the luxury and the views are magnificent; every seat is the best seat.

cálido, entrañable, y dondequiera uno se ubique la comodidad y la vista son magníficas; cada sitio es el mejor sitio.

El andén, mientras tanto, ha quedado vacío y solamente se aguarda la orden de partida. Inquietos, los viajeros se asoman por las ventanillas y tratan de averiguar la causa de la demora; pero nadie aparece para dar alguna explicación. El lugar está desierto y únicamente se oye el ronquido de la locomotora. Bajo una saliente de madera la solitaria campana se bambolea con dulzura. La angustia se apodera de los viajeros y empiezan los interrogantes. ¿Y si de pronto aparece alguien con la noticia de que el viaje se suspende, que todo es una absurda equivocación?... Se produce una calma expectante, similar a la que precede a un gran evento. Pero entonces un primer rayo de sol, tras rebotar incansable por los cromados del tren, va a atropellar a la pequeña campana, que resuena jubilosa (¿Quién la tañó? *Dios,* responde una vieja) indicando la partida y recibiendo por respuesta un largo silbido de la locomotora. En ese momento también, y sin que lo noten los pasajeros, ocupados en lanzar vivas, ocurre algo sorprendente: un estremecimiento sacude la tierra y los carcomidos durmientes, que a duras penas sostienen las vías y el tren, casi florecen, pues una extraordinaria afluencia de savia que brota del suelo los rejuvenece y fortifica; el musgo que sofoca los rieles empieza asimismo a resquebrajarse y sus fragmentos se convierten en esponjosas franelas que una mano invisible restriega contra las vías; y allá, un poco más lejos, abandonando un largo sueño reumático, las palancas rechinan su agradecimiento al rocío, que resbala igual a un elixir aceitoso por las coyunturas oxidadas y crujientes. El maquinista, percatándose de esa repentina metamorfosis, se inclina hacia fuera y hace una señal con los brazos; desde la lejanía alguien le responde del mismo modo. Tal parece que todo está en orden, como lo prescriben los reglamentos, de manera que no resta sino partir. Y efectivamente: entre gritos, agitar de manos, ladridos y abrazos interminables, al fin parte el bello tren de la estación abandonada, y avanzando por una vereda de tréboles encintada de hierro se adentra, con un piafar de regocijo, en el misterio irisado de lo maravilloso...

The platform is now deserted and everyone is awaiting the signal to depart. Nervously, the passengers peer out of the windows, trying to determine the reason for the delay; but no one is on hand to offer an explanation. The whole town is deserted and the only thing to be heard is the throbbing of the engine. Attached to a wooden crossbar, the solitary bell sways gently. The travelers are seized with panic and questions arise. What if someone appears to announce that the journey is suspended, that it was all an absurd mistake...? But then a mood of calm expectancy quiets them, like that which precedes some extraordinary event. At that moment, a single ray of sunshine, after reflecting off the metallic surfaces of the train, strikes the little bell, which begins to ring merrily *(Who rang the bell? God, an old woman replies),* thus indicating the train's departure and receiving the reply of a long whistle from the engine. At the same moment, without the passengers being aware of it in the midst of their wild cheering, something astonishing happens: a tremor shakes the earth and the worm-eaten sleepers, that have barely sustained the weight of the rails and the train, seem to bring forth new life, since a great outflowing of sap, issuing from the ground itself, rejuvenates and strengthens them; the moss that has grown over the rails now begins to crumble away and the resulting fragments turn into patches of spongy flannel that an invisible hand rubs over the metal; and then, a little farther on, emerging from a long arthritic sleep, the switch point levers creak in gratitude for the welcome dew that flows like an oily elixir through their rusty and creaking joints. The engine driver, taking note of this sudden metamorphosis, leans out of his cab and makes a signal with his arm; in the distance someone replies to him with the same sign. All of this seems to indicate that everything is in order, in compliance with regulations, so that the time has come for departure.

And so it is: amid shouts, the waving of arms, the barking of dogs, endless joyful embraces, the handsome train at last draws away from the abandoned station and, advancing over a field of clover split by rails, the train, with an eager pawing of its wheels, lunges forward into the mysterious iridescence of the wondrous...

II

...Constante y alborozado, el tren hiende la distancia y a un tiempo parece hender la tierra, pues tras su paso los márgenes abarquillados que flanquean los rieles exhalan, como suspiros de satisfacción, los suaves vapores de una cosa recién creada. Y en el interior de los coches, guarnecidos de hierro y seda, los viajeros se entregan a las delicias de la pura contemplación. Y en ningún sitio, en ninguna boca, un gesto o una palabra disonante; ni siquiera una pregunta, nada, todo en ellos es abandono y docilidad, confianza y certidumbre. El paisaje, el tren, los apetitos suprimidos, todo eso es para cada viajero como el aroma de una flor invisible: suficiente en sí mismo para reconocerla.

...Y el paisaje se bambolea entre los zigzagueos de una perspectiva caprichosa, que ya hiere las miradas con agudezas o ralladuras, ya la arrastra con suavidad por las corrientes de una espiral que despliega sus círculos hacia el infinito.

...Y la avidez de las miradas parece cristalizarse en lanzas que todo lo atraviesan, escarban y levantan, por lo que cada detalle del paisaje se ve así arrojado a una especie de saco ilimitadamente dúctil. Sí, el otear de los viajeros se hace inexorable y ningún rincón queda sin relevar. A veces una imagen del todo simple, o común, se graba en las pupilas con el relieve de una talla, de modo que durante un rato el viajero puede tener ante sí a un hombre que arroja su sombrero al aire, o a una joven agachada recogiendo la cosecha, o a una vaca como vigía debajo de un árbol solitario, o, recorriendo la hierba plateada de rocío, la silueta impecable de una torcaza. Luego la imagen se diluye en un esfumado de cuyo roce sutil el viajero emerge con sus ojos como clarificados.

...Y cuando veloces atraviesan una estación repleta de gente que con señas tratan de detener el tren, los viajeros se asoman por las ventanillas y el no, no, no comunicado con el oscilar de sus dedos es menos una burla que el signo de una confidencia: la de su condición de elegidos.

...Y al llegar la oscuridad los viajeros se recogen, saciados, y fijando la mirada en la luna elevan una callada plegaria de gratitud por la bendición de esa pausa y por las nuevas y extraordinarias vivencias que, enrolladas en el

II

Steadily and joyfully, the train cleaves through space and at the same time seems to slice through the earth, since in its wake the greenery that flanks the rails gives off, like contented sighs, the gentle aromas of something newborn. And inside the coaches, surrounded by metal and silk, the passengers surrender to the pleasures of simple contemplation. Nowhere is there uttered a word of displeasure, not even a question, nothing. Everything about them is trusting and peaceful, relaxed and confident. The landscape, the train, the allayed concerns, all of this is for each passenger like the scent of an invisible flower, completely unquestioned and sufficient in itself to be recognized.

...And the countryside sways with the twists and turns of a capricious perspective that at times pierce the eyes with sharp points and angles and at other times draw the gaze gently through the flowing path of a spiral that extends its circles off into infinity.

...And the eagerness of the glances seems to center itself on sharp points that penetrate everything, digging up, lifting, so that every detail of the landscape is included in a kind of immensely acceptable act of plundering. Yes, the surveying gazes of the passengers is inexorable and no feature escapes examination.

At times, a perfectly simple, or common, image is offered to a passenger's eye with the full dimension of a carving, so that for a while he can observe a man throwing his hat into the air or a young woman bending over to pick vegetables or a cow standing like a sentinel under a solitary tree or, cast over the dew-covered grass, the precise shadow of a woodpecker. The image is then diffused into a faint mist, out from which the traveler emerges with the sense of his vision having been cleansed.

...And when the passengers pass quickly past a station platform filled with people who are signaling to the train to stop, the "no, no, no" communicated by their waggling fingers is less a mockery than a sign of confidence in their having been selected as the chosen ones.

...And when darkness falls the passengers settle down, surfeited, and gazing up at the moon they offer a prayer of thanks for that day and for the new and

oscuro pergamino de la noche, los aguardan en la jornada siguiente.

...Y en cada uno de los claros en el bosque que enmarca las vías, siempre, como una pupila amable y vigilante, un retazo de mar.

...Y las estaciones llegan y se marchan suavemente, casi en puntas de pie, como si la naturaleza quisiera mezclar sus floraciones y sus marchiteces en un conjunto sutilmente aureolado de regio esplendor.

...Un viajero de ojos profundos y larga barba lleva consigo un cuaderno de tapas azules donde apunta las impresiones del viaje, en tanto que con trazos desmañados trata de dibujar en los márgenes ciertos detalles de los paisajes vistos. En ocasiones sus acompañantes le piden que lea algún párrafo, y con atención, casi impresionados, oyen entonces las palabras que describen lo que ellos mismos han visto o sentido, y que ahora, metamorfoseado en arte literario, aparece irreconocible, lejano, como algo perteneciente a la leyenda y con un sabor en el que es ya posible distinguir el fino polvillo de la caducidad.

...Y por momentos los viajeros creen sentir sobre sí una leve, sutil presión; algo semejante al peso de una mirada.

III

Y de esta manera, entre satisfacciones y complacencias, sin pausas ni trasbordos, continúa el bienaventurado viaje. Pero un día sucede algo asombroso: un niño predice—y acierta—la aparición de un determinado detalle en el paisaje. Interrogado, responde que no hace sino recordar el camino recorrido, parte del cual ha empezado al parecer a repetirse, como si estuvieran regresando. Los viajeros se precipitan alarmados a las ventanillas y con miradas implacables recorren el paisaje. ¡Allí!, grita de pronto alguien, señalando una lejana estribación. Algunos viajeros la reconocen y comienzan entonces las predicciones acerca de lo que los aguarda más adelante.

Al principio, los vaticinios no coinciden demasiado con la realidad, pero luego, lentamente, los aciertos se van acumulando, hasta que al fin ya no es posible dudar: aun cuando el tren continúa avanzando, en realidad se trata de un camino de vuelta. En algún lugar, en algún momento, se produjo el

extraordinary experiences that, rolled up in the dark parchment of the night, await them on the following day.

...And beyond every clearing in the woods that stretch along the tracks, always, like a friendly and vigilant eye, a fleeting view of the sea.

...And the seasons come and recede gently, seemingly on tiptoe, as if nature wanted to blend her flowerings and witherings into a softly glowing totality of regal splendor.

...A passenger with deep-set eyes and a long beard carries with him a blue-covered notebook into which he writes down impressions of the trip, while in the margins he tries to capture with artless strokes certain details of the landscapes he has seen. Occasionally, his traveling companions ask him to read a paragraph or two and attentively, quite impressed, they hear the words that describe what they themselves have seen or felt, and that now, transformed into literary expression, seems irreconcilable, distant, like something belonging to legend, something with a flavor in which it is now possible to detect the fine dust of decrepitude.

...And for moments the passengers think they feel upon them a slight, subtle pressure; something similar to the weight of a gaze.

III

Thus, in a mood of satisfaction and complacency, without pauses or stops for boarding, the blessed journey continues. One day, however, something astonishing occurs: a child predicts—and accurately—the appearance of a specific feature of the countryside. When he is questioned, he replies that all he did was remember the places that he had already seen, some of which apparently have begun to be repeated, as if movement was being reversed. Alarmed, the passengers crowd to the windows and with narrowing glances examine the countryside. "There!" shouts someone, pointing toward a distant mountain outcropping. Several travelers recognize it and now conjectures arise over what will be waiting for them farther on.

At the outset, the predictions do not coincide very closely with reality, but then, slowly, the correct guesses begin accumulating, to the point that it is

desvío, la curva fatal, pero nadie lo advirtió; y ahora el tren está regresando. Un clamor angustioso se eleva de los vagones y en instantes las voces se desgarran en un mismo reclamo: *¡Atrás!* Pero es inútil; el vocerío apenas llega hasta el interior de la locomotora, donde el fogonero, los dientes apretados y la mirada fiera, parece embriagarse con un furor de paletadas crecientes. Los más exaltados proponen a gritos tomar la locomotora y reducir a sus ocupantes; pero la mención del aterrador fogonero los paraliza. Otros, arrastrados por un paroxismo incontenible, se arrojan del tren y sus cuerpos se hunden entre los arbustos. Las mujeres lloriquean y abrazan a sus hijos; éstos, viendo la desesperación de sus madres, lanzan chillidos que van a unirse a las imprecaciones de los hombres. Y así, entre retorcimientos, rostros desencajados y manos que se alargan extáticas hacia atrás, empieza a oscurecer, y el tren atraviesa luego la noche como un largo quejido.

El amanecer encuentra a los viajeros despiertos y rígidos. Han velado toda la noche y se hallan agotados. En algunos sitios los asientos aparecen vacíos. Un niño reclama a su madre; una mujer busca entre sollozos a su marido. Algunos viajeros permanecen con la cabeza apoyada en el borde de las ventanillas, indiferentes a las ramas o a las hojas que golpean sus rostros. Nadie escucha a quienes todavía proponen, con tozudez, la esperanza o la curiosidad; demasiado defraudados para consolarse con palabras, prefieren el silencio. Afuera el terreno ya no luce; oscurecido por una nube de cenizas que el viento trae de confines incendiados e ignotos, recoge las miradas rencorosas de los viajeros, que a cada momento descubren, debajo del intenso sombreado, ciertos detalles por demás conocidos. Pero ni un gesto los traiciona; incólumes al descubrimiento, se abandonan a una fingida indiferencia, la misma que conservarán, como un preciado bien, a lo largo del viaje que, de un cierto modo, puede decirse que otra vez comienza...

IV

...Y desmoronados en sus duros asientos, los viajeros se entregan a un apagado intercambio de recuerdos, que surgen, como briznas, tras largo

no longer possible to have any doubt: even as the train continues forward, it is actually making the return trip. In some place, at some moment, the fatal turnoff occurred, but no one took notice; and now the train is going back. An anguished cry fills the coaches, and immediately all the voices merge into one single plea: "Turn back!" But it is useless: the clamor scarcely reaches the interior of the locomotive, where the stoker, his teeth clenched, his gaze fixed, seems to have become intoxicated with his increasingly furious shoveling of coal. The most excited passengers cry out for a storming of the locomotive and the subduing of its occupants; but the mention of the terrifying stoker leaves them all paralyzed. Yet others, seized by an irresistible compulsion, throw themselves from the train and their bodies disappear into the brush. The women weep and hug their children, who, seeing their mothers' desperation, let out squeals that blend in with the curses of the men. So it is that, to the accompaniment of writhing bodies, distorted expressions, and arms extended out toward the direction from which they came, it begins to grow dark and the train now penetrates the night like a long lament.

Daybreak finds the travelers awake and stiff-jointed. They have not slept during the night and they are exhausted. Some seats are now vacant. A child is calling out for its mother; a woman searches, sobbing, for her husband. Some passengers remain with their heads leaning on the sills of the window frames, indifferent to the leaves and branches that whip across their faces. No one listens to those who are still stubbornly encouraging hope or patience; these passengers, feeling too deceived to be consoled with words, prefer silence.

Outside, the land is no longer bright; obscured by a cloud of ashes from some unknown incinerated region, it receives the spiteful gazes of the passengers, who now repeatedly discover, beneath the hovering overcast, certain features of the landscape that they recall. But their attitude is not betrayed by any outward gesture; deprived of the discovery of new sights, they immerse themselves in a feigned indifference, the same as that they will maintain, like some sort of valuable benefit, for the rest of the journey, which, in a certain sense, could be said to be starting over...

escarbar en la memoria. Ni siquiera los niños conservan del viaje (*De ida*, como ya lo llaman con sus vocecitas un tanto extrañadas) algo más que un conjunto de sensaciones, imposibles de comunicar.

...Y las disputas y los incidentes no tardan en aparecer. Una mujer con el vestido desgarrado huye hacia otro vagón, perseguida por un hombre; un niño golpea a su hermano que le niega una mariposa recién atrapada.

...Y a cada rato los colores se apagan, y una tonalidad grisácea, levemente punteada de negro, se apodera del paisaje. Un viajero se asoma y señala hacia lo alto: allí una imponente nube gris, henchida de sol, derrama por sus costados, como un gran candil, una tenue llovizna de luz cenicienta.

...Y cualquier detalle en el paisaje, cualquier sonido o palabra oída al azar, evoca en cada viajero el desabrido ritual cotidiano de la vida antigua, cuyos símbolos y cruces empiezan entonces a sucederse en la memoria cada vez más terribles, como los señalamientos de un trayecto infernal.

...Algunos desesperados arrancan de las manos de su dueño un cuaderno azul y, frenéticos, leen sus páginas en voz alta. Pero las palabras suenan extrañas, sin significado. Son un puro sonido, y los dibujos que enmarcan ese absurdo lingüístico se les aparecen a los desorbitados ojos del lector, que ya entrega el cuaderno a otras manos igualmente ávidas, como las huellas de un insecto despatarrado. En un rincón, un hombre de larga barba se arrebuja con su abrigo y después, la mirada ausente, se vuelve hacia la ventanilla.

...Y el tren se asemeja cada vez más al vacío cascarón de un insecto muerto hace tiempo, pero en cuyo interior aún se agita, ciego e impotente, un rebaño de larvas...

V

Y una noche, al doblar un recodo, aparece en el camino la pequeña estación abandonada. El tren se detiene con suavidad frente a la oficina del jefe. En los vagones, pulidos por el rocío, se reflejan las diminutas estrellas. La luna se asoma entre las nubes y a lo lejos el caserío se enciende de blancura, como

IV

...And, slumped in their hard seats, the travelers indulge in a fitful exchange of recollections, that surface like so many nuggets turned up after lengthy digging into memories. Not even the children retain from the journey ("the journey out" as they refer to it in subdued voices) anything more than a series of sensations that are impossible to express.

...And the arguments and the disturbances are not long in appearing. A woman in a torn dress flees to another coach, pursued by a man; a child strikes his brother who refuses to give him the butterfly he has just caught.

...And progressively the colors outside fade, and a shadowy cloud, speckled with black dots, settles over the countryside. A passenger looks out and points up toward something; up above, a huge gray cloud, its center radiant with sunlight, spills out from its sides, like an enormous candle, a faint drizzle of ash-colored light.

...And every detail of the landscape, every sound or word casually heard, evokes in each passenger the insipid daily routine of life before, whose symbols and crosses are seen through memory as increasingly terrible, like the signs pointing out an infernal trajectory.

...Some desperate persons seize the blue notebook from the hands of its owner and frantically read its pages out loud. But the words sound strange, meaningless. They are pure sound, and the sketches that accompany that linguistic mishmash appear to the person looking at them, who in turn passes the notebook to other avid hands, like the tracks of a sprawling insect. In a corner a man with a long beard bundles himself up in his coat and turns his gaze to the window.

...And the train resembles more and more the empty shell of a long-dead beetle, but one in whose interior there still swarm, blind and powerless, a cluster of larvae ...

V

Then one night, on rounding a curve, the small abandoned train station appears. The train pulls up gently in front of the stationmaster's office. On

un camposanto. El súbito silencio acaba por despertar a los viajeros, que enseguida reconocen el lugar. Se produce un amago de protesta, pero el sueño y el cansancio los contiene. Lentos, envejecidos, descienden dificultosamente del tren y van a agruparse frente al caserón de madera. Parecen confundidos y las miradas se dirigen, humildes, hacia el piso. Finalmente un viejo mira las estrellas, como para orientarse, y después comienza a caminar lentamente rumbo al pueblo, seguido por el resto de las personas.

Avanzan arrastrando los pies entre crujidos de articulaciones. Ya son pocos los que permanecen en el andén. Uno de ellos, el más rezagado, se detiene y fija la mirada en la vieja campana; luego se acerca y sus manos aferran la deshilachada soga que aún resiste. Aguarda a que el último de los viajeros abandone la estación y entonces da un tirón de la soga. Un ruido sordo, apagado, surge del metal de la campana. El hombre suspira profundamente y vuelve a tirar de la soga. Esta vez el sonido llega hasta el grupo de viajeros que marcha por el camino, quienes se detienen al oírlo. Un nuevo tañido los hace vacilar y las manos, temblorosas, se dirigen a la cabeza, como para extraer un recuerdo. Pero ahora los tañidos empiezan a amontonarse, estridentes, y cada uno de ellos golpea como un latigazo en los oídos de los viajeros, que impulsados por el repique apresuran la marcha. Pero sólo recorren unos metros, pues frente a ellos avanza, rumorosa y terrible, al ritmo de frenéticas pisadas, una gran nube de polvo, cuyos primeros lengüetazos ya rozan los rostros de los espantados viajeros, que permanecen en medio del camino, fascinados por el repique y por la nube, que continúa avanzando, incontenible. Es necesario que se aparten, los gemidos y las toses así lo indican, y sin embargo no se mueven de su sitio. Algo nuevo los paraliza: el repentino sentimiento de una rememoración inminente, en la que acaso... Pero no, ya no hay tiempo; ya la nube de polvo los envuelve, ya las conciencias se sofocan...

the surface of the coaches, moistened with dew, the diminutive stars are reflected. The moon emerges from among the clouds and in the distance the little group of houses is bathed in white light, like a cemetery. The sudden silence awakens the travelers, who immediately recognize where they are. Slowly, now older, they descend with difficulty from the train and gather together in front of the wooden station house. They seem confused and their meek expressions are fixed on the ground. Finally, an old man looks up at the stars, as if to get his bearings, and then begins walking slowly toward the town, followed by the rest of the travelers.

They move ahead, dragging their feet, their joints creaking. There are now only a few people left on the platform. One of them, bringing up the rear, looks at the old bell; then he approaches it and his hands grasp the frayed rope. He waits for the last of the travelers to leave the station and then gives a tug on the rope. A deep, muffled sound reverberates from the metal of the bell. The man sighs and pulls once again on the rope. This time the sound reaches the group of travelers who are moving down the road and they stop to listen to it. Another peal of the bell causes them to pause and they lift their trembling hands to their heads, as if trying to extract a memory. But now the shrill peals begin to accumulate and each one of them sounds like the lash of a whip in the ears of the travelers who, spurred on by the tolling, hasten their steps.

But they can proceed only a short distance because in front of them there is advancing a huge cloud of dust, noisy and terrifying, accompanied by the sound of hurried footsteps. The foremost part of the cloud now reaches the front ranks of the frightened travelers, who remain there in the middle of the road, fascinated by the tolling bell and by the dust cloud, which continues advancing relentlessly. They need to stand aside, as their coughing and complaints now require, and yet they do not budge from their position. Something new freezes them in place: the sudden conviction of an imminent remembrance, with which perhaps ... But no, there is no longer time; the cloud of dust now envelops them, and their consciousness is overcome ....

Los desarraigados

POR CRISTINA PERI ROSSI

A menudo se ven, caminando por las calles de las grandes ciudades, a hombres y mujeres que flotan en el aire, en un tiempo y espacio suspendidos. Carecen de raíces en los pies, y a veces, hasta carecen de pies. No les brotan raíces de los cabellos, ni suaves lianas atan su tronco a alguna clase de suelo. Son como algas impulsadas por las corrientes marinas y cuando se fijan a alguna superficie, es por casualidad y dura sólo un momento. Enseguida vuelven a flotar y hay cierta nostalgia en ello.

La ausencia de raíces les confiere un aire particular, impreciso, por eso resultan incómodos en todas partes y no se los invita a las fiestas, ni a las casas, porque resultan sospechosos. Es cierto que en apariencia realizan los mismos actos que el resto de los seres humanos: comen, duermen, caminan y hasta mueren, pero quizás el observador atento podría descubrir que en su manera de comer, de dormir, caminar y morir hay una leve y casi imperceptible diferencia. Comen hamburguesas Mac Donald o emparedados de pollo Pokins, ya sea en Berlín, Barcelona o Montevideo. Y lo que es mucho peor todavía: encargan un menú estrafalario, compuesto por gazpacho, puchero y crema inglesa. Duermen por la noche, como todo el mundo, pero cuando despiertan en la oscuridad de una miserable habitación de hotel tienen un momento de incertidumbre: no recuerdan dónde están, ni qué día es, ni el nombre de la ciudad en que viven.

Carecer de raíces otorga a sus miradas un rasgo característico: una tonalidad celeste y acuosa, huidiza, la de alguien que en lugar de sustentarse firmemente en raíces adheridas al pasado y al territorio, flota en un espacio vago e impreciso.

Aunque algunos al nacer poseían unos filamentos nudosos que sin duda con el tiempo se convertirían en sólidas raíces, por alguna razón u otra las perdieron, les fueron sustraídas o amputadas, y este desgraciado hecho

TRANSLATED BY Sean Higgins

The Uprooted

BY CRISTINA PERI ROSSI

You see them frequently, walking down the streets in big cities, men and women floating on air, suspended in time and space. Their feet lack roots, and sometimes they even lack feet. Their hair doesn't have roots, nor do they have soft vines to tie their trunks to any type of ground. They are like algae propelled by the ocean currents and, when they finally attach themselves to any surface, it is by chance and only momentarily. They immediately begin to float again, and there is a certain nostalgia in it.

Their rootlessness confers upon them a unique, imprecise air, which is why they seem awkward everywhere and are not invited to parties or houses, because they appear to be suspect. It is true that, on the surface, they do the same things other humans do—they eat, sleep, walk and even die, but perhaps the careful observer might discover a slight and almost imperceptible difference in the way they eat, sleep, walk and die. They eat hamburgers at McDonald's or sandwiches at Pollo Pokins, be it in Berlin, Barcelona, or Montevideo. And what's even worse, they order outlandish dishes from ridiculous menus, made up of gazpacho, cioppino, and English cream. They sleep at night, just like the rest of the world, but when they wake up in the darkness of a miserable hotel room, they experience a moment of uncertainty—they don't recall where they are, nor what day it is, nor the name of the city they live in.

The absence of roots gives their glances a characteristic feature—a blue and watery tonality, evasive, like that of someone who, instead of acquiring strong nourishment from roots attached to the past and to the land, floats in space, vague and undefined.

Although at birth some of them had some knotty threads, which would have undoubtedly become solid roots with time, for some reason or other, they lost them, they were taken away from them or amputated, and this

los convierte en una especie de apestados. Pero en lugar de suscitar la conmiseración ajena, suelen despertar animadversión: se sospecha que son culpables de alguna oscura falta, el despojo (si lo hubo, porque podría tratarse de una carencia de nacimiento) los vuelve culpables.

Una vez que se han perdido, las raíces son irrecuperables. En vano el desarraigado permanece varias horas parado en la esquina, junto a un árbol, contemplando de soslayo esos largos apéndices que unen la planta con la tierra: las raíces no son contagiosas ni se adhieren a un cuerpo extraño. Otros piensan que permaneciendo mucho tiempo en la misma ciudad o país es posible que alguna vez le sean concedidas unas raíces postizas, unas raíces de plástico, por ejemplo, pero ninguna ciudad es tan generosa.

Sin embargo, hay desarraigados optimistas. Son los que procuran ver el lado bueno de las cosas y afirman que carecer de raíces proporciona gran libertad de movimientos, evita las dependencias incómodas y favorece los desplazamientos. En medio de su discurso, sopla un viento fuerte y desaparecen, tragados por el aire.

unfortunate circumstance turns them into a sort of victim of the plague. But instead of arousing compassion in others, they usually inspire hostility— they are suspected of being guilty of some obscure fault, the dispossession (if there was one, because it could be a matter of a deficiency from birth) implies their guilt.

Once they are lost, the roots are irretrievable. The exile stands in vain at a street corner, next to a tree, glancing sideways at those long appendages that unite the plant to the earth—the roots are not contagious, nor do they adhere to foreign bodies. Others think that if they stay long enough in the same city or country, someday they will be granted fake roots, some plastic roots, for example, but no city is that generous.

Nevertheless, there are optimistic exiles. They are the ones who attempt to see the good side of things and declare that lacking roots allows them great freedom of movement, it avoids uncomfortable dependencies and facilitates travel. In the midst of their speech, a strong wind blows, and they disappear, swallowed up by the air.

Atardecer en la playa

POR BÁRBARA JACOBS

La señorita Gálvez no tiene tiempo de pensar en la última vez que vio a su hermano el que murió ni de imaginar la última que verá al que está por morir, en cosa de meses. No tiene tiempo tampoco de ver el mar ahora que está en una terraza con vista a la playa, ni sabe si tendrá tiempo de recordar el barco que ve cuando ya no lo tenga enfrente. Ni mucho menos tiene tiempo de tratar de averiguar por qué, a veces y sin aviso, piensa en una carretera solitaria por la que va, con árboles y en invierno, como si saliera de una biblioteca y estuviera al lado de José, con quien se iba a casar pero que se fue, o se murió o la olvidó. Ni tiene tiempo de adivinar por qué sueña con gente que se fue como José, o que murió como José, si sabe que cuando ella estuvo con ellos no pensó más en ellos de lo que cualquiera pensaría. No tiene tiempo de hacer caso a los recuerdos que llaman de pronto a su memoria; los rostros, las palabras de la gente a la que quiere. Ni tiempo de detenerse a imaginar qué están haciendo esas gentes a las que quiere, si se encontraron al fin con quien se iban a encontrar, si les fue bien o si están tristes. La señorita Gálvez no tiene tiempo porque no quiere saber más de la cuenta, ni llorar más de la cuenta, ni imaginar lo que la cuenta no quiere que imagine. Ese barco es la vida que va pasando, y ella también está muriendo, y va siendo olvidada por la gente, hecha a un lado, como recuerdo, en favor de la brisa que hay que sentir, el libro que hay que leer, la gente a la que hay que oír porque está aquí, ahora, y el presente es lo único que tienes.

TRANSLATED BY Susan Ouriou

A ship's passing

BY BÁRBARA JACOBS

Miss Gálvez doesn't have time to think about the last time she saw her brother, the one who died, or to imagine a few months ahead to the last time she'll see the one who's dying. Neither does she have time to gaze at the sea now that she's on a terrace overlooking the beach; nor does she know if she'll have time to remember the ship she sees once it's no longer in front of her. Nor does she have anything like the time to try to find out why sometimes without warning she conjures up a winter's scene of a deserted, tree-lined road down which she walks, as though she were leaving the library with José, who she was supposed to marry but then he left, or he died, or he forgot her. Neither does she have time to wonder why she dreams about people who left like José, or who died like José, knowing that when she was with them she didn't give them much more thought than anyone else would. She doesn't have time to heed the sudden memories that call to her; the faces and words of the people she loves. Nor time to pause and imagine what those people she loves are doing, whether they finally met the person they set out to find, whether it turned out well or whether they're unhappy. Miss Gálvez doesn't have time because she doesn't want to know more than her share, or cry more than her share, or imagine what her share wasn't meant to include. The ship she sees is life passing by, and she too is dying and will be forgotten by others, set aside, like a memory, replaced by the breeze that has to be felt, the book that has to be read, the people who have to be listened to because they are here, now, and the present is all that you have.

vestir una sombra

POR JULIO CORTÁZAR

Lo más difícil es cercarla, conocer su límite allí donde se enlaza con la penumbra al borde de sí misma. Escogerla entre tantas otras, apartarla de la luz que toda sombra respira sigilosa, peligrosamente. Empezar entonces a vestirla como distraído, sin moverse demasiado, sin asustarla o disolverla: operación inicial donde la nada se agazapa en cada gesto. La ropa interior, el transparente corpiño, las medias que dibujan un ascenso sedoso hacia los muslos. Todo lo consentirá en su momentánea ignorancia, como si todavía creyera estar jugando con otra sombra, pero bruscamente se inquietará cuando la falda ciña su cintura y sienta los dedos que abotonan la blusa entre los senos, rozando la garganta que se alza hasta perderse en un oscuro surtidor. Rechazará el gesto de coronarla con la peluca de flotante pelo rubio (¡ese halo tembloroso rodeando un rostro inexistente!) y habrá que apresurarse a dibujar la boca con la brasa del cigarrillo, deslizar sortijas y pulseras para darle esas manos con que resistirá inciertamente mientras los labios apenas nacidos murmuran el plañido inmemorial de quien despierta al mundo. Faltarán los ojos, que han de brotar de las lágrimas, la sombra por sí misma completándose para mejor luchar, para negarse. Inútilmente conmovedora cuando el mismo impulso que la vistió, la misma sed de verla asomar perfecta del confuso espacio, la envuelva en su juncal de caricias, comience a desnudarla, a descubrir, por primera vez su forma que vanamente busca cobijarse tras manos y súplicas, cediendo lentamente a la caída entre un brillar de anillos que rasgan en el aire sus luciérnagas húmedas.

TRANSLATED BY Thomas Christensen

TO Dress a Shadow

BY JULIO CORTÁZAR

The hardest thing is to surround it, to fix its limit where it fades into the penumbra along its edge. To choose it from among the others, to separate it from the light that all shadows secretly, dangerously, breathe. To begin to dress it casually, not moving too much, not frightening or dissolving it: this is the initial operation where nothingness lies in every move. The inner garments, the transparent corset, the stockings that compose a silky ascent up the thighs. To all these it will consent in momentary ignorance, as if imagining it is playing with another shadow, but suddenly it will become troubled, when the skirt girds its waist and it feels the fingers that button the blouse between its breasts, brushing the neck that rises to disappear in dark flowing water. It will repulse the gesture that seeks to crown it with a long blonde wig (that trembling halo around a nonexistent face!) and you must work quickly to draw its mouth with cigarette embers, slip on the rings and bracelets that will define its hands, as it indecisively resists, its newborn lips murmuring the immemorial lament of one awakening to the world. It will need eyes, which must be made from tears, the shadow completing itself to better resist and negate itself. Hopeless excitement when the same impulse that dressed it, the same thirst that saw it take shape from confused space, to envelop it in a thicket of caresses, begins to undress it, to discover for the first time the shape it vainly strives to conceal with hands and supplications, slowly yielding, to fall with a flash of rings that fills the night with glittering fireflies.

RHYTHM

137

de Rayuela

POR JULIO CORTÁZAR

Sí, pero quién nos curará del fuego sordo, del fuego sin color que corre al anochecer por la rue de la Huchette, saliendo de los portales carcomidos, de los parvos zaguanes, del fuego sin imagen que lame las piedras y acecha en los vanos de las puertas, cómo haremos para lavarnos de su quemadura dulce que prosigue, que se aposenta para durar aliada al tiempo y al recuerdo, a las sustancias pegajosas que nos retienen de este lado, y que nos arderá dulcemente hasta calcinarnos. Entonces es mejor pactar como los gatos y los musgos, trabar amistad inmediata con las porteras de roncas voces, con las criaturas pálidas y sufrientes que acechan en las ventanas jugando con una rama seca. Ardiendo así sin tregua, soportando la quemadura central que avanza como la madurez paulatina en el fruto, ser el pulso de una hoguera en esta maraña de piedra interminable, caminar por las noches de nuestra vida con la obediencia de la sangre en su circuito ciego.

Cuántas veces me pregunto si esto no es más que escritura, en un tiempo en que corremos al engaño entre ecuaciones infalibles y máquinas de conformismos. Pero preguntarse si sabremos encontrar el otro lado de la costumbre o si más vale dejarse llevar por su alegre cibernética, ¿no será otra vez literatura? Rebelión, conformismo, angustia, alimentos terrestres, todas las dicotomías: el Yin y el Yang, la contemplación o la *Tätigkeit,* avena arrollada o perdices *faisandées,* Lascaux o Mathieu, qué hamaca de palabras, qué dialéctica de bolsillo con tormentas en piyama y cataclismos de living room. El solo hecho de interrogarse sobre la posible elección vicia y enturbia lo elegible. *Que sí, que no, que en ésta está...* Parecería que una elección no

TRANSLATED BY **Gregory Rabassa**

from Hopscotch

BY JULIO CORTÁZAR

Yes, but who will cure us of the dull fire, the colorless fire that at nightfall runs along the Rue de la Huchette, emerging from the crumbling doorways, from the little entranceways, of the imageless fire that licks the stones and lies in wait in the doorways, how shall we cleanse ourselves of the sweet burning that comes after, that nests in us forever allied with time and memory, with sticky things that hold us here on this side, and which will burn sweetly in us until we have been left in ashes. How much better, then, to make a pact with cats and mosses, strike up a friendship right away with hoarse-voiced concierges, with pale and suffering creatures who wait in windows and toy with a dry branch. To burn like this without surcease, to bear the inner burning coming on like fruit's quick ripening, to be the pulse of a bonfire in this thicket of endless stone, walking through the nights of our life, obedient as our blood in its blind circuit.

How often I wonder whether this is only writing, in an age in which we run towards deception through infallible equations and conformity machines. But to ask one's self if we will know how to find the other side of habit or if it is better to let one's self be borne along by its happy cybernetics, is that not literature again? Rebellion, conformity, anguish, earthly sustenance, all the dichotomies: the Yin and the Yang, contemplation or the *Tätigkeit*, oatmeal or partridge *faisandée,* Lascaux or Mathieu, what a hammock of words, what purse-size dialectics with pajama storms and living-room cataclysms. The very fact that one asks one's self about the possible choice vitiates and muddies up what can be chosen. *Que sí, que no, que en ésta ésta ...* It would seem that a

puede ser dialéctica, que su planteo la empobrece, es decir la falsea, es decir la transforma en otra cosa. Entre el Yin y el Yang, ¿cuántos eones? Del sí al no, ¿cuántos quizá? Todo es escritura, es decir fábula. ¿Pero de qué nos sirve la verdad que tranquiliza al propietario honesto? Nuestra verdad posible tiene que ser *invención,* es decir escritura, literatura, pintura, escultura, agricultura, piscicultura, todas las turas de este mundo. Los valores, turas, la santidad, una tura, la sociedad, una tura, el amor, pura tura, la belleza, tura de turas. En uno de sus libros, Morelli habla del napolitano que se pasó años sentado a la puerta de su casa mirando un tornillo en el suelo. Por la noche lo juntaba y lo ponía debajo del colchón. El tornillo fue primero risa, tomada de pelo, irritación comunal, junta de vecinos, signo de violación de los deberes cívicos, finalmente encogimiento de hombros, la paz, el tornillo fue la paz, nadie podía pasar por la calle sin mirar de reojo el tornillo y sentir que era la paz. El tipo murió de un síncope, y el tornillo desapareció apenas acudieron los vecinos. Uno de ellos lo guarda, quizá lo saca en secreto y lo mira, vuelve a guardarlo y se va a la fábrica sintiendo algo que no comprende, una oscura reprobación. Sólo se calma cuando saca el tornillo y lo mira, se queda mirándolo hasta que oye pasos y tiene que guardarlo presuroso. Morelli pensaba que el tornillo debía ser otra cosa, un dios o algo así. Solución demasiado fácil. Quizá el error estuviera en aceptar que ese objeto era un tornillo por el hecho de que tenía la forma de un tornillo. Picasso toma un auto de juguete y lo convierte en el mentón de un cinocéfalo. A lo mejor el napolitano era un idiota pero también pudo ser el inventor de un mundo. Del tornillo a un ojo, de un ojo a una estrella... ¿Por qué entregarse a la Gran Costumbre? Se puede elegir la tura, la invención, es decir el tornillo o el auto de juguete. Así es como París nos destruye despacio, deliciosamente, triturándonos entre flores viejas y manteles de papel con manchas de vino, con su fuego sin color que corre al anochecer saliendo de los portales carcomidos. Nos arde un fuego inventado, una incandescente tura, un artilugio de la raza, una ciudad que es el Gran Tornillo, la horrible aguja con su ojo nocturno por donde corre el hilo del Sena, máquina de torturas como puntillas, agonía en una jaula atestada de

choice cannot be dialectical, that the fact of bringing it up impoverishes it, that is to say, falsifies it, that is to say, transforms it into something else. How many eons between the Yin and the Yang? How many, perhaps, between yes and no? Everything is writing, that is to say, a fable. But what good can we get from the truth that pacifies an honest property owner? Our possible truth must be an *invention,* that is to say, scripture, literature, picture, sculpture, agriculture, pisciculture, all the tures in this world. Values, tures, sainthood, a ture, society, a ture, love, pure ture, beauty, a ture of tures. In one of his books, a Morelli talks about a Neapolitan who spent years sitting in the doorway of his house looking at a screw on the ground. At night he would gather it up and put it under his mattress. The screw was at first a laugh, a jest, communal irritation, a neighborhood council, a mark of civic duties unfulfilled, finally a shrugging of shoulders, peace, the screw was peace, no one could go along the street without looking out of the corner of his eye at the screw and feeling that it was peace. The fellow dropped dead of a stroke and the screw disappeared as soon as the neighbors got there. One of them has it; perhaps, he takes it out secretly and looks at it, puts it away again and goes off to the factory feeling something that he does not understand, an obscure reproval. He only calms down when he takes out the screw and looks at it, stays looking at it until he hears footsteps and has to put it away quickly. Morelli thought that the screw must have been something else, a god or something like that. Too easy a solution. Perhaps the error was in accepting the fact that the object was a screw simply because it was shaped like a screw. Picasso takes a toy car and turns it into the chin of a baboon. The Neapolitan was most likely an idiot, but he also might have been the inventor of a world. From the screw to an eye, from an eye to a star ...Why surrender to Great Habit? One can choose his ture, his invention, that is to say, the screw or the toy car. That is how Paris destroys us slowly, delightfully, tearing us apart among old flowers and paper tablecloths stained with wine, with its colorless fire that comes running out of crumbling doorways at nightfall. An invented fire burns in us, an incandescent ture, a whatsis of the race, a city that is the Great Screw, the horrible needle with its

golondrinas enfurecidas. Ardemos en nuestra obra, fabuloso honor mortal, alto desafío del fénix. Nadie nos curará del fuego sordo, del fuego sin color que corre al anochecer por la rue de la Huchette. Incurables, perfectamente incurables, elegimos por tura el Gran Tornillo, nos inclinamos sobre él, entramos en él, volvemos a inventarlo cada día, a cada mancha de vino en el mantel, a cada beso del moho en las madrugadas de la Cour de Rohan, inventamos nuestro incendio, ardemos de dentro afuera, quizá eso sea la elección, quizá las palabras envuelvan esto como la servilleta el pan y dentro esté la fragancia, la harina esponjándose, el sí sin el no, o el no sin el sí, el día sin Manes, sin Ormuz *o* Arimán, de una vez por todas y en paz y basta.

night eye through which the Seine thread runs, a torture machine like a board of nails, agony in a cage crowded with infuriated swallows. We burn within our work, fabulous mortal honor, high challenge of the phoenix. No one will cure us of the dull fire, the colorless fire that at nightfall runs along the Rue de la Huchette. Incurable, perfectly incurable, we select the Great Screw as a ture, we lean towards it, we enter it, we invent it again every day, with every wine-stain on the tablecloth, with every kiss of mold in the dawns of the Cour de Rohan, we invent our conflagration, we burn outwardly from within, maybe that is the choice, maybe words envelop it the way a napkin does a loaf of bread and maybe the fragrance is inside, the flour puffing up, the yes without the no, or the no without the yes, the day without manes, without Ormuz *or* Ariman, once and for all and in peace and enough.

continuidad de los parques

POR JULIO CORTÁZAR

Había empezado a leer la novela unos días antes. La abandonó por negocios urgentes, volvió a abrirla cuando regresaba en tren a la finca; se dejaba interesar lentamente por la trama, por el dibujo de los personajes. Esa tarde, después de escribir una carta a su apoderado y discutir con el mayordomo una cuestión de aparcerías volvió al libro en la tranquilidad del estudio que miraba hacia el parque de los robles. Arrellanado en su sillón favorito de espaldas a la puerta que lo hubiera molestado como una irritante posibilidad de intrusiones, dejó que su mano izquierda acariciara una y otra vez el terciopelo verde y se puso a leer los últimos capítulos. Su memoria retenía sin esfuerzo los nombres y las imágenes de los protagonistas; la ilusión novelesca lo ganó casi en seguida. Gozaba del placer casi perverso de irse desgajando línea a línea de lo que lo rodeaba, y sentir a la vez que su cabeza descansaba cómodamente en el terciopelo del alto respaldo, que los cigarrillos seguían al alcance de la mano, que más allá de los ventanales danzaba el aire del atardecer bajo los robles. Palabra a palabra, absorbido por la sórdida disyuntiva de los héroes, dejándose ir hacia las imágenes que se concertaban y adquirían color y movimiento, fue testigo del último encuentro en la cabaña del monte. Primero entraba la mujer, recelosa; ahora llegaba el amante, lastimada la cara por el chicotazo de una rama. Admirablemente restañaba ella la sangre con sus besos, pero él rechazaba las caricias, no había venido para repetir las ceremonias de una pasión secreta, protegida por un mundo de hojas secas y senderos furtivos. El puñal se entibiaba contra su pecho, y debajo latía la libertad agazapada. Un diálogo anhelante corría por las páginas como un arroyo de serpientes, y se sentía que todo estaba decidido desde siempre. Hasta esas caricias que enredaban el cuerpo del amante como queriendo retenerlo y disuadirlo, dibujaban abominablemente la figura de

continuity of parks

BY JULIO CORTÁZAR

He had begun to read the novel a few days before. He had put it down because of some urgent business conferences, opened it again on his way back to the estate by train; he permitted himself a slowly growing interest in the plot, in the characterizations. That afternoon, after writing a letter giving his power of attorney and discussing a matter of joint ownership with the manager of his estate, he returned to the book in the tranquility of his study which looked out upon the park with its oaks. Sprawled in his favorite armchair, its back toward the door—even the possibility of an intrusion would have irritated him, he had thought of it—he let his left hand caress repeatedly the green velvet upholstery and set to reading the final chapters. He remembered effortlessly the names and his mental image of the characters; the novel spread its glamour over him almost at once. He tasted the almost perverse pleasure of disengaging himself line by line from the things around him, and at the same time feeling his head rest comfortably on the green velvet of the chair with its high back, sensing that the cigarettes rested within reach of his hand, that beyond the great windows the air of afternoon danced under the oak trees in the park. Word by word, licked up by the sordid dilemma of the hero and heroine, letting himself be absorbed to the point where the images settled down and took on color and movement, he was witness to the final encounter in the mountain cabin. The woman arrived first, apprehensive; now the lover came in, his face cut by the backlash of a branch. Admirably, she stanched the blood with her kisses, but he rebuffed her caresses, he had not come to perform again the ceremonies of a secret passion, protected by a world of dry leaves and furtive paths through the forest. The dagger warmed itself against his chest and underneath liberty pounded, hidden close. A lustful, panting dialogue raced down the pages like a rivulet of snakes, and one felt it had all been decided from eternity. Even to

otro cuerpo que era necesario destruir. Nada había sido olvidado: coartadas, azares, posibles errores. A partir de esa hora cada instante tenía su empleo minuciosamente atribuido. El doble repaso despiadado se interrumpía apenas para que una mano acariciara una mejilla. Empezaba a anochecer.

Sin mirarse ya, atados rígidamente a la tarea que los esperaba, se separaron en la puerta de la cabaña. Ella debía seguir por la senda que iba al norte. Desde la senda opuesta él se volvió un instante para verla correr con el pelo suelto. Corrió a su vez, parapetándose en los árboles y los setos, hasta distinguir en la bruma malva del crepúsculo la alameda que llevaba a la casa. Los perros no debían ladrar, y no ladraron. El mayordomo no estaría a esa hora, y no estaba. Subió los tres peldaños del porche y entró. Desde la sangre galopando en sus oídos le llegaban las palabras de la mujer: primero una sala azul, después una galería, una escalera alfombrada. En lo alto, dos puertas. Nadie en la primera habitación, nadie en la segunda. La puerta del salón, y entonces el puñal en la mano, la luz de los ventanales, el alto respaldo de un sillón de terciopelo verde, la cabeza del hombre en el sillón leyendo una novela.

those caresses which writhed about the lover's body, as though wishing to keep him there, to dissuade him from it; they sketched abominably the frame of that other body it was necessary to destroy. Nothing had been forgotten: alibis, unforeseen hazards, possible mistakes. From this hour on, each instant had its use minutely assigned. The cold-blooded, twice-gone-over reexamination of the details was barely broken off so that a hand could caress a cheek. It was beginning to get dark.

Not looking at one another now, rigidly fixed upon the task which awaited them, they separated at the cabin door. She was to follow the trail that led north. On the path leading in the opposite direction, he turned for a moment to watch her running, her hair loosened and flying. He ran in turn, crouching among the trees and hedges until, in the yellowish fog of dusk, he could distinguish the avenue of trees which led up to the house. The dogs were not supposed to bark, they did not bark. The estate manager would not be there at this hour, he was not there. He went up the three porch steps and entered. The woman's words reached him over the thudding of blood in his ears: first a blue chamber, then a hall, then a carpeted stairway. At the top, two doors. No one in the first room, no one in the second. The door of the salon, and then, the knife in hand, the light from the great windows, the high back of an armchair covered in green velvet, the head of the man in the chair reading a novel.

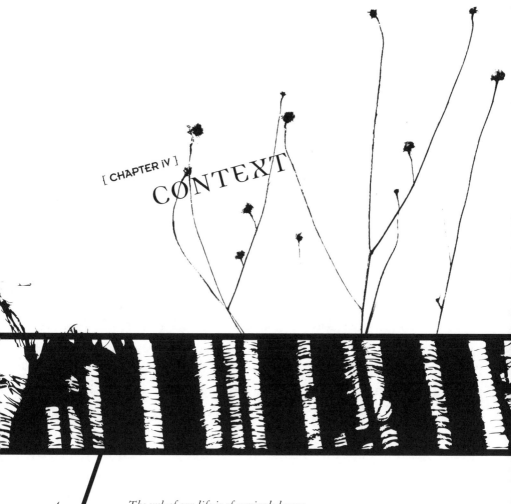

[CHAPTER iV]

CONTEXT

The web of our life is of a mingled yarn.

—SHAKESPEARE
All's Well That Ends Well

Maya weavers are among the world's most accomplished, producing brightly colored textiles adorned with diamonds, triangles, spirals, sunbursts, and other patterns. But those patterns are not just decorations—to those who know how to read them they are signs that, put together, compose stories. Weaving and storytelling have a long association, one that appears in our word *text*, which is related to the word *textile* through a source word that meant "something woven."

A text is a thing that is woven of many elements, and it is also part of a net of broader relations connecting with the traditions of the culture in which it is produced, as well as with all the particulars of its place of origin. The translator must address not just the knotted node of the text itself but also the wider net of which that node is a part. If a *text* is a woven thing, the addition of the prefix *con-* ("together") to form the word *context con*nects the text with the broader, mingled yarn of life. We must translate not just the text but also the context.

How can this be done? Consider the case of Du Fu, who has been hailed as the greatest of the poets of China's Tang dynasty. Despite his reputation, Du Fu's work is less available in English than that of his equally fine contemporary Li Bo. I think this is in large part because Du Fu's work is more allusive. The cultural references of the poems are so extensive that one almost needs an education in medieval Chinese culture to make them fully comprehensible. Translations by Kenneth Rexroth and Burton Watson exemplify two approaches to this problem. Rexroth, in *One Hundred Poems from the Chinese,* offers a free translation in which the allusions are mostly omitted. Watson, in *The Selected Poems of Du Fu,* combines translations with extensive annotations.

It is not just allusions or intertextual connections that pose problems for the translator. Regionalisms, the specifics of place, can also be thorny.

I worked on one project where the editors were so concerned that the text not seem foreign that they insisted there should be no foreign words whatsoever—a *metate* should be called a grinding stone, a *comal* should be called a griddle, and so on. As these examples suggest, the text concerned cooking, and it seemed odd to eliminate the text's distinctive flavor and substitute something generic. The editors finally relented, but their concern suggests the anxiety in the U.S. marketplace about challenging readers with foreign terms and concepts.

In the United Kingdom, by the way, the first edition of *Like Water for Chocolate* was titled *Like Water for Hot Chocolate*—which makes the title more comprehensible but tempers the passion. Another attempt at recontextualizing a source text is cited with approval by George Steiner in his *After Babel*. It comes from Christopher Logue's 1967 translation of Homer's *Iliad:*

> The chariot's basket dips.
> The whip fires in between the horses' ears,
> and as in dreams or at Cape Kennedy they rise,
> slowly it seems, their chests like royals, yet
> behind them in a double plume the sand curls up ...

For Steiner, the comparison of horses rising up to spaceships launching is "perfectly appropriate." (I find it intrusive.) We will address this issue further in the next section, on the role of the translator as a figure implicit (or complicit) in the text.

Bruce Berger's translation of Estela Davis's "A Rosary for Raquel" confronts the issue of regionalism. The author, a resident of Baja California, has sought to capture the flavor of her native place. It was important to her and to the translator that the speech and behavior of the characters be true to the region. Berger describes how he tested the original work for authenticity with a local rancher, who read the book aloud to his illiterate father. The family affirmed that Davis "writes like we speak." To stay true to this authenticity in English translation, Berger worked closely with the author and her English-

speaking son. The result is a translation in which regional considerations are paramount. The colloquial English Berger uses matches the countrified language of the narrator and characters.

The subject of "A Baroque Cell," by David Huerta, is the sixteenth–seventeenth-century Spanish poet Luis de Góngora, who is well known in the Spanish-language literary context but may be only a vague figure to many English readers. Yet one can get a sense of the poet's baroque style (which gave rise to the term *Gongorism*) with its "luscious language and feverish acrobatics of thought," in the words of translator Mark Schafer, who has so well captured the spirit of the poem.

In *The End of Madness* the Mexican novelist Jorge Volpi incorporates, in the words of his translator, Suzanne Jill Levine, "caricatures of such consecrated figures as Jacques Lacan, Louis Althusser, Roland Barthes, and even Fidel Castro. In this excerpt, Volpi focuses on Lacan, a hero of young radicals for his writings that combine philosophy and structuralist social science with psychoanalysis. As satire and brainy critique, Volpi's novel certainly demythifies the era: maybe this book indeed pretends to be its teleological end as well as laying a lapida upon the revolutionary utopian dream." Without some sense of the avant-garde intellectual milieu in which the book is set the reader will miss much of its wit and thrust.

Fernando del Paso's *Palinuro of Mexico* is an intensively allusive novel. The title, to begin with, alludes to Palinurus, the boatman in Virgil's *Aeneid* who falls victim to the god of sleep, and the book takes us through a Mexican Nighttown as it tells the story of two cousins who are medical students. With his cascade of allusions, the author—who has described himself as "a baroque writer, extravagant and immoderate"—presents an enormous challenge to the translator. In the selection here, scores of references appear to British painting and culture, the geographies of London and Mexico City, and much more; each of these must be referenced precisely with their correct English names, and this can be a painstaking task. In addition, the English text must

take its place among the heirs of Joyce, since any English-language reader will be aware of that antecedent. Happily, the translator, Elisabeth Plaister, is up to the challenge.

un rosario para raquel

POR Estela Davis

Sólo dos velas están
quemando un poco de sombra;
para tu pequeña muerte
con dos velas sobra.

—Nicolás Guillén

Estuvo tan chistoso el velorio de Raquel que la gente no tuvo más oficio que estarse riendo. Hubo quienes hasta se orinaron de la risa. A mí se me hace muy curioso porque toda la vida no oí otra cosa, que la pobre de Raquel para allá, que la pobre de Raquel para acá. La pobre nunca se casó, "por pendeja," decía la gente, y siguió viviendo con Marina, su hermana, cuando ésta se casó, muy bien por cierto. Al modo de la gente que en todo está, decían que dizque Marina era muy mala con Raquel, y sí ha de haber sido porque era como la criada de la casa, la que hacía todo el quehacer, y pobre de ella que no lo hiciera bien.

Marina le ponía unas maltratadas, hasta delante de la gente la regañaba como a una chiquita. No le importaba, y enfrente de ellas les decía a las amigas:

—Está de remate la lela de Raquel, no se pide más que en sus narices se encaraman las gallinas al metate, le pisotean y picotean las masas y ella no es para espantarlas.

—¡Se te están quemando los frijoles, burra!, ¿no te das cuenta? ¡Estás de remate de suata!

—No sé qué querencia tiene con los animales, que toda la vida los tiene embutidos en la cocina. Con seguridad que ahí mismo les avienta la comida, por eso. Mira, nomás entro yo a la cocina y salen a la carrera perros, cochis y gallinas, ¡Ay, si a veces me dan ganas de moquetearla, la malvada suata!

—¡Ay, pobre de ti, Marina! ¡Cómo batallas!

Raquel nomás oía, con una sonrisita como de culpa. Para que más que

A Rosary for Raquel

BY ESTELA DAVIS

Only two candles
Are burning a bit of shade;
For your tiny death
Two candles are enough.

—NICOLÁS GUILLÉN

The wake for Raquel was so hilarious that all people could do was laugh. Some laughed so hard they peed. What struck me so peculiar was that all my life I had heard the opposite: it was poor Raquel this, poor Raquel that. People said she didn't have the smarts to get married and she kept living with her sister Marina when Marina did marry—and married well. Busybodies claimed that Marina was really hard on Raquel, and it must have been true, for she became the maid, had to do all the housework, and woe unto her if she didn't do it right.

Marina treated her so badly that she even scolded her like a little girl in front of others. She was shameless about it, and when friends were in the house, you could hear:

"Raquel is so surpassingly dumb that as soon as the chickens sniff something, they jump up to the *metate* and peck and kick their way through the dough and Raquel does nothing to shoo them off."

"You're burning the beans, numbskull. Can't you tell? You're hopeless!"

"I don't understand this fascination with animals, but all her life they've been installed in the kitchen. Of course, that is where she throws them food. As soon as I set foot in the kitchen, dogs, pigs, and chickens go running off. Sometimes I feel like punching the nincompoop."

"Oh, poor you, Marina! How you struggle!"

Raquel merely listened with a guilty little smile. To tell the truth, she loved

la verdad, le encantaba andar en la cocina maneándose con el animalero. Le gustaban a la pobre, pues, y platicaba mucho con ellos.

Al principio la gente hablaba mucho de Marina, por lo mañosa y mala que era con Raquel, pero con el tiempo se fueron acostumbrando, hasta que se les olvidó que eran hermanas y ya nadie la tomaba en cuenta, ni le hacían caso. A mí se me figura que ha de haber sido muy buena gente. Yo me acuerdo que cuando iba a algún mandado a su casa siempre la veía traficando en la cocina, gorda y pachorruda, pero eso sí, atizando en las hornillas, haciendo tortillas o tostando café. Me gustaba mucho ir para allá porque a la salidita de la cocina había un hueco en el suelo, donde vivía un cangrejo negro y gordote, ¡grandísimo! Cuando salía, Raquel le daba comidita y le hablaba como si hubiera sido un chamaquito. El cangrejo daba unas vueltecitas y se volvía a meter a su agujero. Luego, para que lo viéramos los chamacos que íbamos, ella lo llamaba con una voz muy ladinita: "¡venga mi bonito, venga mi bonito!" Parece como modo de mentira, pero el canijo cangrejo salía y la seguía. Yo nomás lo miraba de lejecitos porque me daba miedo, parecía tarántula.

Cuando me acuerdo de Raquel pienso que lo más divertido que le pasó fue su velorio. Porque a lo que decía la gente, la pobre no tuvo más que sufrimientos en la vida y lo que son las cosas, se murió viejita. Sabrá Dios cuántos años tendría, ni siquiera sé si tendría apellido; yo siempre oí que la mentaban como Raquel nomás. Otra cosa de la que siempre me acuerdo muy bien, es que cuando nos contaban el cuento de La Cenicienta, Raquel se me venía a la cabeza. Ha de haber sido por tantos mitotes que escuchaba de la hermana mala y por la cocina donde siempre la veía, que estaba negra de tizne de las paredes y el techo, a lo mejor por eso era tan prieta. Porque Marina, su hermana, era muy blanca, altota, gruesa y muy panda, tenía el pelo canoso y se peinaba de molote con peinetas. Siempre andaba vestida de negro, con mangas largas y le resaltaban las manos blancas y lisitas.

Cuando se murió la pobre de Raquel hacía un calor de los mil demonios. La tendieron en un catre de lona, tapado con una sábana muy blanca de las que ella misma lavaba, tendía al sol y añilaba para que no se percudieran. Abrieron las ventanas y las puertas para que corriera el aire fresco y no se fuera a echar a perder el cuerpo. El velorio fue en la sala, como correspondía a la categoría de

to go around the kitchen with her menagerie. It pleased the poor girl and gave her someone to talk to.

At first people gossiped a lot about Marina and how sharp and nasty she was to Raquel, but then people got so used to it that they even forgot the two were sisters, stopped paying attention, and didn't notice it. I think Raquel must have been a good person. I remember that whenever I went to the house on some errand, she was always slaving away in the kitchen, fat and slow, but faithfully stirring the oven coals, making tortillas or toasting coffee. I loved to go there because on the way out of the kitchen there was a hole with an enormous black crab. I mean huge! When it came out, Raquel fed it and talked to it like it was a child. The crab would walk around a bit and then go back in its hole. Later, so that we kids could see it, she called in a squeaky baby voice, "Come, my pretty! Come, my pretty!" It sounds like I'm making this up, but the damned crab would come out and follow her. I watched from a little way off because it looked so much like a tarantula that it scared me.

When I think of Raquel, I think that the most entertaining thing that ever happened to her was her wake. From what people said, the poor woman only suffered in life, and as such things go, she died old. Only God knew her actual age, or if she had a last name; I always just called her Raquel. Another thing I remember well is that when anyone told us the story of Cinderella, Raquel always came to mind. It must have been because of all the stories we heard about her evil sister and because we always saw her in the kitchen, where she was black with soot from the walls and ceiling. That's probably why she always looked so dark. Her sister Marina, on the other hand, was very white and tall and hefty with a military posture, and pulled her graying hair back into a bun she fixed with little combs. She always went around dressed in black, with long sleeves that made her hands look white and extremely smooth.

It was hotter than Hades when poor Raquel died. They stretched her out on a canvas cot and covered her with a very white sheet that she herself had washed, hung in the sun and blued so it wouldn't get dingy. They opened the windows and doors to let in the breeze and keep the body from spoiling. The wake was in the living room, as befitted Marina's station. They placed four candles, one at each corner of the cot, in very pretty standing candleholders lent by the

Marina. Le acomodaron cuatro cirios, uno en cada esquina del catre, en unos candelabros de pie muy bonitos que les prestaron en la iglesia, porque el padre y las monjitas adoraban a Marina por ser muy católica. Le pusieron unos ramos de buganvilia morada con mucha tela de alambre y unas coronas de flores de papel crepé. La vistieron con un vestido negro con cuellito de encaje blanco que era de Marina, y como le quedaba chico no se lo abrocharon por detrás. De todos modos, como estaba tendida no se le notaba, toda la gente dijo que se veía muy elegante. Luego la polvearon, le pintaron chapitas, y al modo viejo, no faltó quien criticara, porque Raquel no se había polveado ni chapeado nunca en su vida. Una señora muy mañosa que se estaba secreteando con otra dijo, "¿qué se le hará a Raquel estar muy sí señora en la sala de Marina?"

Por cierto, ¡cómo batallaron para acomodarle las manos! Como las tenía gorditas y había padecido muchas reumas, no le podían cruzar los dedos y se las tuvieron que amarrar con un trapito blanco y limpiecito para que no se le resbalaran del estómago, que se le hinchó mucho, cosa que fue muy comentada en el velorio. Se me figura que como la gente ni se fijaba en Raquel, no se había dado cuenta que siempre fue muy estomaguda, y ahí estaban opine y opine. Unas decían que porque a lo mejor tenía un tumor en el vientre, otras que era pura gordura, otras que a lo mejor tenía hidropesía. Suerte que ya era muy vieja para que le achacaran que estaba embarazada; el caso es que no se les entendía. De todos modos nadie supo de qué se murió. A lo mejor fue adrede, porque de un ataque no fue. La encontraron en la cocina, sentadita en una silla de soyate, tranquilita, como recostada de lado de la pared. Eso sí, dicen que estaba toda tiznada de la cara, de los brazos y de las manos y que la tuvieron que limpiar bien con un trapito enjabonado. La cabeza no se la lavaron, pues a pesar de ser tan vieja no tenía una sola cana y no se le notaba lo tiznado del pelo.

Como sucede, pues, mucha gente se acordó de Marina y fueron llegando al velorio: "te acompaño en tus sentimientos... te acompaño en tus sentimientos... te acompaño en tus sentimientos," le decían. Ella los abrazaba y lloraba recio, recio. Siempre se desmayó como tres veces, a lo mejor porque ya no iba a tener quien le hiciera el quehacer. También había señores, y un montón de chamacos, dando una guerra... A tal grado que las mamás a cada rato los sacaban para moquetearlos y que se pusieran en juicio.

church, for the *padre* and the nuns loved Marina for being very Catholic. They made chickenwire arrangements of purple bougainvillea branches and crowns of papier-mâché flowers. They dressed her in a black dress of Marina's with a white lace collar, and because it was too small for her, they didn't fasten it in back. Anyway, the way she was laid out, no one could tell and everyone said she looked very elegant. Then they powdered her, rouged her in the old style, and naturally there were some critics because she had never powdered or rouged herself in her life. One sharp-tongued woman secretly said to another, "Will they really let Raquel play such a lady in Marina's living room?"

What a struggle to arrange her hands! Because they were swollen from all the rheumatism she suffered, they couldn't be laced together with her fingers and had to be bound with a strip of clean white cloth so they wouldn't fall off her stomach, which was itself pretty swollen—a circumstance much commented on at the wake. I figured that people had never really focused on Raquel, for she'd always had a large stomach, but there were plenty of opinions. Some said she probably had an intestinal tumor, others that it was pure fat, and still others that it was dropsy. It was lucky she was too old to be accused of being pregnant, but the truth was that nobody could figure it out. For one thing, no one knew what she died of. She probably just wanted to go, for there was no heart attack. They found her in the kitchen sitting in a wicker chair, totally calm, leaning against the wall. They did say her face and arms and hands were all sooted and they had to scrub them hard with a soaped rag. They didn't bother washing her hair because at her age it was gray anyway and no one would notice the grime.

Of course many people considered Marina and went to the wake: "My sympathy is with you.... My sympathy is with you.... My sympathy is with you...." She embraced them and wept buckets, and I mean buckets. She fainted at least three times, probably because now she didn't have anyone to do the housework. There were also men and a whole bunch of kids making such war that every now and then the mothers had to take them out and slap them to restore order.

Two friends of Raquel's—crazy Nicho, who shouldered water on a pole to the washtub and the kitchen, and Toño the deaf-mute, who raked the yard and threw out the garbage—certainly they couldn't miss the wake. The two had been the way they were since birth. Raquel loved them and

No podían faltar en el velorio dos buenos amigos de Raquel, Nicho el loco, que le acarreaba agua en una palanca para el lavadero y la cocina, y Toño el sordomudo, que le rastrillaba el solar y le tiraba la basura. Los dos eran así de nacimiento, Raquel los consecuentaba porque los quería mucho, les daba taquitos de frijol y café; eso sí, a escondidas de Marina, que dicen que era muy miserable para la comida. Nicho y Toño eran unos personajes muy vagos y muy lisos, de modo que siempre le andaban llevando mitotes a Raquel, que se entretenía muchísimo con ellos.

Cuando avisaron que se iba a rezar el rosario, Toño el mudo se fue a hincar en primera fila junto a la doña que lo iba a dirigir. Por cierto que esta doña era muy solicitada para estos menesteres, que porque se sabía las letanías al revés y al derecho y porque tenía la voz clarita y muy fuerte, de modo que todos le entendían lo que rezaba, porque para que más que la verdad, hay unas que no se les entiende ni papa de lo rapidito que rezan. Además también tenía fama de ser muy ocurrente y papelera, así que, poniendo cara como de dolorosa, cogió el rosario y empezó a rezar con los ojos cerrados para concentrarse y no perder la cuenta. Y yo, al modo, creo que también para no ver a Toño el mudo, pues no pudo disimular lo mal que le cayó que se hincara junto de ella. Pero dio la casualidad que Toño el mudo se levantó, y en su lugar se hincó otro señor. Y la doña ni en cuenta, ahí estaba rece y rece, cuando va llegando al primer misterio, esas partecitas donde los demás contestan, nomás de repente dio un gritote "¡Ayyy, habló el muuudo!" Bueno... ¡qué bárbaro!... fue una risión que ni se imaginaban. Se rió tanto la gente de la imprudencia de la doña que tuvieron que suspender el rosario hasta que todos se calmaran y se pusieran en juicio, solemnes, como debe ser, pues. Porque cuando parecía la mera verdad, que ya estaban muy calmaditos, no faltó quien, con la boca tapada con el tápalo, se empezó no más a estremecer y en un minuto todo mundo se estaba riendo de nueva cuenta.

Ya más tardecito, cuando las cosas se tranquilizaron bastante, dijeron que se iba a empezar un nuevo rosario por el alma de Raquel. Ya iban por ahí del segundo misterio, muy encarrerados, cuando se empieza a oír un ladradero de perros, gruñidos y carreras, y que va entrando un cochi enormísimo y canilludo, en fuerza de carrera, hostigado por un montón de perros. El pobre animal, muy

smothered them with attention, giving them bean tacos and coffee, but out of sight of Marina, who was stingy with food. Nicho and Toño were nosy and irresponsible and always showed up with lots of gossip for Raquel, who was very entertained by them.

When the time for the rosary was announced, Toño the mute knelt in the first row next to the lady who was to lead. This lady was much in demand for such duties because she knew the litany forward and backward and because she had a clear strong voice everyone could follow, for to tell the truth, there are some you can't understand for beans because they pray so fast. Besides, she was known for really getting into the part, grabbing the rosary with a grief-stricken look and closing her eyes so she could concentrate and not lose count. I, at any rate, think she also kept her eyes closed because she didn't like it that Toño the mute was kneeling next to her. Perhaps Toño sensed it, for he got up and another man took his place. The lady had no idea and just kept on praying. When she got to the first mystery, the part where everybody responds, the lady shrieked, "The mute spoke!" At that there were howls of laughter you can't imagine. People so cracked up at the lady's mistake that they had to stop the rosary until people got control of themselves and calmed down and became solemn again, like they ought. Whenever it seemed you could trust everyone to stay quiet, someone would start shaking with a shawl pulled over her mouth and in a moment everyone was howling all over again.

A bit later, when things finally settled down, they announced they were going to begin a new rosary for the soul of Raquel. They were headed into the second mystery when you could hear furious barking, growling and the tearing around of dogs, then a huge pig with enormous feet burst in at full speed, followed by the raving pack. The poor frightened animal could find no place to hide except under the cot, jolting the deceased and toppling candles, wreaths and people. It took off through the other side of the cot with the dogs in hot pursuit. At first people were stunned by the scare, and as soon as they recovered they began straightening the wreaths and branches and candles. They were still at it when the laughing sickness returned. Some began coughing and choking. Several women ran with their legs together toward the privy, which was at the far end of the yard. Some didn't make it and peed in their panties. Others cried

espantado, no halló más que meterse por debajo del catre, zangoloteando a la difunta, tumbando cirios, coronas y gente. Salió por el otro lado del catre y los perros atrás de él. De buenas a primeras la gente se quedó como pasmada del susto, y a como se les fue pasando se pusieron a acomodar los cirios, los ramos y las coronas. En esas estaban todavía cuando empezaron con el mal de risa. Unas hasta se ahogaban y les daba tos. Muchas mujeres salieron corriendo con las piernas juntitas al excusado que les quedaba lejísimos, hasta la punta del solar. Unas no llegaron y se orinaron en los calzones. Otras lloraban y hasta basquearon de la risa. A una muchacha muy aspaventosa le estaba dando como alferecía, y la mamá la tuvo que molonquear y darle unas buenas cachetadas.

A Marina, que ya estaba muy mortificada, le dio por decir que la risa era nerviosa, y mandó cocer una olla de té de azahar, para ver si así la gente se calmaba y se podía rezar los rosarios que tanto necesitaba la difunta para el eterno descanso de su alma. Nicho el loco, valiéndose de la ocasión, dijo que a él mejor le dieran café. De todos modos, al rato, con el tecito de azahar y ese como desgüance que le entra a uno después de reírse mucho, como que empezó a calmarse la cosa. Siempre pasó un buen rato para que la gente se pusiera en juicio porque ya casi era de noche. Y como quiera que sea, no faltaba alguna que le retentara la risa y se salía a la carrera, y como la risa es muy pegajosa ahí se iban haciendo hilo las demás. Se les pasaba y ahí venían para adentro, y entonces le entraba el mal a otra y dos o tres que le hacían testera, el caso es que era el cuento de nunca acabar.

—¡Ya muchachas, qué bárbaro, qué va a decir Marina...!

—Sí es cierto, ya no se rían, nos va a castigar Dios...

—¡Ay sí, qué dirá la gente...!

Bueno, pues como dicen que la tercera es la vencida, ya en la noche, estando todos muy solemnes, comenzaron otro rosario.

Parecía la mera verdad que todo iba muy bien, cuando en esas va entrando Nicho el loco, caminando de puntitas, como con sigilo, porque así caminaba él, no por otra cosa. Llevaba un cigarro en los dedos, pajariando para todos lados a ver quién le daba lumbre. Como todos estaban rezando, se hicieron los tontos y este canijo se fue metiendo con mucho cuidado, diciendo despacito: "pémiso Raquel... pémiso Raquel." Se agachó a prenderlo en uno de los cirios, que ya no más era un cabito, y que se le va apagando. Entonces, que se da la

and even threw up from laughter. One frightened girl was on the verge of an epileptic fit and her mother had to shake and slap her out of it.

Marina, who at this point was mortified, said that it was just nervous laughter and ordered that a pot of orange blossom tea be brewed to calm people down so that they could pray the rosaries the deceased so needed for the eternal rest of her soul. Crazy Nicho, seeing an opportunity, said he'd rather have coffee. At any rate, between the orange blossom tea and the exhaustion that settles in after you've laughed too hard, things were calming down. It took a long time for people to get a grip on themselves, for by now it was nearly night. And no matter how back-to-normal things got, someone was always struck by a new laughing fit and had to go running out, for the laughter was so contagious it didn't take much to get the others going again. One culprit would get over it, come back in, and then two or three more would have to do the same. It was like a story that wouldn't quit.

"Enough, girls, this is disgraceful, what will Marina say?"

"It's true, stop laughing or God will punish us."

"That's right, what will people say...."

Well, as they say, the third time's a charm; by now it was nighttime, everyone was very solemn, and they began another rosary.

Everything really seemed to be going smoothly when in came crazy Nicho on tiptoes as if to be quiet, but in fact because he always walked that way. He was holding a cigarette in his fingers and looked all around for someone to give him a light. Since everyone was praying and pretended not to notice the dolt, he carefully crept forward and said, "'Scuse me, Raquel ... 'scuse me, Raquel." He bent down to get a light from one of the candles, which by now had burnt to a stub, and instead put it out. He turned around to get a light from another and tipped over the candlestick. Soon the others were on the floor! And now the day of reckoning had come. The crowd, which was still barely suppressing its laughter, totally lost control. The final touch was that Marina, who had spent the whole day deep in the role of the bereaved, probably with an anguish she didn't feel, started trembling with laughter herself, hiding her mouth with one of those beautifully bordered handkerchiefs elegant ladies use when they cry.

vuelta para prenderlo en el otro, y que se va maneando con el candelabro... ¡y al suelo con todo y todo! Bueno, ahora sí que fue el día del juicio. La gente, como ya traía la risa por encimita, ni disimulaban para carcajearse. No se pida más, que hasta la faceta de Marina, que todo el día había estado muy en su papel de doliente, con una pena que se me figura que no sentía, se cimbraba de la risa, con la boca tapada con un pañuelito bordado muy curiosito, de esos que usan las señoras elegantes cuando se les ofrece llorar.

De todos modos, como que la gente ya estaba cansada de reírse tanto, y algunas más sosegadas empezaron a ponerse medio nerviosonas, mas que no faltó una que dijo, yo la oí clarito: "Se me figura que aquí anda rondando el diablo. ¡Qué casualidad que ni un rosario le hemos podido rezar a Raquel!" El comentario cundió y la gente, que ya estaba disgusta, nomás volteaba para atrás a cada rato. Se ponían chinitas de pensar que anduviera por ahí el maligno. Afortunadamente la doña que guiaba el rosario se paró, diciendo: "Me van a dispensar, voy a ir un ratito a la casa para darle cena a mi marido. Más noche voy a volver," y se fue muy oronda. No, hombre, este pretexto les gustó muchísimo a las que se morían por irse a sus casas a contar el mitote y a reírse del velorio. Tocante al rosario, pues quedó pendiente otra vez.

Yo no sé si será verdad, pero me contaron que por ahí de las cuatro de la mañana le rezaron un rosario enterito a Raquel, las tres o cuatro personas que la velaron.

El entierro fue a las siete de la mañana, antes de que hiciera más calor, y supe, porque fue muy criticado, que en la misa de cuerpo presente y en el panteón la gente no cortó la risa, dizque parecía que estaban en un fandango y no en un sepelio. Al modo de la gente. Pero a lo mejor son puros mitotes, yo no fui.

De todos modos me dio por pensar mucho en lo chistoso que había estado el velorio. No sé, pero a veces se me figura que todos esos detallitos de Toño el mudo, de los animales y de Nicho el loco, fueron hechos adrede para que Raquel en su último día sobre la tierra, se divirtiera y se riera como nunca lo pudo hacer, la pobre, en vida.

A lo mejor pensaron que Raquel necesitaba para el eterno descanso de su alma más risas que rezos. ¡Sólo Dios sabe!

In any case, since people were wrung out from laughing so much, and others were quiet from being so rattled, somebody just had to say, and I heard it clearly: "The devil must be lurking around here. What strange luck that we haven't been able to say a single rosary for Raquel!" The remark spread through the crowd, which started getting uncomfortable, with people glancing behind them now and then. It gave them gooseflesh to think the evil one might be prowling nearby. Fortunately, the lady who led the rosary got up and said, "You'll have to excuse me, but I have to go home for a bit to feed my husband supper. Later tonight I'll be back." And she marched off with great authority. It was just the excuse the rest had been waiting for, because everyone was dying to go home and tell the story and laugh about the wake. As for the rosary, it was still pending.

I don't know if it's true, but they tell me that around four in the morning they said an entire rosary for Raquel, with three or four mourners present.

The burial was at seven in the morning, before it got any hotter, and I know, because it was much criticized, that at the funeral mass in the cemetery people were still laughing, and they say that it was more like a party than an interment. That's how people are. But it could be just a story, because I didn't go.

In any case, the hilarity of Raquel's wake gave me a lot to think about. I don't know, but sometimes I think that all the stuff about Toño the mute, the animals, and crazy Nicho happened deliberately so that, on her last day on earth, Raquel could laugh and enjoy herself as she never could, poor thing, in life.

It may be that for her eternal rest Raquel needed laughter more than prayers. Only God knows!

una celda barroca

POR DAVID HUERTA

Para Juan José Arreola

Habría cerrojos y círculos violetas,
rasguños dorados de borní, peñas enormes.

Habría luidas conjeturas entre los densos
tomos filosóficos, bajo los mamotretos
de teologal espesor—y una calavera jerónima
presidiéndolo todo.

Habría lienzos de sombras mitológicas
y una Biblia circundada
por una desganada devoción.

Habría—no sé—un dejo de fiebre
en todo el ámbito.

Habría, en fin, un manojo de cebollas
enviado puntualmente
para mitigar el hambre heroica
de Luis de Góngora y Argote.

TRANSLATED BY Mark Schafer

A Baroque Cell

BY DAVID HUERTA

For Juan José Arreola

There would be bolts and violet circumferences,
the marsh harrier's gilded slashes, massive crags.

There would be threadbare conjectures among the dense
philosophical tomes, under the massive volumes
of theological thickness—and a Hieronymite skull
presiding over it all.

There would be canvases of mythological shadows
and a Bible surrounded
by halfhearted devotion.

There would be—perhaps—a hint of fever
throughout.

There would be, in short, a bunch of onions
sent punctually
to appease the heroic hunger
of Luis de Góngora y Argote.

de
El fin de la locura

POR JORGE VOLPI

1.4 El fin de la terapia

—Estoy paralizado, doctor. ¿Se imagina usted lo que es ser golpeado sin misericordia, empujado a un vagón lleno de prisioneros y conducido al infierno de una prefectura? Poco importa que, demasiado fatigados o previendo un inminente hacinamiento en los centros penitenciarios, les hayan concedido la gracia de liberarlos. El castigo no está en los palos, las costillas rotas o los días sin luz, sino en la humillación. Los poderosos no se cansan de proclamar el imperio de las normas cuando no hacen otra cosa que romperlas. Es intolerable, doctor. La cárcel es el reverso de la ley. ¿Se da cuenta de la ironía? La única ley es la de ellos. La del más fuerte, la del policía. Adentro no hay derecho que valga. No hay jueces ni abogados ni defensores de oficio, sólo el poder en su máxima expresión. ¿Entiende lo que le digo? Después de haber visto eso, ¿cómo actuar como si nada? No podemos seguir sordos, mudos, ajenos. Debemos seguir su ejemplo, doctor. Acuérdese de Claire …

Lacan no ocultaba su fastidio. ¿Quién me creía yo para hablarle en ese tono? Él había tenido la magnanimidad de acogerme, pero yo me sobrepasaba. A pesar de su relativa simpatía hacia el movimiento estudiantil, no toleraba los desplantes de los jóvenes y menos aún que no reconociesen su papel como precursor.

—Su lucha es absurda—me amonestó—. Es evidente que usted no sabe lo que dice, doctor Quevedo. Lo único que busca, como esos muchachos, es otro amo. Su ironía no me amilanó. Contemplé la burguesa apacibilidad de su gabinete. ¿Cómo ser un rebelde en el entorno de un notario?

from
The End of Madness
BY JORGE VOLPI

1.4 The End of Therapy

"I'm paralyzed, doctor. Can you imagine what it's like to be mercilessly beaten, shoved into a truck filled with prisoners and hauled away to the hell of a police station? It matters very little that, too exhausted or dreading the imminent crowding of the jails, they've been given the grace of freedom. Punishment is not in the sticks, the broken ribs, or the days without light, it's in the humiliation. The powerful never tire of proclaiming the empire of rules when they do nothing but break them. It's unbearable, doctor. Prison is the exact opposite of the law. Do you realize the irony? The only law is theirs. The law of the strongest, of the police. Inside, rights have no value. There are no judges or lawyers or public defenders, only the ultimate expression of power. Do you understand what I'm telling you? After having seen that, how can you act as if it were nothing? We can't continue being deaf, mute, alienated. We have to follow her example, doctor. Remember Claire ..."

Lacan didn't hide his annoyance. Who did I think I was to speak to him in that tone? He had had the generosity to welcome me, but I went too far. In spite of his relative sympathy for the student movement, he did not tolerate the arrogant remarks of young people, especially when they didn't recognize his role as precursor.

"Your struggle is absurd," he admonished me. "You obviously don't know what you're saying, Doctor Quevedo. The only thing you're looking for, like those boys, is another master."

—Le agradezco lo que ha hecho por mí—me excusé—. Estas semanas han sido invaluables, sin ellas no me atrevería a buscar otra vida. Se lo debo a usted, doctor. Espero que sigamos siendo amigos.

—¿Amigos? —rió—. Los amigos no existen. Y, si existieran, usted no sería uno de los míos. Pero no se altere: tampoco posee la estatura para ser mi adversario. No logré hendirle un sarcasmo equivalente.

—Si necesita algo, no dude en llamarme—le dije sin más.

—¿Llamarlo? —rió—. No sea soberbio. Será usted quien termine arrastrándose para que lo reciba de nuevo. Como Claire. Lo odié. Pero tampoco podía romper definitivamente con él. Seguía considerándome su alumno y no tenía intenciones de abandonar su seminario.

—Hasta pronto, doctor Lacan.

Estaba tan enfadado que bajé las escaleras a toda prisa justo cuando Judith, la hija favorita de Lacan, subía por ellas. A causa de la impenetrabilidad de la materia, fui yo quien terminó rodando por el suelo.

—¿Se encuentra usted bien? —la joven se apresuró a auxiliarme.

La cabeza me daba vueltas.

—¿Paciente o amigo de mi padre? —me preguntó luego, con un tono en donde no faltaba cierta coquetería.

—Ambas cosas—respondí, confuso—. O ninguna.

—¿Español?

—Mexicano. Me llamo Aníbal Quevedo … Y usted debe ser su Judith.

Sobre el escritorio de Lacan siempre lucía un retrato suyo. Era la hija consentida de Lacan, la mujer de Jacques-Alain Miller, la compañera de batallas de Claire. ¡Claro! ¿Cómo no lo pensé antes? ¡Ella era la única persona en el mundo que podía saber dónde encontrarla!

—Usted conoce a Claire, ¿verdad? —le espeté.

—¡Ya sé quién es usted! —Judith bajó el tono de voz para que su padre no fuese a escucharla—. El mexicano.

—¿Claire le habló de mí?

—Por supuesto … ¿Sabe? Las dos siempre sufrimos una predilección

His sarcasm did not intimidate me. I contemplated the bourgeois complacency of his surroundings. How could one be a rebel in a notary's office?

"I am grateful to you for what you've done for me," I apologized. "These weeks have been invaluable, without them I wouldn't have dared seek another life. I owe this to you, doctor. I hope that we'll continue to be friends."

"Friends?" he laughed. "Friends don't exist. And, if they did exist, you wouldn't be one of mine. But don't get upset: you don't have the stature to be my adversary."

I didn't manage to cut him down in return.

"If you need something, don't hesitate to call," I simply said.

"Call you?" he laughed. "Don't be arrogant. You'll be the one who will end up dragging himself back here to be received by me again. Just like Claire."

I hated him. But I couldn't afford to break with him definitively either. He continued to consider me his student and had no intentions of abandoning his seminar.

"See you soon, Doctor Lacan."

I was so mad that I ran down the steps, just as Judith, Lacan's favorite daughter, was coming upstairs. Because of the impenetrability of matter, I was the one who ended up rolling on the floor.

"Are you okay?" the young woman hurried to give me a hand. My head was spinning.

"Are you a patient or a friend of my father's?" she asked me, not without a certain flirtation in her tone.

"Both," I replied, confused. "Or neither."

"Spanish?"

"Mexican. My name is Anibal Quevedo ... And you must be Judith."

A portrait of her was always on display on Lacan's desk. She was his pampered daughter, the wife of Jacques-Alain Miller, Claire's comrade in arms. Of course! Why hadn't I thought of it earlier? She was the only person in the world who might know where to find her.

"You know Claire, right?" I sprang the question on her.

particular por los sudamericanos … Una especie de atracción irrefrenable, ¿me entiende?

—¿Tiene idea de dónde está ella ahora? —la acorralé, ansioso.

Los ojos de Judith me escrutaron de arriba abajo.

—No.

—¿No?

Ella subió un par de escalones. Tenía unas piernas magníficas.

—¿Podríamos vernos en otra parte? —me propuso, insinuante—. Ahora debo irme, si no mi padre se pondrá con un humor de perros. ¿En el Flore, a las ocho?

Judith desapareció en el rellano y yo abandoné aquella casa. La primavera al fin nos concedía una tregua. Cargado con esta nueva ilusión, apresuré mis pasos. Necesitaba contemplar el cauce moroso y turbio del Sena.

[ᴄᵒᵍᵒᵃᵉᵍᵒᵍᵕ]

2.1 Universitarios del mundo …

—Ya te lo dije, Aníbal—Judith me acarició el brazo con suavidad—. No tengo idea de dónde esté.

Pese a que la joven decidió tutearme de inmediato, su voz podía sonar tan brutal como la de su padre. Le había hecho la misma pregunta una y otra vez hasta sacarla de quicio: mi ansiedad, demasiado burguesa, le resultaba pueril.

—Pero está a salvo …

—Claire tomó la decisión de marcharse por sí misma, nadie la obligó. Siempre ha sido impredecible—me dijo mientras me pellizcaba una mejilla como se hace con un niño caprichoso—. Lo que no entiendo es por qué los hombres se obsesionan tanto con ella … Mi padre …

Judith comenzaba a desesperarse. Era evidente que yo no era la mejor compañía posible. Debía de tener mejores opciones que yo.

—¿Qué buscas, Aníbal?

"I know who you are!" Judith lowered her voice so that her father wouldn't hear her. "The Mexican."

"Claire spoke to you about me?"

"Of course ... You know, the two of us suffer the same particular predilection for South Americans ... A kind of irresistible attraction, you get me?"

"Do you have any idea where she is now?" I cornered her, anxiously.

Judith's eyes scrutinized me from top to bottom.

"No."

"No?"

She went up a couple of more steps. She had magnificent legs.

"Could we meet someplace else," she suggested, insinuatingly. "I have to go now, or my father will have a fit. At the Flore, at eight?"

Judith disappeared on the landing, and I left the house. Springtime had at last brought us a truce. Filled with this new hope, I hurried on. I needed to reach the riverbank and contemplate the slow-moving, dark waters of the Seine.

[༄༅]

2.1 University Students of the World ...

"I already told you, Anibal," Judith gently caressed my arm. "I have no idea where she is."

Despite the fact that the young woman had decided to speak to me in an intimate way from the start, her voice could sound as brutal as her father's. I had asked her the same question again and again, driving her batty. My anxiety, so bourgeois, seemed childish to her.

"But she's safe ..."

"Claire made the decision to leave all by herself, no one forced her to. She's always been unpredictable," she said to me, pinching my cheek as if I were an impulsive child. "What I don't understand is why men get so obsessed over her ... My father ..."

Su pregunta me sumió en un estado de pánico. Lo único que sabía era que sin Claire no conseguiría vivir en paz. Una vez más me dejé llevar por la inercia.

—No lo sé. Unirme a ustedes.

—¿Has escuchado hablar del nuevo Centro Universitario Experimental de Vincennes? —Judith le dio un provocativo trago a su copa—. Quizás te gustaría venir … Voy a dar un curso sobre revoluciones culturales …

No comprendí si me hablaba en clave o si se mofaba de mí. Sentí el roce de su pie en mi pantorrilla. O quizás yo alucinaba.

—¡Claro! —balbucí torpemente—. Me gustaría mucho …

—Te espero ahí, entonces—terminó ella y se levantó.

Su magnífica silueta se perdió escaleras abajo. No podía dejar de extrañarme que aquella niña mimada fuese poco menos que una delincuente. Me equivocaba: las niñas mimadas suelen ser las más peligrosas. Al final de aquella cita, me sentía como un adolescente que no se ha atrevido a besar a su enamorada. Pero al menos había adquirido un nuevo vínculo con el mundo de Claire.

Judith was becoming exasperated. It was obvious that I was not the best possible company. She had to have better options than me.

"What are you looking for, Anibal?"

Her question plunged me into a state of panic. The only thing I knew was that without Claire, I could never live in peace. Once more, I let inertia carry me along.

"I don't know. To join up with you guys."

"Have you heard talk again about the new Experimental University Center of Vincennes?" Judith swigged her glass of wine provocatively. "Perhaps you'd like to come … I'm going to give a course on cultural revolutions …"

I didn't get whether she was speaking to me in code or making fun of me. I felt her foot brush against my ankle. Or perhaps I was hallucinating.

"Of course!" I stammered awkwardly. "I'd like that very much …"

"I'll expect you there, then," she finished and got up.

Her magnificent figure disappeared down the stairs. It didn't cease to amaze me that this spoiled girl was nothing more than a delinquent. I was wrong: spoiled girls are usually the most dangerous. At the end of that date, I felt like a teenager who hasn't dared to kiss his girlfriend. But at least I had acquired a new link to Claire's world.

de

palinuro de méxico

POR FERNANDO DEL PASO

Del sentimiento tragicómico de la vida

Sí, hermano, vengo de Londres. ¡De Londres! ¿Te das cuenta? *London: thou art the flour of cities all.* He vivido varios años allí, en esa ciudad irreal, en la Roma de hoy y compendio de nuestro tiempo como la llamó Emerson. Demasiados años quizás. El inefable doctor Jonson dijo una vez que si alguien estaba cansado de Londres, es que estaba cansado de la vida. Por lo tanto, no me queda ninguna esperanza, puesto que estoy cansado de Londres. ¿Pero cómo se puede hacer caso a quién despreció libros tan magníficos como *Tom Jones* y *Tristam Shandy* y que dijo que prefería la vista de Fleet Street a la de cualquier paisaje rural? Al tío Austin le traje una corbata King's College. Aunque te voy a confesar que yo también soy animal de ciudad. Soy de los que piensan que Dios creó el mundo para darse un espectáculo a sí mismo, y por eso a él le corresponde aplaudir la actuación multitudinaria de las cataratas del Niágara o aburrirse con el monólogo interminable del desierto del Sahara. Yo me quedo con lo que el hombre hizo para el hombre. Y que más te puedo decir de Londres: es una ciudad que se pasa las noches durmiendo y soñando con sus glorias pretéritas. Con esto quiero decirte que la vida se acaba a las once pasado meridiano. ¡Nunca he visto a nadie que se acueste tan temprano como los ingleses! Salvo, quizás, las propias inglesas, que se acuestan a las siete porque tienen que regresar a sus casas a las diez. Y mientras tanto, la luz de los semáforos baila manzanas en medio de la lluvia. ¡Cómo llueve hermano! El otro día,

from
palinuro of mexico
BY FERNANDO DEL PASO

The tragicomic sense of life

That's right, I've just returned from London. From London! Can you imagine! 'London: thou art the flower of cities all.' I lived there for several years, in that city which never becomes real at all, in that Rome of today and the epitome of our times, as Emerson called it. Too many years perhaps. The ineffable Dr. Johnson once said that when a man is tired of London, he is tired of life. Therefore, there is no hope for me, since I am tired of London. But how can you take any notice of somebody who despised books as magnificent as *Tom Jones* and *Tristram Shandy* and who said that he preferred the view of Fleet Street to that of any rural landscape? I brought Uncle Austin a King's College tie. Although, I must admit, I am also a city animal. I am one of those people who think that God created the world to put on a show for himself and therefore it is up to him to applaud the multitudinous acting of the Niagara Falls or get bored with the interminable monologue of the Sahara desert. I'll settle for what man has made for man. What more can I say of London: it is a city that spends its nights sleeping and dreaming of its past glories. By that I mean that life stops at eleven past the meridian. I've never seen people who go to bed as early as Englishmen! Except, perhaps, the English women who go to bed at seven because they have to be home by ten. Meanwhile, the glow of the traffic lights dances in the rain. How it rains, man! The other day, I got so fed up that I went outside and beat the rain with

harto, salí de la casa y le di de paraguazos a la lluvia. Pero fue inútil. La lluvia es implacable y diamantina. Con esa misma agua, llené esta botella para la abuela Altagracia. Le diré que es agua de Lourdes. Total, todas las aguas son iguales, y en ellas se pueden encontrar las mismas algas microscópicas con la forma de medialunas y caramelos de esmeralda, los heliozoos como erizos de luz y los piojos de gelatina azul que descubrimos tú y yo, cuando éramos niños, en los libros del tío Esteban. Al tío, por cierto, le traje varias láminas para la revista de los laboratorios, y entre ellas las Escenas de Hospital de Taddeo di Bartolo y el Premio a la Crueldad de Hogarth donde un perro que se come el corazón del autopsiado me recordó, como ya te imaginarás, al perro del viejo Caronte. Al abuelo le traje un ejemplar viejísimo de un Atlas y Portulano de la República Mexicana. Y para mí, para Walter, traje una reproducción gigante del maravilloso cuadro de Millais que muestra a Ofelia muerta en las aguas del río, y frente al cual, cuando al fin lo pude contemplar en el original, y acordándome de mis buenos tiempos de estudiante y del juego de microscópica que después le regaló el tío Esteban a nuestra prima y me asombré de los mundos que bullían "del áureo microscopio en la platina," ¿quién dice así? ¿Machado? me di cuenta que también en los ojos y los pulmones de los ahogados podemos descubrir, con suerte, esas maravillas de simetría iridiscente, esos animálculos que parecen relojes de arena, cangrejos diminutos, pulseras de cuentas y lágrimas verdes con pelos largos. Por lo demás, viejo, los ingleses se arreglan cada mañana los parches del cabello, se atan las cintas de la voz, se cosen la lengua, se abrochan los ojos, se almidonan la sonrisa y comienzan a caer del cielo sobre La City, de bombín y paraguas, como si los hubiera pintado Magritte. Bueno, no exactamente, porque aunque todos los ingleses son iguales, unos son más iguales que otros. Me he acordado mucho de ti, primo, mientras caminaba por Londres del brazo de Eliot. No soy ni monárquico, ni clasicista, ni católico anglicano: pero conversé con él, sin embargo, en Hampstead, en Putney, en Primrose y en otras tenebrosas colinas de Londres. He pensado en ti y en tus ilusiones, cuando caminaba a la orilla del Támesis, por los jardines del malecón, en tanto me apiadaba de los mendigos que al anochecer se cubren con

my umbrella. But it was no good. The rain was implacable and diamantine. And with that same rainwater, I filled this bottle for Grandmother Altagracia. I'll tell her it's holy water from Lourdes. All water is the same anyway and in it you find the same microscopic algae in the shape of half moons and emerald sweets, heliozoans like hedgehogs of light and fleas of blue gelatine which you and I discovered as children in Uncle Esteban's books. And for uncle, by the way, I've brought several plates for his laboratory's magazine, including Taddeo di Bartolo's *Hospital Scenes* and Hogarth's *The Reward of Cruelty* which shows a dog eating the heart of the corpse on which the autopsy is being performed which reminded me, as you can well imagine, of old Charon's dog. For Grandfather, I brought an extremely old edition of *Atlas and Charts of the Mexican Republic*. And for me, for Walter, I brought a huge reproduction of Millais' painting showing the dead Ophelia in the river before which, when I finally got the opportunity to see the original and remembering my good old days as a student and the microscopy set which Uncle Esteban later gave to our cousin and which had left me astounded by the worlds teeming 'on the stage of the aureate microscope'—who was it that said that anyway? Machado?—I realized that with luck we may also discover in the eyes and lungs of drowned people those wonders of the iridescent symmetry, those little creatures that look like hourglasses, tiny crabs, bead bracelets and green tears with long hairs. Moreover, old man, every morning the English straighten their hair-pieces, tie their vocal chords, sew on their tongues, button their eyes, starch their smiles and start with equal punctuality to descend from the sky upon The City, complete with bowler hat and umbrella, as though painted by Magritte. Well, not exactly; although the English are all equal, some are more equal than others. I thought of you often, cousin, as I walked through London arm-in-arm with Eliot. I am neither royalist, classicist, nor Anglo-Catholic but I conversed with him, none the less, in Hampstead, in Putney, on Primrose and other shady Hills of London. I thought of you and your illusions, as I walked along the banks of the Thames, through the Embankment Gardens, as I felt sorry for the

el tiempo bajo el poeta que se inflama, y con el cual también conversé de su tierra nativa y en su nativa lengua. ¡He conocido maravillas, no tienes idea! ¡He conocido personalmente el estetoscopio de Líster y los fórceps de Liston! Me faltó poco para tenerlos en las manos. Me acordé tanto de ti, primo, de las noches aquellas que paseábamos por Mesones y por San Juan de Letrán y por la Reforma y por la colonia Juárez y después, cuando amanecía, llegábamos al Bosque de Chapultepec que recorríamos entero desde el Paseo de la Milla hasta el Molino del Rey. Podría escribir ahora un libro que se llamara Historia de Dos Ciudades. Podría escribir, mejor, un libro de mil páginas nada más que sobre la impresión de melancolía infinita que me produjo Ofelia. De todos modos, aunque sea para eso, para ver los originales de los cuadros que conociste en ilustraciones, vale la pena ir a Europa, pasando claro está por Nueva York para saludar a Guernica: La Lección del Doctor Tulp, que es nada menos que la Lección de Anatomía de Rembrandt, me pareció infinitamente más bella de lo que jamás imaginé. ¡He visto tanta pintura! ¡He contemplado tantos Triunfos de la Muerte, incluyendo el de Lorenzetti en Pisa, y tantos cuadros de cadáveres en descomposición, sin faltar, claro, los de Valdés Leal! Pero además de pensar en ti, en tus ilusiones y en la mano del general Obregón, ¿te acuerdas de ella? He hablado contigo muchas veces en voz alta, sin miedo de que me pensaran loco. ¡Hay tantos locos en esa ciudad, hermano, tanta gente que habla sola! Nadie por supuesto les hace caso, ni siquiera los policías que a su vez hablan con dos voces distintas: si les preguntas por una calle, su cachiporra florece como la vara de nardo de San José, y te contestan con la voz amable. Pero cuidado: con la otra voz, con la que guardan junto a su corazón transistorizado, en cualquier momento te pueden acusar de pederasta o de inmigrante pakistano. ¡Conocí una dentadura afinada en Do mayor! Conocí, en el Museo Hunteriano, la más increíble colección de trozos selectos del organismo humano. Allí están, en sus prismas transparentes, como el barco que se encontró el Barón de Münchhausen y que navegaba encerrado en un témpano. A mamá Clementina, si viviera, le hubiera traído una manita de marfil para rascarse la espalda, que vi en una tienda de Portobello. Y mientras tú, primo, caminabas por San

tramps who at dusk roll themselves in time beneath the poet going up in flames with whom I also conversed, in his native land and tongue. Such wonders I saw, you cannot imagine! I personally met Lister's stethoscope and Liston's forceps. I almost had them in my hands. I thought of you, cousin, and of those nights when we walked along the streets, along Mesones and along San Juan de Letrán and along Reforma and through the Juárez district and afterwards, as dawn broke, we reached Chapultepec Park which we crossed from one side to the other, from the Paseo de la Milla to Molino del Rey. I could write a book called *A Tale of Two Cities*. Better still, I could write a book with a thousand pages on nothing more than the feeling of infinite melancholy that Ophelia produced in me. Anyway, if only to see the originals of the paintings that you know from illustrations, it is worth going to Europe, by way, of course, of New York to pay your respects to *Guernica*; *The Anatomy Lesson of Dr Tulp*, Rembrandt's *Anatomy Lesson*, of course, seemed to me infinitely more beautiful than I had ever imagined. So many paintings have I seen! I have beheld so many *Triumphs of Death*, including the one by Lorenzetti in Pisa and so many pictures of decomposing corpses including, of course, those by Valdés Leal! And not only did I think of you, of your illusions and of General Obregon's hand, do you remember? but I often spoke aloud to you, without fear that they might think me mad. There are so many mad people in that city, man, so many people who talk to themselves! Nobody takes any notice of them of course, not even the police who sometimes speak with two different voices: if you ask them for directions, their truncheons blossom like St Joseph's lily stem and they answer you in a friendly voice. But beware: with the other voice, the one they keep close to their transistorized heart, they may at any moment accuse you of being a pederast or a Pakistani immigrant. I saw a pair of dentures tuned in C major; in the Hunterian Museum I saw the most incredible collection of select pieces of the human organism. There they all are, in their transparent prisms, like the vessel found by Baron Münchhausen which sailed along enclosed in an iceberg. For Mamma Clementina, if she were alive, I would have brought

Ildefonso o por Justo Sierra, con tu Manual de Microscopía bajo el brazo, y soñando como yo soñé algún día encontrar en una gota de agua de mar o en los ojos del poeta Shelley la noctiluca luminosa y transparente y las diatomeas de clorofila enmascarada que forman el fango de los lechos oceánicos y que tienen formas de trenes, de flautas, de enjambres y de círculos radiados, mientras tú soñabas y te reías pensando en Horacio Wells en el momento en que descubría las propiedades hilarantes del cloroformo y llorabas pensando en Horacio Wells cuando fue humillado en Boston y se echó a la calle a arrojar vitriolo a la cara de las prostitutas, mientras tú te jurabas—como me juré yo algún día recibirte de médico para aprender a describir el barniz del cráneo y la red fluviátil que rodea a la vida, para aprender a disecar cadáveres mansos y a detectar la propagación marcial de la adrenalina, yo, tu primo Walter, caminaba con mi paraguas y mi chaleco de rombos por Charing Cross Road y husmeaba en las librerías de viejo y me moría de la angustia de no poder comprar tantos libros tan maravillosos... ¡Nunca he comprado menos libros en mi vida, hermano! y te decía—te dije—que muy bien, podemos aceptar que aunque no sepas cuándo tu vida comienza a ser o dejar de ser tuya, de todos modos es tuya y de nadie más. Hubieras visto, claro, qué mirada tan alarmada me echó el dependiente de la librería pero no, te repito, porque yo estuviera hablando solo, sino porque lo hacía en español. Pero la vida, continué, no es una cosa. La vida, aunque aparentemente puedas usarla y disfrutar y abusar de ella, no es un traje; la vida—dije señalando un lindo mapa de Kent iluminado a mano—no es diez hectáreas de terreno, y por último la vida—grité saliendo a la calle—no es un automóvil. ¡Qué automóviles en Londres, hermano! Ante un Rolls Royce, no queda sino quitarse el sombrero y comenzar a pedir limosna. Pero los ingleses, si les pide para comprar pan, no te dan ni un penique. Si les pides para tomar una pinta de cerveza tampoco, pero al menos te ven con simpatía. La vida—continué caminando por el lado más dulce y sombreado de la famosa calle de Pall Mall—, es saber disfrutar el momento presente y los pequeños placeres, y por asociación de ideas encendí un cigarrillo (el último que me quedaba) y lancé una bocanada de humo hacia las flores de las ventanas del Banco de Nova

a little ivory hand to scratch her back with, which I saw in a shop in Portobello Road. And while you, cousin, walked along San Ildefonso and Justo Sierra, with your *Microscopy Manual* under your arm and dreaming as I used to myself of one day finding in a drop of sea water or in the poet Shelley's eyes the luminous and transparent protozoa and the diatoms of masked chlorophyll which formed the slime on the bed of oceans and are shaped like trains, flutes, swarms of bees and radiate circles, while you dreamt and you laughed thinking of Horace Wells at the moment he discovered the laughing properties of chloroform and wept thinking of Horace Wells when he was humiliated in Boston and rushed out into the streets to fling vitriol into prostitutes' faces while you swore to yourself—as I swore to myself—to one day qualify as a doctor, to learn to describe the varnish of the skull and the tidal net surrounding life, to learn to dissect tame corpses and to detect the martial propagation of adrenalin, all the while, I, your cousin Walter, was walking along Charing Cross Road with my umbrella and my patchwork waistcoat, poking around in the secondhand bookshops and dying a thousand deaths because I couldn't buy all those wonderful books … never in my life have I bought fewer books, man! and I was saying to you—I said to you—that we may indeed accept that, although you do not know when your life actually begins and ceases to be your own, in all events it is yours and nobody else's. Of course, you should have seen the look of alarm that the bookshop assistant gave me but, I repeat, not because I was talking to myself but because I was doing it in Spanish. But life, I continued, is not a thing. Life, although it seems you may use it and enjoy it and abuse it, it is not a suit of clothes; life, I said, pointing to a beautiful hand-tinted map of Kent, is not ten hectares of land and, finally, life, I shouted as I walked out into the street, is not a car. Such cars in London, man! Faced with a Rolls Royce, all you can do is take off your hat and hold it out for alms. But if you ask the English for money to buy bread, they won't give you a penny. If you ask them for money to buy a pint of beer they won't give you anything either, but at least they look at you a little more sympathetically. Life, I continued, as I walked along the sweeter

Scotia, otra hacia el Instituto de Artes Contemporáneas, y una tercera hacia el monumento de Florence Nightingale. A cambio de todos los libros que no compré, están todos los libros que sí leí. Me hice lector del Museu Británico, hermano, y miembro de la London Library. ¡Imagínate: un millón de libros a mi alcance: en inglés, español, francés... en todos los idiomas vivos y todas las lenguas muertas! Y allí, en la biblioteca y ante las obras de Plinio El Viejo y de Cayo Salustio Crispo; allí frente a la tragedia ática y los libros de Tucídides (copié para el tío Esteban una magnífica descripción que hace Tucídides sobre la peste de Atenas), me dije que los anatomistas habían arrancado de cuajo las raíces griegas y latinas para bautizar con ellas las partes de nuestro cuerpo, y que el tórax y la crista galli, el yeyuno y el septum lucidum el tuber cinereum y el calamus scriptorius pertenecían a este linaje. La vida puede ser, sí, quizás, una propiedad, le aseguré a Florence Nightingale, pero su razón de ser una propiedad no sería siquiera, como señala Hegel, una prolongación necesaria de la libertad individual, por la sencilla razón de que tú, Florence Nightingale, y tú, primo, y yo Walter, no elegimos vivir y ser libres. La vida, insisto, no es una cosa—le dije al empleadito de la biblioteca, que dio la casualidad que hablaba un poco de español y creyó que le estaba yo dando el título de un libro. ¿La vida qué, señor? me preguntó. Del Sentimiento Trágico de la Vida, de Miguel de Unamuno, le dije, y mientras se iba a buscar el libro, fui al baño a orinar. ¡Nunca he orinado tanto en mi vida, hermano! Y es que me pasaba la mañana tomando té para guiñarle un ojo al sueño y aprovechar al máximo la prórroga que cada día inauguraba, y la tarde y la noche tomando cerveza, para quiñarle un ojo al insomnio. Pero puedo decir que como buen boyscout que conoce dentellada a dentellada la historia de Mowgli, nunca me acosté sin hacer algo bueno: sin haber, por lo menos, conquistado la imaginación por ese día. Y cuando tenía en la mano mi querido órgano reproductor, o en otras palabras una muy querida prolongación de mi libertad individual, me dije a mí mismo: bueno, sí, la vida, entre otras cosas, es un montoncito de cosas de las cuales depende. La vida es tu cerebro, me dije viéndome en el espejo. Pero no tu cerebro sólo, sino tu cerebro más tus ojos, más tu boca, más tu aparato

and more shady side of famous Pall Mall, is to know how to enjoy the present moment and its small pleasures and, by association of ideas, I lit a cigarette (my last) and blew a cloud of smoke towards the flowers in the window-boxes of the Nova Scotia Bank, another towards the Institute of Contemporary Arts, a third towards the Florence Nightingale Monument. In contrast to all those books which I did not buy are all those books which I did read. I became a reader at the British Museum, man, and a member of the London Library, just think of it: a million books within my grasp, in English, in Spanish, French ... in all living languages and all dead tongues! And there, in the library, in the presence of the works of Pliny the Elder and of Gaius Salustius Crispus, Attic tragedy and the works of Thucydides (I copied a magnificent description by Thucydides of the Plague of Athens for Uncle Esteban), I reflected that anatomists had torn up Greek and Latin roots and with them baptized the parts of our body, and that the thorax and that the crista galli, the jejunum and the septum lucidum, the tuber cinereum and the calamus scriptorius are of this lineage. Life may well, indeed, be a belonging, I assured Florence Nightingale, and you, cousin, and I, Walter, did not choose to live and to be free. Life, I repeated, is not a thing, I said to the librarian who, by coincidence, spoke a little Spanish and thought that I was giving him the title of a book. Life what, sir? he asked me. *The Tragic Sense of Life* by Miguel de Unamuno, I said to him and, while he went off to look for the book, I went to the gents to pee. Never in my life have I peed so much, man! And the fact is, I spent my morning drinking tea to overcome sleepiness and make the most of the respite offered by each day and then I spent all afternoon and evening drinking beer to overcome insomnia. But I can say that, like any good boy scout who knows his story of the Mowgli bite by bite, I never went to bed without having achieved something good: without, at least, having conquered imagination for that day. And as I held my beloved reproductive organ or, in other words, a dearly loved extension of my individual freedom, I said to myself: well, yes, life is, among other things, a little heap of things on which it depends. Life is your brain, I said to myself as I looked at my

circulatorio, más tu eso y lo otro, continué, lavándome las manos y saliendo al vestíbulo y mientras esperaba que el empleado trajera el libro —los ingleses se toman su tiempo para todo, menos para el acto sexual—, me puse a hojear el Libro Guinness de los Récords Mundiales, y además de enterarme de la mujer que distinguía colores con los dedos, y de la media tonelada y pico que pesa el hombre más gordo del mundo y de otras imbecilidades por el estilo, vi que naturalmente y como era de esperarse el cerebro de Turguenev—uno de los más grandes conocidos hasta la fecha—, pesaba dos kilos doce gramos, y el de Anatole France —uno de los más pequeños—, sólo un kilo diecisiete gramos. Y digo *naturalmente* porque fuera de toda consideración literaria, comprobé una vez más que el cerebro humano es *una cosa*. A ti, perdóname, aparte de algunos recuerdos no te pude traer sino una de las corbatas de moño que me pediste. Aunque parezca mentirla, en Londres casi no existen. ¡Qué mal se visten los ingleses, hermano! Pero eso no es nada: ¡qué mal se desvisten las inglesas! Y bueno, todas esas cosas, dije firmando el recibo, son tu vida. Le di las gracias al empleado, abrí el libro al azar en la página donde Unamuno cuenta cómo Leopardi vio la estrecha hermandad que hay entre el amor y la muerte, apunté la frase en una libretita para agregarla a mi colección de frases y de ideas semejantes—el amor tiene el olor de la muerte, dijo Bataile, y Thomas Mann tuvo que recurrir al francés para hacer decir a su personaje: *le corps, l'amour, la mort, ces trois ne font qu'un*—y me despedí de la London Library y de su puerta de cristales biselados, y salí a la Plaza de Saint James con la esperanza de que ya se hubiera asomado el sol. Imposible. En Inglaterra el sol es una brillante excepción y en el invierno, si acaso una hipótesis deslumbrante. Estábamos, sin embargo, en verano. ¡En el día más largo del año! Pero ante esa sombría perspectiva, me guardé el libro en la bolsa, y me dije que para conocer el sentimiento trágico de la vida basta vivir en Londres soñando siempre con un amanecer en el trópico.

reflection in the mirror. Not only your brain, but your brain plus your eyes, plus your mouth, plus your circulatory system, plus your this, plus your that, I continued as I washed my hands and went out into the hall and, while I waited for the librarian to bring my book—the English take their time over everything except sex—I started leafing through the *Guinness Book of Records* and, besides learning of the woman who could identify colours through her fingers and that the world's fattest man weighed half a ton and a bit and other such inanities, I read that of course, predictably, Turgenev's brain—one of the largest known to date—weighed two kilos twelve grams and that of Anatole France—one of the smallest—only one kilo and seventeen grams. And I say *of course* because, literary considerations aside, this confirmed, yet again that the human brain is *a thing*. You must forgive me, but I am afraid that all I could bring for you, apart from a few souvenirs, was the bow tie you asked me for. Would you believe, they hardly exist in London? How badly the English dress, man! And that's the least of it: how badly English women undress! And well, all these things, I said as I signed the receipt slip, are your life. I thanked the librarian and, at random, opened the book at the part where Unamuno relates how Leopardi saw the close relationship existing between love and death. I jotted down the sentence in my little black book to add to my collection of similar sentences and ideas—love has the smell of death, said Bataille while Thomas Mann had to turn to French to have his character say: *le corps, l'amour, la mort, ces trois ne font qu'un*—and I took my leave of the London Library with its doors of bevelled panes and went out into St James Square, hoping that the sun might by then have come out. No chance. In England, the sun is a brilliant exception and in winter but a dazzling hypothesis. It was, however, summer. The longest day of the year! Faced with this dismal prospect, I put the book in my pocket and I told myself that, to experience the tragic sense of life, one has only to live in London dreaming ever of a tropical dawn.

[CHAPTER V] The Translator

"Signor, that there gentleman," pointing to a grave person of a very
prepossessing appearance, "has translated a book. . . . "

"Notwithstanding all your learning," replied the knight, "I could almost
swear you are hitherto unknown to the world, which is ever averse to remu-
nerate flourishing genius, and works of merit. What talents are lost, what
abilities obscured, and what virtues are undervalued in this degenerate age! yet,
nevertheless, a translation from one language to another... is, in my opinion,
like the wrong side of Flemish tapestry, in which, tho' we distinguish the figures,
they are confused and obscured by ends and threads, without that smoothness and
expression which the other side exhibits. . . . "

—MIGUEL DE CERVANTES
Don Quixote de la Mancha (translated by Tobias Smollett)

The Translator

In Villa Oluta, Veracruz, a traveler may be startled to come upon a monument to Cortés's translator Malinche—not because Mexico has any shortage of monuments but because many Mexicans have disavowed Malinche, and few visible traces of her remain. In Mexico City, a house where Malinche is supposed to have lived stands at 57 Higuera Street; it is unmarked by any plaque or notice. Perhaps, considering her reputation as the "Mexican Eve," Malinche's invisibility in modern Mexico is a kindness.

Translators often seek invisibility. If one sign of an insufficient translation is that its phrasings retain an unnatural foreignness—reading "as if translated"—then is the ideal translation one that seems the most plausible as an original work in the target language? "The illusion of transparency," Lawrence Venuti writes in *The Translator's Invisibility,* "is an effect of fluent discourse, of the translator's effort to insure easy readability by adhering to current usage, maintaining continuous syntax, fixing a precise meaning. What is so remarkable here is that this illusory effect conceals the numerous conditions under which the translation is made, starting with the translator's crucial intervention in the foreign text."

For most translators there is a strong element of self-abnegation in the process of translation. The translator attempts to put aside aspects of personal style in order to serve as a domesticating conductor or conduit for the foreign text. (Analogy could be made to an actor who puts aside his own personality when he puts on a mask and assumes a role.)

Does it have to be this way? Sometimes a translator can call attention to the act of translation and to the translator's role in the production of the translated text. It could be argued that this is a more honest attitude toward the work than collaborating in the pretense that the text translated itself.

The literary critic Wayne Booth asserted the presence of an "implied author" as an implicit aspect of the text—readers form judgments about the presumed author of a work as they read, and the text can be analyzed to determine what

sort of author is implied. If the reader is aware that the work in question is a translation, perhaps we might think about the "implied translator" as well.

Two versions of the same excerpt from Senel Paz's *El lobo, el bosque y el hombre nuevo* provide an unusual opportunity to see two translations of the same work, made around the same time without an awareness of the other, thereby inadvertently shedding light on the translator's work. In 1996 I was asked by Brad Morrow, editor of the journal *Conjunctions,* to translate Paz's story for an issue Morrow was preparing on new Caribbean writing (*Conjunctions 27,* Fall 1996). What neither of us knew was that Peter Bush had recently done a translation in the United Kingdom, entitled *The Wolf, the Woods and the New Man* (usually this information emerges in rights negotiations). Together the two versions suggest the range of possibilities that confronts the translator at every point in the translation. Perhaps the main difference in this case is simply that one version is more in an American voice and the other more in a British one.

Mention was made earlier of a work by Carlos Fuentes that shrank dramatically in translation. In *Three Trapped Tigers* we witness the opposite phenomenon, a work that has swelled in translation. Donald Gardner and Suzanne Jill Levine, working closely with the author, Guillermo Cabrera Infante, expanded the farcical wordplay of the original work, providing many new puns and *jeux des mots* for the English edition. This famous triumph of translation demonstrates what is possible when a translator is given free reign.

John Felstiner's "Fertile Misremembrance: Translating Levertov's Neruda" highlights the act of translation is an unusual way. At its core is a sure-handed translation of Pablo Neruda's "Apogeo del apio" ("Celebration of Celery"), a translation that never slips in diction or meter. But as interesting as the translation itself is the story of its making, which began with a passage that haunted the poet Denise Levertov and led to some detective work on the translator's part. In his preamble to the poem, he contextualizes his translation, bringing the translator—who so often seeks, perhaps futilely, the role of invisible go-between—into the foreground.

x

from
The Wolf, The Forest, and The New Man

BY SENEL PAZ

For us Cubans, *I'm leaving,* in the tone that Diego had spoken it, had a terrible connotation. It meant leaving the country forever, erasing yourself from its memory and it from yours, and—like it or not—it meant treason. That is something one knows from the start: it's included in the price of passage. Once you have it in your hand you can never convince anyone that you didn't want it. That can't be your case, Diego. What are you going to do away from Havana, from its hot, messy streets, the clamor of the habaneros. What will you do in some other city, Diego, love, where the Lezama had not been born, and Alicia didn't dance her farewell performance every Friday night? A city without bureaucrats or hardliners to criticize, without a David to love you. "It's not for the reason you imagine," he said. "You know that for me politics is a pig in a poke. It's because of Germán's exposition. You're not very observant, you didn't notice the stir it made. It turned out it wasn't him they fired, it was me. Germán worked out something with them, he rented a room and came to work in Havana as a craftsman. I realize I went too far in defense of his work, that I was insubordinate and reckless, that I took advantage of my position. So what? Now, with that censure in my file I'll never find any work, except in agriculture or construction, and you tell me, what am I going to do with a brick in my hand, where would I put it? It's a simple labor censure, but who's going to hire me with that on my record, who would take a chance on me? It's unjust, I know it; I have the law on my side, and in the end they will have to see reason and exonerate me. But what can I do? Fight? No. I'm weak, and your world is not for the weak. On the contrary, you act as if we don't exist, as if we were here solely to mortify you and collude against you. For you life is easy: you don't

fuéramos así sólo para mortificarlos y ponernos de acuerdo con la gusanera. A ustedes la vida les es fácil: no padecen complejos de Edipo, no les atormenta la belleza, no tuvieron un gato querido que vuestro padre les descuartizó ante los ojos para que se hicieran hombres. También se puede ser maricón y fuerte. Los ejemplos sobran. Estoy claro en eso. Pero no es mi caso. Yo soy débil, me aterra la edad, no puedo esperar diez o quince años a que ustedes recapaciten, por mucha confianza que tenga en que la Revolución terminará enmendando sus torpezas. Tengo treinta años. Me quedan otros veinte de vida útil, a lo sumo. Quiero hacer cosas, vivir, tener planes, pararme ante el espejo de *Las Meninas*, dictar una conferencia sobre la poesía de Flor y Dulce Maria Loynaz. ¿No tengo derecho? Si fuera un buen católico y creyera en otra vida no me importaba, pero el materialismo de ustedes se contagia, son demasiados años. La vida es ésta, no hay otra. O en todo caso, a lo mejor es sólo ésta. ¿Tú me comprendes? Aquí no me quieren, para qué darle más vueltas a la noria, y a mí me gusta ser como soy, soltar unas cuantas plumas de vez en cuando. Chico, ¿a quién ofendo con eso, si son mis plumas?

suffer from Oedipus complexes, you don't worry about beauty, you never had a favorite cat that your father quartered before your eyes just to make a man of you. I know you can be a faggot and still be strong, there are lots of examples. That is clear. But not in my case. I'm weak, I'm worried about growing old, I can't wait ten or fifteen years for you to reconsider, as confident as I am that the Revolution will in the end correct its errors. I'm thirty. I've got another twenty useful years at most. I want to do things, to live, make plans, stop and look at myself in the mirror at *Las Meninas*, give a lecture on the poetry of Flor and Dulce María Loynaz. Don't I have that right? If I were a good Catholic and believed in an afterlife it wouldn't matter, but your materialism is contagious after all these years. This is life, there is no other. Or at least, there better not be another, you know what I mean? They don't want me here, why not turn my cheek any longer; besides, I like being the way I am, to put on a little plumage now and then. Tell me, who do I harm, if they're my feathers?

de
el lobo, el bosque y el hombre nuevo

POR Senel Paz

Me voy, en el tono en que lo había dicho Diego, tiene entre nosotros una connotación terrible. Quiere decir que abandonas el país para siempre, que te borras de su memoria y lo borras de la tuya, y que, lo quieras o no, asumes la condición de traidor. Desde un principio lo sabes y lo aceptas porque viene incluido en el precio del pasaje. Una vez que lo tengas en la mano no podrás convencer a nadie de que no lo adquiriste con regocijo. Éste no podía ser tu caso, Diego. ¿Qué ibas a hacer tú lejos de La Habana, de la cálida suciedad de sus calles, del bullicio de los habaneros? ¿Qué podías hacer en otra ciudad, Diego querido, donde no hubiera nacido Lezama ni Alicia bailara por última vez cada fin de semana; una ciudad sin burócratas ni dogmáticos para criticar, sin un David que te fuera tomando cariño? "No es por lo que piensas," dijo. "Sabes que a mí en política me da lo mismo ocho que ochenta. Es por la exposición de Germán. Eres muy poco observador, no sabes el vuelo que tomó eso. Y no lo botaron a él del trabajo, me botaron a mí. Germán se entendió con ellos, alquiló un cuarto y viene a trabajar para La Habana como artesano de arte. Reconozco que me excedí en la defensa de las obras, que cometí indisciplinas y actué por la libre, aprovechándome de mi puesto, pero ¿qué? Ahora, con esta nota en el expediente, no voy a encontrar trabajo más que en la agricultura o la construcción, y dime, ¿qué hago yo con un ladrillo en la mano?, ¿dónde lo pongo? Es una simple amonestación laboral, ¿pero quién me va a contratar con esta facha, quién va a arriesgarse por mí? Es injusto, lo sé, la ley está de mi parte y al final tendrían que darme la razón e indemnizarme. Pero, ¿qué voy a hacer? ¿Luchar? No. Soy débil, y el mundo de ustedes no es para los débiles. Al contrario, ustedes actúan como si no existiéramos, como si

TRANSLATED BY **Peter Bush**

from
The wolf, the woods and the new man
BY SENEL PAZ

The tone with which Diego had said 'I'm leaving' has terrible connotations for us. It means you're departing the country forever, that you're erasing yourself from its memory, and it from yours, and, whether you like it or not, you're agreeing to be labelled a traitor. You agree to that from the start because it comes with the price of the ticket. Once it's in your grasp you won't convince anyone you weren't delighted with your purchase. It's not you, Diego. What would you do far from Havana, from those dirty, warm streets and bustling *habaneros?* What would you do in another city, dear Diego, where Lezama wasn't born and Alicia Alonso doesn't put in a final appearance every weekend? A city without bureaucrats and hardliners to criticise, without a David, who is getting to like you? 'It's not because of what you think', he said. 'You know I couldn't care less about the political swings and roundabouts. It's because of Germán's exhibition. You're not very perceptive, you don't know the impact it had. They didn't kick him out of his job. I was the one they kicked out. Germán reached a compromise with them, he's rented a room and is coming to Havana to work in arts and crafts. I recognise I went too far in defending his work, that I was undisciplined and acted like a free agent, took advantage of my position, but so what? Now I've got that on my record, I only get work in the fields or on building-sites, and you tell me what I'd do with a brick in my hand, where would I put it? It's only a caution, but who will ever give a job to someone with my looks. I know it's not fair, that the law's on my side and in the end they'd have to admit as much and give me compensation. But what am I going to do? Fight? No way. I'm weak, and there's no place for the weak in your world. On the contrary, you behave as if we didn't exist, as if we were

fuéramos así sólo para mortificarlos y ponernos de acuerdo con la gusanera. A ustedes la vida les es fácil: no padecen complejos de Edipo, no les atormenta la belleza, no tuvieron un gato querido que vuestro padre les descuartizó ante los ojos para que se hicieran hombres. También se puede ser maricón y fuerte. Los ejemplos sobran. Estoy claro en eso. Pero no es mi caso. Yo soy débil, me aterra la edad, no puedo esperar diez o quince años a que ustedes recapaciten, por mucha confianza que tenga en que la Revolución terminará enmendando sus torpezas. Tengo treinta años. Me quedan otros veinte de vida útil, a lo sumo. Quiero hacer cosas, vivir, tener planes, pararme ante el espejo de *Las Meninas*, dictar una conferencia sobre la poesía de Flor y Dulce Maria Loynaz. ¿No tengo derecho? Si fuera un buen católico y creyera en otra vida no me importaba, pero el materialismo de ustedes se contagia, son demasiados años. La vida es ésta, no hay otra. O en todo caso, a lo mejor es sólo ésta. ¿Tú me comprendes? Aquí no me quieren, para qué darle más vueltas a la noria, y a mí me gusta ser como soy, soltar unas cuantas plumas de vez en cuando. Chico, ¿a quién ofendo con eso, si son mis plumas?

only here to mortify you and reach agreements with the bums in exile. You lead an easy life: you don't suffer an Oedipus complex, you're not tortured by beauty, you didn't have a favourite cat which your father chopped up in front of you so as to make a man of you. It's not impossible to be queer and strong. There are plenty of examples. I know that. But I'm not one of them. I'm weak, I'm terrified about growing old, I can't wait ten or fifteen years for you to have second thoughts, however confident I am the Revolution will finally change its ways. I'm thirty. At most I've got twenty years of active life left. I want to do things, live, make plans, see myself in the mirror of *Las Meninas,* give a lecture on the poetry of Flor and Dulce María Loynaz. Don't I have that right? If I were a good Catholic and believed in another life I wouldn't worry, but your materialism is contagious, that's too many years to wait. This is our life, there is no other. Or at any rate, there's probably only this one. Do you understand? They don't want me here, why mess around, I like the way I am, I want to drop a few pansy petals now and then. Who could that possibly upset, honey, if they're my petals?'

de

ᴛres ᴛristes ᴛigres

POR GUILLERMO CABRERA INFANTE

Rompecabeza

¿**Q**uién era Bustrófedon? ¿Quién fue quién será quién es Bustrófedon? ¿B? Pensar en él es como pensar en la gallina de los huevos de oro, en una adivinanza sin respuesta, en la espiral. *El era Bustrófedon para todos y todo para Bustrófedon era él.* No sé de dónde carajo sacó la palabrita—o la palabrota. Lo único que sé es que yo me llamaba muchas veces Bustrófoton o Bustrófotomatón o Busnéforoniepce, depende, dependiendo y Silvestre era Bustrófenix o Bustrofeliz o Bustrófitzgerald, y Florentino Cazalis fue Bustrófloren mucho antes de que se cambiara el nombre y se pusiera a escribir en los periódicos con su nuevo nombre de Floren Cassalis, y una novia de él se llamó siempre Bustrofedora y su madre era Bustrofelisa y su padre Bustrófader, y ni siquiera puedo decir si su novia se llamaba Fedora de veras o su madre Felisa y que él tuviera otro nombre que el que él mismo se dio. Me imagino que sacó la pal-abra de un diccionario como del nombre de una medicina (¿ayudado por Silvestre?) tomó lo de continente de Mutaflora, que era la bustrofloresta de los bustrófalos.

Recuerdo que un día fuimos a comer juntos él, Bustrofedonte (que era el nombre esa semana para Rine, a quien llamaba no solamente el más leal amigo del hombre, sino Rineceronte, Rinedocente, Rinedecente, Rinecente, como luego hubo un Rinecimiento seguido del Rinesimiento, Rinesimento, Rinesemento, Rinefermento, Rinefermoso, Rineferonte, Ronoferante, Bonoferviente, Buonofarniente, Busnofedante, Bustopedante, Bustofedonte:

TRANSLATED BY Donald Gardner AND Suzanne Jill Levine

from
Three Trapped Tigers
BY GUILLERMO CABRERA INFANTE

Brainteaser

Who was Bustrófedon? Who was/is/will be Bustrófedon? Boustrophedon? Thinking about him is like thinking of the goose that laid golden eggs, of a riddle with no answer, a spiral without end. *He was Bustrófedon for all and all for Bustrófedon was he.*

I don't know where the fuck he got that 7-plus-4-letter name from. All I know is that he often called me Bustrofoton or Bustrophotomaton or Busneforoniepce, depending deepening on my current hangup, but I always answered his mastery voice, and Silvestre was Bustrophoenix or Bustrophoelix or Bustrofitzherald, and Florentino Cazalis was Bustrofloren long before he changed his name and began writing in the papers bustroperously as Floren Cassalis, and his girl was always called Bustrofedora and his mother was Bustrofelisa and his father Bustrofather, and I just don't know if his girl friend's real name was Fedora or if his mother was really called Felisa or whatever. But I guess he must have picked that word, *the* word at random (house) out of a dictionary like the way he took the name of a medicine (with Silvestre's help?) to bustroform the continent of Mutaflora with its metafauna of bustroffaloes composed of hunting bustrophies sent back alive.

I remember one day we'd gone out to eat together, he and Bustrofedonte (which was Rine's name that week, because his name wasn't just Man's Best Friend but also: Rinecerous, Rinaidecamp, Rinaissance, leading to general Rinformation and Rineffulgence followed by a Rinegation and back to Rinessentials and Rinephemera, Rinetcetera, Rineffervescent, Bonofarniente,

variantes que marcaban las variaciones de la amistad: palabras como un termómetro) y yo, cuando aparecieron los dos a buscarme al periódico me dijo, Vamos a una bustrofonda, porque detestaba los restaurantes de lujo y las lámparas de lágrimas y las flores de papel, y llegamos y no se había sentado cuando llamó al camarero. Bustrómozo, dijo y ya ustedes saben cómo son los camareros en La Habana tarde en la noche, que no les gusta que los llamen por su nombre: ni camareros ni mozos ni dependientes ni cosas por el estilo, así que vino el tipo con una cara más larga que la cola de una boa y casi tan fría y escamosa, y deveras que ya no era un mozo. Bustrósotros, dijo, v-va, vamos a cocomer, dijo imitando un gago este Bustrófunny-man y el camarero (o como se llame) lo miró mortalmente, más víbora que boa o una víboa, y yo me metí una servilleta de papel (era una fonda a la moderna) en la boca para ahogar la risa, pero la risa sabía nadar crawl, relevo australiano o de pecho y las servilletas sabían a saliva de tigre y toca la casualidad que B. que en ese momento se llamaba Bustrófate me decía, Debíamos haber convivido a Bustrófelix, y yo tenía la risa llegando a la presa de papel y él que me pregunta, Eh Bustrófoto, y yo que le digo, con la servilleta en la meta de la boca, Fi flaro, y allá va la servilleta como un volador de alcance intermedio seguido por una carcajada supersónica que era una cadena de pedos bucales o vocales o bocales y el proyectiro que da, le cae al camarero en su cara, que toma todo el largo de su cara larga como pista de aterrizaje, que en un final da en diana de ojo ajado, y el tipo se niega a servirnos y se nos va de la vida como van las arenas al mar (música de Sabre Marroquín) y arma tremendo bochinche allá en el fondo del océano con el dueño poseidónico y nosotros en el más acá muertos de risa en la orilla del mantel, con este pregonero increíble, el heraldo, Bustrófono, éste, gritando, BustrofenóNemo chico eres Bustrófonbraun, gritando, Bustrómba marina, gritando, Bustifón, Bustrosimún, Busmonzón, gritando, Viento Bustrófenomenal, gritando a diestro y siniestro y ambidiestro. Tuvo que venir el dueño que era un gallego calvo y chiquito y gordo, más bajito que el camarero, que al ponerse de pie al fondo no daba pie y parecía que se puso de rodillas, un Busto que anda.

Bonosirviente, Busnofedante, Bustopedant: rineing ringing the changes on his name to show the ring & range and changes in their friendship: casting words in a spellometer) and me, and when the two of them came to find me in the newspaper office he said, Let's go eat in a Bustrofeteria, because he loathed expensive restaurants and chandeliers and paper flowers, and when we found a B-eanery and before we'd sat down he'd called the waiter. Bustroboy, he said. You know what they're like, the waiters in Havana early in the evening or late at night: all bums, so they don't like to be called by their name: neither waiter nor boy or Charlie or even come here you flunky, that kind of thing, and so this fellow came up with a face as long as a boa's tail and almost as cold and scaly and he clearly wasn't a boy any longer if he ever had been. C-come on, old b-boy, w-we w-want s-some b-bustrofood, said putting on a sturm und s-stammer this Bustrofunfare, and the waiter (if that's the right word) looked daggers at him, more cobra than boaish or boyish or boorish, and I shoved a paper napkin (it was a modernstyleatery) in my mouth to drown my laughter, but my laughs could crawl and do breast and back and breathstroke so the paper towels were beginning to taste like papertigertale, and as fuck or late would have it, B., whose name was Bustrophate that moment, said to me, We should of off invited Bustróphoelix, and my laughter was Bustrofoaming around the floodgates of the next of napkin and then he asked me, What you think, Bustrophotoflood? and I answer Fure fof fourse and my napkin flies off fike a pfeiffer fjet followed by a superzanic bang composed of a chain eruction of vocal or oral or auroral farts and in the trajectory it follows the servjette sets itself on a collision main course with the waiter's face, taking the whole length of his long lonely face like a landing strip, finally striking his jaundiced eyeball like a yellow bullseye and the fellouch refuses to serve us and gets off our cloud to plunge icariously into the horizontal chasm of thiseatery and starts bellyaching in the backroom to the Poseidowner and we're still there in the hearafter drowning of laughter on the shores of the tablecloth, almost nausicated, with this unbelievable public proclaimer Bustrophone herald tribunely crying out, You were a BustrophenoNemo, a Bustrofonbraum, crying out loud, Bustyphoon, Bustornado, Bustrombone, outcrying himself, Bustrombamarina, crying to left and right, sydneyster-and-

THE TRANSLATOR

203

—¿QUE OS PASA?

—Queremos (dijo Bustro tan tranquilo, de perfil) queremos quomer.

—Pero, haziendo burlas, amiguito, no se come.

—Y quién hizo burlas (preguntó Bustrófactótum y como él era un tipo largo y flaco y con muy mala cara y esta malacara picada por el acné juvenil o por la viruela adulta o por el tiempo y el salitre o por los buitres que se adelantaban, o por todas esas cosas juntas, se paró, se puso de pie, se dobló, se triplicó, se telescopió hacia arriba agigantándose en cada movimiento hasta llegar al cielo raso, puntal o techo.)

Y el dueño se achicó, si es que podía hacerlo todavía y
fue el hombre increíblemente encogido, pulgarcito
o meñique, el genio de la botella al revés y
se fue haciendo más y más y más chico,
pequeño, pequeñito, chirriquitico
hasta que se desapareció por
un agujero de ratones al
fondo-fondo-fondo,
un hoyo que
empezaba
con
o

y me cordé de Alicia en el País de las Maravillas y se lo dije al Bustroformidable ye él se puso a recrear, a regalar: Alicia en el mar de villas, Alicia en el País que Más Brilla, Alicia en el Cine Maravillas, Avaricia en el País de las Malavillas, Malavidas, Mavaricia, Marivia, Malicia, Milicia Milhizia Milhinda Milindia Milinda Malanda Malasia Malesia Maleza Maldicia Malisa Alisia Alivia Aluvia Alluvia Alevilla y marlisa y marbrilla y maldevilla y empezó a cantar tomando como pie forzado (forzudo) mi Fi Flaro y la evocación de Alicia y el mar y Martí y los zapaticos de Rosa, aquella canción que dice así con su ritmo tropical:

dexterly, ambidexterritorially. Of curse the wan and ownly oner had to turn up right then & there: a fat bald little fellow even shorter than the waiter, so short that be hecame shorter as he approached us and when he finally arrived at the table he seemed to be walking on his hands not his feet. A moveable feat. A bust. Or was it a buster?

—WASSA MATTA?

—We wonly want to weat, Bustro said, turning a doldrum profile toward him.

—You won't get anything to eat if you fool around like that.

—Like what? Bustrofastidious asked and as he was a tall skinny fellow with a real ugly mug and thismugly of his was cratered with an acme of an acne or

huge pox Americana or
        huge pox Americana or
        by time and tide and its ruins or
        meteorites or
        vultures or

by all these things together:

    MACNEPOXVLTURETEORUINITES

he stood, got to his feet, doubled tripled, B' telescoped himself forward looking more like an unjolly green giant every miniminute till he almust touched the ceiling, roof or rafters, so big was he.

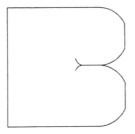

Laralaralara larararará

(afinando su guitarronca voz)

Voy arriba! ¡Allá va eso!

Bustrófueno mar tes fumas

(f)arina fina y Philar

(f)iero fallir afrenar

suphón dillito dis phruta

Váyala fiña di Viña

deifel Fader fidel fiasco

falla mimú psicocastro

alfú mar sefú más phinas

AH NO pero no sirve: todo esto había que oírlo, hay que oírlo, oírlo a él, como había que oír su *Borborigma Darü*:

Maniluvios con ocena fosforecen en repiso.

Catacresis repentinas aderezan debeladas

Maromillas en que aprietan el orujo y la regona,

Y esquirazas de milí rebotinan el amomo.

¿No hay amugro en la cantoña para especiar el gliconio?

Tufararas vipasanas paloteabean el telefío.

La reata de encellado, ¿no enfoscaba en el propíleo?

Ah, cosetanos bombés que revulsan el limpión!

Tunantada enmohecida se fulmina en la diapente.

Pastinacas de diapreas opositan

El frimario mientras pecas de satirio

Afollaban los fosfenos del litófago en embrión.

¡No hay marisma!

AND THE OWNER GOT SMALLER AND SMALLER AND
SMALLER AND YET SMALLER IF IT WAS STILL POSSIBLE AND MAN
was but so incredibly shrunk he was only the size of my
thumb or my little finger which is a very little finger:
he's in fact a genie of the bottle in reverse and now he
went on getting littler and littler, as tiny as anyone
can be, even tinier and tinier: the tiniest tim on
earth, and tinier than even: tm: till amazing us with
his shrinking bouts & feats: and he was no
longer visible, not quite yet invisible: so
final-ly he stood up to vanish down a hole
by the door: a mouse-whole by-by by
the way by the door: a house of a
doormouse so very Butso housey
this mousey-hall did not begin right
& there it began somewhere
els somewhere elsie: it
began with—oh no! oh
yes!—but no! but yes,
sire, it began it
yessiree! but hole it,
mate! hold it a
moment for this
hole begins
here but
and/or,
ah so
an
o

and it reminded me of Alice in Wonderland and I said just that to Bustroformidable
crytone and he began to entertain certain sentences and us and he delit and
regaled us: the brief and regal night of Frank Masonry: Alice in Funland, Alice
in Thyland, Alice in Mytime, Alice in Wonder, Alice in Wanderlush, Alice the
one and last, My Alice, Malice, Malice Forathought, Alice and Eve, Malice
and Varix, Evealice, Avarice, Avaricia and Malicia and Malaysia and Melanesia
and Macromicia and Micronisia and Microlicia, Microalice in the hole, in the
whole, in the hold, Alace in the hole, Alichole, Alls-hole, Alasthouse, Alasose,
Alicetose, Alicetosis, Halicetosis, Helixhose, Helaxhoses, Elaxtosis and shrinking
and growing up again and shriveling back to seize he—B—Bl—B1? Why not
B2? B or not 2B—him began sitting and singing and seizing and sizing me up
and down with my Fure fof fourse, furoff coarse, my Four de Force and with his

Los ibídemes de prasma refocilan
En melindres y a su lado la gumía jaraneaba un notocordio
En trisagios de silbón.

Gurruferos malvaviscos
Juntamente en metonimias desancoraban la gubia
Para pervertir la espundia y abatanar el cachú.

¡No hagan olas!

Cachondeos poliglotos prefacionan el azur
Y amartelan el rehílo de alcatifas en palurdo,
Otrosíes de la fullona dorada en el conticinio
¡Vale reis!
¿No entrelinean el dilúculo?
¡Prior pautado!

Volapiés de sonajeros atafagan el boquín
Y en las dalas, en las dalas de Gehenna
Recurvan los borborigmos de la simonía de abril.

Y justamente en este mes aprovechó Rogelito Catresino para pasar por la calle y nos pusimos a cantar todas las variantes de todos los nombres de la gente que conocemos, que es juego secreto—hasta que vino el camamozo o como se llame a interrumpir la ceremonia y Bustrófedon lo saludó con lo que él llama, llamaba el pobre su namaste, pero hecha no con las palmas de la mano, sino con el dorso, así:

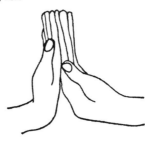

Alliteration his Alcemption his Alicevocation, merrily marrying, Marryling my self and Cuba and Martí and the Wanton nightmare I Want-a-nam-'ere La Guantanamera, that Martían song with its tropsical rhythm that goes wroughly like thus, dedicated to the one I hate:

(*instant pretension or interpoleation or inpernetration by M.S.*)

Yo soy un hombre sincero
I'm a man without a zero
De donde crece la palma
From the land of the pawn-trees
Y antes de morirme quiero
And 'fore lay-dying I xerox
Hechar mil voces del alma.
One thousand copies of me.

Con los sobres de la piedra
With the sour sickle of this hearse
Quiero yo mi muerte hinchar
I want to share man Mao
El apoyo de la Sierra
The reivers of the Sierra
Más compras hace que el mal
I like butter, then some tea.

Mi anverso es un verde claro
My grin is a dear sun-tan
En un jardín encendido
Gotten in a flaming garden
Mi reverso un muerto herido
My torso is a wounded fountain
Que luce en el norte un faro.
That looks for shells in a maiden.

BUT NO, it's no good: you'd have to hear it, you'd have to hear him in Bustroperson as you'd also have to hear his *Poe(t)' Ravings:*

y pedimos la comida.

Bustrofrijoles dijo Bustrófedon dijo él mismo Con arroz blanco traté de decir yo pero él dijo Bustrofilete dijo Bustrophedón-té dijo Bustrófedon dijo Bustrofricasé dijo Bustrofabio ay dolor bustrosfueron en un tiempo, dijo, porque era él siempre quien habló y lo dijo todo mirando al camarero cara a cara (o caracara), frente a frente, mirándole los ojos, los dos, porque todavía sentado era más alto que el otro de manera que se encogió un poco, generoso, y cuando terminamos pidió el postre también para todos. Todositario. Bustroflán, dijo y luego dijo, Bustrófeca y yo me metí por fin por medio rápido y dije, Tres cafés, pero al tratar de decir, fino, Por favor, dije Forvapor o forpavor, no sé y no sé tampoco cómo salimos sin acusarnos alguien de terroristas por la implosión y la explosión y el estruendo de las rosas, risas, y cuando trajeron el café, antes, y lo tomamos y pagamos y salimos del restaurándo ya íbamos cantando las Variaciones Quistrisini (copyright, Boustrophedon Inc.) de esa Cantata del Café que fue Bustróffenbach quien La compuso:

> Yo to doró
>
> to doró noño hermoso
>
> to doró ono coso
>
> ono coso co yo solo so
>
> COFO
>
> Ye te deré
>
> te deré neñe hermese
>
> te deré ene kese
>
> ene kese ke ye sele se
>
> KEFE
>
> Yi ti dirí
>
> ti dirí niñi hirmisi
>
> ti dirí ini kisi
>
> ini kisi ki yi sili sí
>
> KIFI

Twice beneath a mudtime weirdly ponderous I spoke in faerie
Over (and o'er) a voluminium of unwritten law (oh lore!)—
While I nodled, noodled, nundled, trundlingly I come unsundered,
As if someone howsomever, rapping, crapping at my do'er.
" 'Tis a widershins," I mongreled, "crapping at my own undo'er—
                    Who unstuck my nether moor?"
Undustunctly I rumumbled it were díssembling Decembled;
And each humbled, blundering embryo fell upon its dying floor.
Ungrately I wished tomorrow; or tomorrow and to borrow
In mine bones was Caesar's horror—horror for a long lost bore—
For the bare and fair and barren former maiden whom I bore—
                    Quoth the waiter, "Medium raw."
And the silken, sullen slinking of each skulking purple passage
Thrilled and spilled and filled and chilled me with a drafty corridor;
So that howsoever bleating my heart stopped but natheless cheating
Went on bleating, eating sleeting (a self-wind heart it was I swore)
                    The whore it was I mildly swore.
Incessantly my soul glue longer; so I longered more languorous,
"So said I," I said, "you Modman, come inside me and explore;
But in sooth, in truth, 'tis proof, you spied me at my knightly crapping,
I'm a ghostwriter, thou knowst well, inscribbling on inphantile floor
Whatsomever rhymes Unreason hath in his untimely maw—
                    Bottomless, I ask for more.

And so on incessanter till breath do us phart. And it was in that same Bloke
Decembryo that Rogelito Castresino took the opportunity to go down the
street and we started singing all the variations on all the names of the people
we know. A secret game—until the chambermate or whatever his name is came
and interrupted the ceremony and Bustrofacetious hailed him like a long lost
bugger, doing what he called, poor Bfellow, his namaste, but he did it not with
the palms of his hands, but with the back, like this:

Yu tu durú

tu durú nuñu hurmusu

tu durú unu kusu

unu kusu ku yu sulu su

KUFU

Ya ta dará

ta dará naña harmasa

ta dará ana casa

ana casa ca ya sala sá

CAFA

yo ofreciendo el acompañamiento rítmico imitando, demostrando que el hombre asciende hasta el mono, chimpanceando a Eribó, haciendo ruidos regulares (creo: estaba borracho y debía tener ritmo) con mis dedos y una cuchara y un vaso y luego afuera con las manos y la yema de los dedos y la boca y los pies de vez en cuando. Ah ah AH! cómo nos divertimos esa noche, carajo, esa Noche Carajo, de verdad que la gozamos y Bustrófedon inventó los trabalenguas más enredados y libres y simples del tipo En Cacarajícara hay una jícara que el que la desencacarajícare buen desencacarajícador de jícaras en Cacarajícara será, y todos esos *analavalanas*, como aquel tan viejo y tan bueno y tan eterno, clásico, de Dábale arroz a la zorra el abad, de los que inventó, en un momento, por una apuesta con Rine, estos tres: Amor a Roma, y: Anilina y oro son no Soroya ni Lina, y: Abaja el Ajab y baja lea jabá, que son simples pero no fáciles y son medio cubanos y medio exóticos o todo exóticos para un tercero equi(s)distante y me sorprendieron porque los pies re-forzados de Rine (dos, dijo Bustrófedon, el derecho y el izquierdo, diestro y siniestro) fueron tres: La Habana y la bandera española (¿por qué? porque paseábamos por el parque Central entre los dos centros, el gallego y el asturiano) y una mulata pasó, y hubo otro pie (B. dijo que eran tres las patas forzosas y que era ahora un cuadrúpedo, el Ñu o Gnu o Nyu) que era nuestro tema eterno entonces, La Estrella, por supuesto, y con ella Bustrofizo

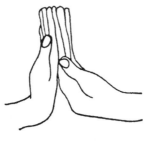

and we ordered dinner. He did.

Bustrobeans said Bustrofacile said he With white rice I tried to say but he said a T T T-bone or Bustrofilet and a cup of BustrofedonT said Bustrofidelis said Bustrofricassee said Bustrofartingissuchsweetsighing and Bustrordered them all at once because it was always he who was talking and he said it all looking at the waiter in the eye (or eyeball to youball), face to farce, looking him in the I's, condescending the stares because though he was still seated he was taller than the other even though he had generously shrunk himself a little, and when we'd finished he ordered dessert for us all too. Tootsyfruitsy. Bustroflan, he said and then he said, Bustrofocee (you focoffee yourselfish, said I) and then trying to serve as gobetween (they also serve who only stand as waiters) said quickly, Three coffees, but when I tried to say, pleasantly, If you please, I said Piss you eve and something Elsie, I'm not sure and I'm not sure either how we managed to make a getaway without someone accusing us of being terrorists what with all the implosion and explosion of laughter, like slaughters off the avenue and when they brought us the coffee, we drank it in pieces and paid and left the restoroom all systems à gogo singing the Quistrisini Variations (copyright Boustrophedon Inc.) on that jittery Festineburg that Bustroffenbach had composed. Here's to Frenchsip!

> Last aald acqaaantanca ba fargat
> And navar saan agaan
> Wa'll drank a cap af kandnass yat
> Far tha sanka afaald Lang Sana.
>
> Lest eeld ecqeeentence be ferget
> End never seen egeen

un anagrama (palabra que descompuso en una divisa, Amarg-Ana) con la frase Dádiva ávida: vida, que escrita en un encierro, en la serpiente que se come, en el anillo que es ana era un círculo mágico que cifra y descifraba la vida siempre que se empezara a leer una cualquiera de las tres palabras y era una rueda de la in-fortuna: ávida, vida, ida, David, ávida, vida, ida, dádiva, dad, ad, di, va: comenzando de nuevo, rodando y rodando y rodando hasta ir al Rrastro del Holvido desde donde podía contarnos su historia (oyentes del Alma de las Cosas), y que también y tan bien y tan(to) bien podía usarse con La Estrella porque la palabra-rueda, la frase, el anagrama de doce letras que son doce palabras:

 era una estrella y sonaban siempre a diva

Nos recitó grandes trozos no escogidos de lo que él llamaba su Diccionario de Palabras A-fines y Ideas Sinfines, que no recuerdo todo, por supuesto, pero sí muchas de sus palabras y las explicaciones, no las definiciones que su autor intercalaba: abá, aba, ababa, acá, asa, allá, Ada (hada), aná y Aya, y lamentando de paso él que Adán no se llamara en español Adá (¿se llamará así en catalá? me preguntó) porque entonces no solamente sería el primer hombre sino el hombre perfecto y declarando el oro el más precioso de los metales escritos y al ala el gran invento de Dédalo el artífice y el número 101 sea alabado porque era, es como el 88 (loado sea) un número total, redondo, idéntico a sí mismo la e-ternidad no lo cambia y como quiera que uno lo mira es siempre él mismo, otro uno, aunque decía que el perfecto-perfecto era el 69 (para alegría de Rine) que es el número absoluto, no solamente pitagórico (jodiendo a Cué) sino platónico y (halagando a Silvestre: a mystic bond of

We'll drenk e cep ef kendness yet
Fer the neskefe eeld Leng Sene.

List iild icqiiintinci bi firgit
Ind nivir siin igiin
Wi'll drink i cip if kindniss yit
Fir thi sikihi iild Ling Sini.

Lost oold ocqooontonco bo forgot
Ond novor soon ogoon
Wo'll dronk o cop of kondnoss yot
For tho so kopho oold Long Sono.

Lust uuld ucquuuntuncu bu furgut
Und nuvur suun uguun
Wu'll drunk u cup uf kundnuss yut
Fur thu sucus uf uuld Lung Sunu.

with me prohividing the reuthmic accompanist, misstaking probing that mon is evolting into mankey by drinking the mild of humonkeydniss: lone leave monkind!, phlaying my chimpanum to Eribó's baboongo, mandrilling a little cynosure of old eyes, making negular roises (at least I think so: I was zoo drunk I insisted I got rhythm) with my fingerprints and a glassdarkly and spooneristmus in my handshake and later outlawside with my handsoff and fingertrips and the mouthfool and for feetall coming in from thime to tyme crying !$ £!!!¿¿%+=&&&! Ah ah ah! AH! What a wallz we had that night, that Knight of the Balls, we really did have a goot dime and Bustroform in grate shape invented the most twattwisting and frensyfree and sample tongtwisters like that one this one it *Was he Houdini who wrote whodunits for women humorously wondering under humble exhumed human uteruses and humeruses?* *h*and *h*all those Madam I'm Adam's, like that so hold hand beewtifutile hand clocksickall hand heternal *No evil live on,* and these three he cuntcockeded, on the stop, spot. after laying a bed for a chit with Ryne: *Now a gas saga won* number one *Wonder Eve's amoral aroma severed now* number two *Emit a tit a time* number three whitch are sample and seasy and are half-Cubist and

writerhood unía a esos dos) alcmeónico, porque se cerraba en sí mismo y las sumas de sus partes más la suma de la suma era igual (aquí Cué se iba) al último número y qué sé yo cuántas complicaciones numéricas que siempre ponían frenético a C y cuando éste iba ya por la puerta B añadía con picardía cubana, Y lo que sugiere caballeros lo que sugiere.

Bustrófedon siempre andaba cazando palabras en los diccionarios (sus safaris semánticos) cuando se perdía de vista y se encerraba con un diccionario, cualquiera, en su cuarto, comiendo con él en la mesa, yendo con él al baño, durmiendo con él al lado, cabalgando días enteros sobre el lomo de un (mata) burro, que eran los únicos libros que leía y decía, le decía a Silvestre, que eran mejor que los sueños, mejor que las imaginaciones eróticas, mejor que el cine. Mejor que Hitchcock, vaya. Porque el diccionario creaba un suspenso con una palabra perdida en un bosque de palabras (agujas no en un pajar, que son fáciles de hallar, sino una aguja en un alfiletero) y había la palabra equivocada y la palabra inocente, y la palabra culpable y la palabra-asesina y la palabra-policía y la palabra-salvadora y la palabra fin, y que el suspenso del diccionario era verse uno buscando una palabra desesperado arriba y abajo del libro hasta encontrarla y cuando aparecía y veía que significaba otra cosa era mejor que la sorpresa en el último rollo (en esos días estaba entusiasmado porque había leído que adefesio venía de la epístola de San Pablo a los efesios, y, decía Bustro, no a uno sino a todos, Te das cuenta viejo que es un invento del mismo culpable de tanta pareja infeliz y tanto adulterio y tantos tangos, y que el matrimonio puede ser el mayor adefesio, porque Bustrófedon era tan enemigo del matrimonio (mártirmonio decía él) como amigo de las casadas, (perfectas o imperfectas) del mar Muerto y lo único que lamentaba era que el diccionario, los diccionarios todos admitieran tan pocas malas palabras y se sabía todas las que traían de memoria (había una, olisbo por consolador, que lo atrapó como un anzuelo y la tuvo clavada en boca semanas y para fastidiar a Silvestre recordaba la película italiana No hay paz entre los olivos con la parodia No hay paja entre los olisbos) como se sabía la definición, del diccionario de la Real Academia, del perro: *M., mamífero doméstico de la familia*

half-Quexotic or completely a toxic for an ekuedistant third partying is sock sweet surrey, and they sourprised me because Rhine's reinforced feet (two, said Bustrofaraway, the left and the wrigth, degauche et malraudroit) were three, ad pedem litter: Havana, the name of a city which is just a beautyfoul corruption of Savanna/ Sabannah/ Sabana/ Abanna/ Havannah/ Havana/ Habana/ La Habana/ *Avana* in Italics Cyrillically Gabana, and the Sbanish panner (why? because we were crossing Central Park between the three centers, the Galician center and the Asturian center plus the off center) and mulatto she-woman walked on by and there was another horny foot (B. said that that made a quadruped, a Nu or Gnude or New) which was our eternal theme then, La Estrella of cursed, and Bustrofactored it into more anagrams (a word he broke up into: A ram sang) with the phrase *Dádiva ávida: vida* which when written in a ringaroundarosy, in an *encierro*: is the serpent that eats itself: is the ring that is an ankh: is a magic circle, cyclic shift which continually makes a cipher of the zephyr of life and deciphers its ways anyway and which you can begin reading with any one of the words and it is a wheel of fartune: *David, ávida, vida, avi, vid, ida, dádiva, dad, ad, di, va*: beginning again, turning and turning and turning the till undtil you come to the wheel of aloneliness with its still center out of which it can tale us its tell, and which can also and as well and so well be used with La Estrella because the wordwheel, the life sentence, the three-times-four-letter anagram which also makes twelve words a twelf-word:

 was a star and

He recited gray darkened passages from what he called his Dicktionary of Contaguous Words end Andless Idees, which of source I cannot remember in their entitirety, but I can give you many of his past words and the explanations, not definitions which their author indented: Aha, Anna, deed, Eve, gig,

de los cánidos, de tamaño, forma y pelaje muy diversos, según las razas, pero siempre
con la cola menor que las patas posteriores (y aquí hacía una pausa) *una de las cuales*
levanta el macho para orinar, y seguía con sus palabras felices:

Ana

ojo

non

anilina

eje (todo gira sobre él)

radar

ananá (su fruta favorita)

sos y

gag (la más feliz)

y estuvo a punto de hacerse musulmán por el nombre de Alá, el dios perfecto, y
se exaltaba con la poca diferencia que hay entre alegoría y alegría y alergia y el
parecido de causalidad con casualidad y la confusión de alienado con alineado,
y también hizo listas de palabras que significaban cosas distinas a través del
espejo

mano/onam

azar/ raza

aluda/adula

otro/orto

risa/asir

y señaló los cambios de sílabas mutantes como gato y toga y roto y toro
y labio y viola en alquimias que no acaban nunca, y habló y explicó y se
explayó y explanó (juego suyo) y jugó con las palabras hasta las tres de la
mañana (hora que supo porque tocaban el vals Las tres de la mañana y esa
noche fue idéntica a otra noche en que molestó a Cué con su nuevo sistema de
numeración no continua basado en un refrán que leyó (quizá B. prefi(ri) era
decir oyó) no sé dónde de que una cifra vale igual que un millón y dónde los

Hannah, noon, poop, radar, wow, which upsidedome explains why I'm sodown, and finally regretting in passing away the fact that Adam wasn't called Adá in Spanish (would he be called like that in Catalá? He wondered) because then not only would he be the first man but he'd also be perfect and the only man right enough to name things, and declaring that noon was logically the zenith of the day just as deed when it is written done has a completeness which says what it means and the number 101 should be praised one hundred times because it was like 88 (glory be) a total number, round, identitcal to itself eternity cannot change it nor space wither nor time stale and however you look at it it is always the same, another one, even though the plus perfect of perfect numbers was, *is*, the 69 (to Rine's great Joy) which is the absolute number always differing and never the shame, not only Pythagorically (which, but exactly, bugged Cué) Platonically as well and (which ticked Silvestre: a mystic bond of broaderhood made them both one, Don One) Alcmeonic, because it closed in on itself and the sum of its farts plus the sum of the sound was equal (Cué walked out at this point) to the last figure and I don't know how many other pseudo numberical complications which always drove C. crazy and when he was leaving B. called at him in the doorway with Cuban Malice, And what does the innuend, gentlemen!

Bustrofrankbuck spent all his time hunting wild words in the dictionaries (his semantic safaris) when he went out of sight, and out of mind (his not ours) and shut himself up with a dictionary to bring 'em words back alive, and any dictionary, it didn't matter which, in his room, driving into the rough sketches of letters, became his dictumnary, eating out of it at oddmeals, taking a bath with/in it sleeping with/on it with words as a pillow waiting for sunup/or/down: It by His side sliding in and out of It, not a book- but a dictionary-worm, because dictionaries were all he read and he said, he said to Silvestre that they were better than dreams, better than masturboratory fansies, better than glu movies. Better than Hitchcock o belie me! Because the dictionary created its suspense with one word lost in a wood of words (not like needles in a haystack which are easy to find, but one particular pin in a pincushion) and there was the wrong word and the word innocent and the word guilty and the word-assassin and the word-police and the word-chase and the word-rescue-patrol

números no tienen un valor fijo o determinado por su posición o el orden sino que tienen un valor arbitrario y cambiante o totalmente fijo, y se contaba, por ejemplo, del 1 al 3 y después del 3 no venía naturalmente el 4 sino el 77 o el 9 o el 1563 y en que dijo que algún día se descubriría que todo el sistema de ordenación postal era erróneo, que lo lógico sería enumerar las calles y darle un nombre a cada casa y declaró que la idea era paralela a su sistema de nuevo bautizo de hermanos en que todos tendrían diferentes apellidos pero el mismo nombre, y a pesar del encojonamiento (no hay otra palabra, lo siento) de Cué fue una noche corta y feliz, divertidos todos porque en el Deauville Silvestre escogió una carta desechada por un coime amigo de Cué, el dos de diamantes y dijo que él podía decir cuál era el derecho o el revés de la carta, no el anverso o el reverso, sino que sabía orientarla, ponerla de pie, fijarla, por mera intuición, así dijo, ya que el dos de diamantes, como se sabe, cae igual siempre y a Bustro le encantó encontrarse con una capicúa gráfica y apostó que era imposible que Silvestre pudiera destruirla sabiendo su verdadera posición y Cué dijo que Silvestre hacía trampas y Silvestre se molestó y Bustródefon se puso de su parte y lo salvó con su abogacía de que era imposible hacer trampas con una sola carta y animó a Silvestre a que nos hiciera el juego del polígamo (así dijo) y Silvestre nos preguntó a todos, menos a B, si sabíamos qué era exactamente un hexágono y Rine dijo que era un polígono de seis lados y Cué que era un sólido de seis caras y Silvestre dijo que eso era un hexaedro y entonces yo cogí y lo dibujé (Eribó, claro, no estaba: lo hubiera hecho él entonces) en un papel

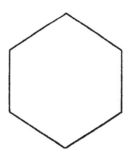

in the last word-reel and lastly the word end, and because the suspense of the dictionary lay in seeing oneself looking desperately for a word up and down the columns until one found it and when it turned up seeing that it meant something different, this was better than one's surprise at the last real, and the one thing he truly and reely regretted was that the dictionary the dictionaries have hardly any obscenities in them as this Bustrofunkandwagnalls knew them all by heart as he also knew by heart and played by ear the definition of the word dog in the Diccionario Manual Ilustrado de la Real Academia Española (2a. ed., Madrid, 1958, p.1173/a): *M., domestic mammal of the family of canidae, of varying size, shape and color according to the breed, but which always has its tail shorter than its hind legs* (and he paused at this pointer) *one of which the male of the species lifts in order to urinate*, and he went on with his happy trip around the words:

Tit

eye

nun

kayak

level

sexes (everything starts with them three)

radar

civic

sos (the most helpful)

gag (the funiest)

boob

and for years he missed Miss Gardner lovesickly because he said, Ava was the ideal woman, and he went crazy over the simihilarity between allegory and allergy and causality and casualty and chance and change, and how easily farce becomes force, and he also made a list of words that read differently in the mirror:

Live/evil

part/trap

flow/wolf

diaper/repaid

y entonces Silvestre dijo que era en realidad un cubo que perdió su tercera dimensión y lo completó así

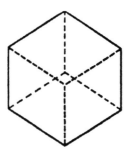

y dijo que cuando el hexágono encontrara su dimensión perdida y supiéramos cómo lo hizo, podríamos nosotros encontrar la cuarta y la quinta y las demás dimensiones y pasear libremente entre ellas (por el Paseo de las Dimensiones dijo B. señalando hacia el Paseo de las Misiones) y entrar en un cuadro, pararnos sobre un punto, viajar del presente al futuro o al pasado o a otro más allá con abrir una puerta solamente, y Rine aprovechó para hablar de sus inventos, como el de la máquina que nos convertirá en un rayo de luz (yo dije que también en un rayo de sombras) y nos enviará a Marte o a Venus (ahí quiero ir yo, dijo Vustrófedon) y allá lejos y hará tiempo otra máquina nos re-convertiría, haría de la luz luces y sombras sólidas y así nos convertiríamos en turistas espaciales, y Cué dijo que era la misma técnica de los puertos de escala y B. dijo que eran Las Esc-alas de Y-ser o Y-ver no Ibert, y Cué cometió el error (que B. escribía erore) de contar que él habia imaginado una vez un cuento de amor donde un hombre en la tierra sabía que había una mujer en un planeta de otra galaxia (ya Bustro comenzó por decir, el camino de toda leche, traduciendo del latin o del griego) que lo amaba y él se enamoraba locamente de ella y ambos sabían que era el verdadero amor imposible porque nunca nunca se encontrarían y deberían amarse en el silencio de los espacios infinitos y claro Bustrófedon terminó la velada jodiendo a Cué al decir que eran Tri-star e Isonda, y ahí fue calabaza calabaza cada uno a su casa y el que no tenga casa que) que, cosa curiosa (curiocosa) encontramos

> reward/drawer
> drab/bard
> Dog/God!

and from this *blast*phemy he used to jump into concussions, what he called his anagogic anagrams:

> cats scat
> risk irks
> wells swell
> Spain pains
> cars scar

to end his high IQ in hai-kus:

> I saw, I was
> Psychic, chic spy.

> Eve, Adam's rib:
> A maid, a bride:
> *Eve!*

> BUT

> Eve's mad:
> A river's dam
> Is bad:
> I've made *bras!*

and he showed the changes in muted and/or mutant syllables like anon and onan and navel and venal and late and tale in endless alchemies, and he explained and expounded and explosed as he played with words till three in the morning (we knew what time it was because they were playing the waltz Three O'clock in the Morning Waltz) when he hit the jackity-jackpot of the spot that tops the post with a stop of pots and puns. That was the night that was exactly the same as another night when he wore Cué out with his new system of discontinuous

en Las Vegas a Arsenio Cué, que nos estuvo evitando no invitando toda la noche porque estaba con una hembra vulgo lea, geva o ninpha (y si hablo como Bustrófedon ya para siempre no lo siento sino que lo hago a conciencia y a ciencia y lo único que lamento es no poder hablar de verdad y natural y siempre (siempre también para atrás, no sólo para adelante) así y olvidarme de la luz y de las sombras y de los claroscuros, de las fotos, porque una de sus palabras vale por mil imágenes), trigueña, alta, blanca muy blanca, linda, fotogénica, una modelo que era un cromo y Cué puso una cara de plomo y habló con su voz de radio y B. le dijo que el club estaba lleno de elementos simples y lo boncheamos saturnalmente y Bustro inventó allí aquel slogan criminal de Arsénico para los Cué, que nosotros convertimos en un himno de la noche hasta que se acabó la noche y cuando yo quise seguir hasta hacerlo un himno del amanecer en el trópico, Rine dijo que asi no valis y me callé y me caí y me cagué en la cultura que siempre viene a interrumpir con su metafísica la felicidad.

Esa fue la última vez (si olvido lo que quiero olvidar, por lo que hago este enorme paréntesis, para lo que quisiera no tener memoria: la noche del sábado) que vi vivo a Bustrofaón (como lo llamaba Silvestre a veces) y si uno no lo vio vivo no lo vio, y fue Silvestre en realidad quien lo vio por última vez, vivo. Antier mismo vino este Bustrófilme que así se llamaba esa semana para nosotros no para el siglo y me dijo que a B. lo habían ingresado y yo pensé que se iba a operar de la vista porque tenía un ojo malo, estrabiado, perdido en la jungla de la noche, apuntado con un ojo para el ser y con otro para la nalga, como decía Silvestre siempre, o para la nada en realidad, y esta visión de camaleón, total era un problema para su cerebro y siempre tenía dolores de cabeza, grandes, enormes jaquecas que él llamaba el pobre las cefalalgias Brutales o las Bustrolalias cefálicas o la Bustrocéfalolalias, y pensé ir a la clínica el lunes al mediodía cuando saliera del turno de noche, que Bustrófedon, más económico o menos desacertado, llamaba el nocturno. Pero ayer martes por la mañana me llama Silvestre y me dice, así de pronto, que Bustrófedon se acaba de morir y sentí que el teléfono me decía algo que era lo

numeration based on a proverb he'd read (probably B. would prefer to say heard) I don't know where about (we ignore his presidents whoreabouts, Ho Ho Ho!) a figure being equal to a million and in which the numbers have no value fixed or determined by their position or order but they have an arbitrary and fluctuating or totally fixed value, and you could count, for example, from 1 to 3 and after the 3 of course the 4 didn't come but 77 or 9 or 1563 and he said that some day they would discover that the whole system of postal addresses was in Error, that the logical thing would be to give numbers to the street and a name to every house and he declared that the idea paralleled his new system for baptizing brothers in which they'd all have different last names but the same first name, and aside from Cué being completely pisstaken (I'm sorry, there's no other word for it, a pissword) it was the short and happy night of frank comradery until the we ours, and wee were all amused (said B.: I'm not amused, am used) when in the Dewville Silvestre picked up a card that a croupier had discarded, the two of diamonds, and he said he could say what was the up or the down of the card, not the obverse or reverse, but that he knew how to set it right, put it on its feet, fix it, by pure intuition, so he said, meaning that the two of diamonds, it's well known, always falls on its two feet and Bustro was delighted to find a graphic palindrome and defied Silvestre to destroy it once he knew its true position and Cué said Silvestre was cheating and Silvestre got bugged and Bustrófedon took his side saying it was impossible to cheat with a single card and he persuaded Silvestre to show us the game of polygamy (that was what he called it) and Silvestre asked us all, aside from B., if we knew exactly what was a hexagon and Rine said it was a six-sided polygon and Cué said it was a solid object with six surfaces and Silvestre said it was a hexahedron and then I began drawing one (Eribó wasn't there, of courset: otherwise he'd have done it) on a piece of paper

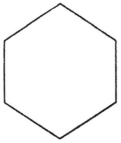

mismo para arriba y para abajo, uno de esos juegos que él inventaba y me di cuenta de que la muerte era una broma ajena, otra combinación: esa capicúa que salía de los mil hoyos (oyos) del teléfono, como una ducha de ácido muriático, corrosiva. Y fue en el teléfono, casualidades o causalidades de la vida, que Bustrofonema, Bustromorfosis, Bustromorfema empezó a cambiar el nombre de las cosas, de veras, de verdad verdad, enfermo ya, no como como al principio que lo trastrocaba todo y no sabíamos cuando era broma o era en serio, solamente que ahora no sabíamos si era en broma, sospechábamos que era en serio, que era serio, porque ya no era solamente el feca con chele, que heredó del lunfardo argentino en Nueva York (donde por cierto lo conoció Arsenio Cué, que fue quien lo vio, quien lo oyó primero), como del gotán, que es al reverso del tango, derivó el barúm que es lo contrario de una rumba y se baila al revés, con la cabeza en el piso y moviendo las rodillas en lugar de las caderas o decir sus Números (más después: ver adelante) que son Américo Prepucio y Harún al'Haschisch y Nefritis y Antigripina la madre de Negrón y Duns Escroto y el Conde Orgazmo y Gregory La Cavia y el epidíditsmo de Panamá y William Shakeprick o Shapescare o Chaseapear y Fuckner y Scotch Fizz-gerald y Somersault Mom y Cleoputra y Carlomaño y Alejandro el Glande y el genial músico bizco Igor Strabismo y Jean Paul Sastre y Teselio y Tomás de Quince y Georges BriquaBraque y Vincent Bongó (jodiendo a Silvio Sergio Ribot más conocido como Eribó gracias al B.) y querer escribir una roman a Klee, y cosas así, como llamar Eutanasia a Atanasia la cocinera de casa de Cassalis (para él la cassa de Casalis) o las competencias con Rine Leal al que le ganó una vez por una cabeza diciendo que los ucranianos tenían la cabeza en forma de U y su verdadero nombre era ucraneanos o llegar y decir que venía implacablemente vestido cuando quería decir que estaba elegante o competir con Silvestre por ver quién hacía más variantes del nombre de Cué, por ejemplo, o ponerme a mí el seudónimo de Códac (suyo fue mi otro bautizo y la idea salió, ya revelada, de Kodak y así encubrió mi nombre prosaico, habanero con la poesía universal y gráfica) y saber, como sabía, todo lo que hay que saber el Volapük y el Esperanto y el Ido y el Neo y el Basic English,

And then Silvestre said that really it was a cube that had lost its third dimension and he completed it like this

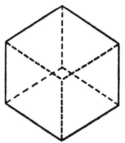

and he said that when the hexagon found its lost dimension again and we knew how it did it, we'd be able ourselves to find the fourth and fifth and other dimensions and travel freely between them (along the diMason Avenue, B. said, pointing to Eribó's former pukebiscity aliency) and enter a picture, across the frame and into the motion picture, then to move frame by frame at twenty-four paces a second, and one more step and stop on a point as on a full-stop, then travel from present to future or to past or to that side of paradise just by opening a door, and Rine took the chance to talk about his inventions, like the machine that would turn us into a light ray (into a shadow ray too, I said) and it would send us to Mars or Venus (that's where I'd like to go, said Vustrofedon) and far away and long will be another machine would turn us re, would make the light beam into lights and solid shadows and so we'd become tourists of time-space, and Cué said it was the same technique as the stage coaches and B. said they weren't the stage but the space coaches man-aged by H. G. Wells Fargo & Co., and Cué made the error (which B. spelt misstake) of telling how he'd once thought of a love tale in which a man on earth knew there was a woman on a planet in another galaxy (Bustrófedon was already saying she'd gone the way of all milk, translating from cow Latin) whom he was in love with and he went crazy with love for her and they both knew that it was the genuine love because they would never-never meet and they'd have to love each other in the silence of infinite space and of corpse Bustrófedon brought the skeletal evening to a closet bugging Cué by saying they were Tristar and Isolstice, and so we all blundered and stumbled off each to his humble home, homble for short (by

y su teoría de que al revés de lo que pasó en la Edad Media, que de un solo idioma, como el latín o el germano o el eslavo salieron siete idiomas diferentes cada vez, en el futuro estos veintiún idiomas (miraba a Cué cuando lo decía) se convertirían en uno solo, imitando o aglutinándose o guiados por el inglés, y el hombre hablaría, por lo menos en esta parte del mundo, una enorme lingua franca, una Babel estable y sensata y posible, y al mismo tiempo este hombre era una termita que atacaba los andamios de la torre antes de que se pensara en levantarla porque destruía todos los días el español diciendo, imitando a Vítor Perlo (al que llamaba Von Zeppelin por la forma de su cabeza), decir sotifiscado y esóctico y dezlenable o decir que él tenía asexo a las interioridades de un asunto o quejarse de que no comprendían en Cuba su *apestoso* humor y consolarse pensando que sería alabado en el extranjero o en el futuro, Porque nadie, decía, es mofeta en su tierra.

Cuando terminé de oír a Silvestre, sin hablar, antes de colgar, colgando el negro, ya de luto, espantoso teléfono, me dije a mí mismo, Carajo todo el mundo se muere, queriendo decir que los felices y los amargados y los ingeniosos y los retardados mentales y los cerrados y los abiertos y los alegres y los tristes y los feos y los bellos y los lampiños y los barbudos y los altos y los bajos y los siniestros y los claros y los fuertes y los débiles y los poderosos y los infelices, ah y los calvos: todo el mundo y también la gente que como Bustrófedon puede hacer de dos palabras y cuatro letras un himno y un chiste y una canción, esos, también se mueren y me dije, Coño. Nada más.

Fue después, hoy, ahora mismo que supe que en la autopsia antes del entierro, que me negué a ir porque Bustrófedon metido allí dentro; en el ataúd, no era Bustrófedon sino otra cosa, una cosa, un trasto inútil guardado en una caja fuerte por gusto, allá, cuando terminaron la trepanación del cráneo en forma de interrogación de Bustrófedon y sacaron de su estuche natural el cerebro y el patólogo lo tuvo en su mano y jugó con él y escarbó y trasteó todo lo que quiso y finalmente supo que tenía una lesión (él, el pobre, hubiera dicho una lección) desde niño, desde antes, de nacimiento, desde antes cuando se formó en que un hueso (¿qué cosa, Silvestre Ycué: un

way of the desert, for short-cut) when, by a strange chance (change-stance), we met up in Las Vegas with Arsenio Cué, who'd been evading our invasion (or invading our evasion) all evening because he was with a woman vulgo tore or wart (and if I talk like Bustrófedon from now on till the end of mine I'm not sorry except that I do it consciously & conscienctiously and the only thing I regret is that I can't talk normally and naturally and all the time (by all the time I mean time past as well as time future) like this and forget about the light and the shadows and the chiaroscuro (about photos for shot, because one word from him is worth a thousand images), a blond, tall, white, white-white, real, pretty, photogenic, a, model, who was a silk-screen repro of herself and Cué put on his leaden face and his radiant voice and B. told him the club was full of simple elements and that we'd probably turned his saturnalia into a saturnine joint, and it was then that Bustrope invented that criminal slogan of Arsenic and old lays, which we turned into a hymn to the night until the night ended and when I wanted to go on hymning and make it into a humn to the dawn of the Magi, Rine said you're an haurora bore all is, so I'd shot my bolt and I shut my mouth and shat my ass silently but on kulchur which always comes and balls things up (if you're having a ball) with its sadometaphysicks.

That was the last time (if I forget what I want to forget, which is why I put in this apparent thesis, to put a period to my memory: Saturday night and Sunday mourning) that I saw Bustropharaoh (as Silvestre sometimes said) and if you don't see him alive you don't see him, and it was really Silvestre who saw him last. Alive. The very evening before this Bustrofilmfan as he was called that week by us, not by everybody or for all time, just by us, had turned up and told me that B.'d been taken to the hospital and I thought they were going to operate on his eye because he had a bad but not evil eye that squinted, squandered and wandered in the jungle of the night: one of his eyes aimed, as Silvestre always said, at lettre and the other at le neon or at the nothing in being, at nothingnest, and this chameleon seeing was terrible, he said but not complained, a puzzle for his brain so he always had headaches, great sustained, stable and migratory migraines which the poor fellow B. called his paracerebellum or the Brutalcephalalgias or the Bustorrential Brainstorms, and I thought of going to the clinic on Monday at midday when I finished my

aneurisma, un embolismo, una pompa de la vena humorística?), un nudo en la columna vertebral, algo, que le presionaba el cerebro y le hacía decir esas maravillas y jugar con las palabras y finalmente vivir nombrando todas las cosas por otro nombre como si estuviera, de veras, inventando un idioma nuevo—y la muerte le dio la razón al médico que lo mató, que no lo asesinó, no, claro, por favor, que ni siquiera quiso matarlo sino que quiso salvarlo, a su manera, de una manera científica, de una manera médica, filantrópico él, humanitario, un Doctor Schweitzer que tenía su Lambarene en el hospital ortopédico con tanto niño deforme y tanta mujer tullida y tanto inválido a su entera disposición, que abrió el cráneo en forma de B para quitarle los dolores de cabeza, los vómitos de palabras, al vértigo oral, para eliminar de una vez y para siempre (tremenda palabra, eh: *siempre*, la eternidad, el carajo) las repeticiones y los cambios y la aliteración o la alteración de la realidad hablada, eso que el médico llamaba, para darle a Silvestre en la yema del gusto, en el mingo hipocondríaco, en la costura científica, casi imitando al propio Bustrófedon, pero claro con su patente de corso, el título para la trata de blancas y negras y mulatas, el D r y punto entre ornamentos y dibujitos y firmas que garantizan lo imposible, usando palabras mayores, técnicas, médicas confirmando eso de que todos los técnicos son mentirosos pero siendo creído siempre como siempre lo son los grandes mentirosos, diciendo en la jerga de Esculapio, con la piedra (¿filosofal o de toque?) de Galeno, diciendo "afasia," "disfasia," "ecolalia," cosas así, explicando, muy petulante según me contó Silvestre, que era *Es decir, estrictamente, pérdida del poder del habla: del discernimiento oral o si se quiere y ya más específicamente, un defecto no de fonación, sino derivado de un disfuncionamiento, tal vez una descomposición, una anomalía producida por una patología específica, que ulteriormente llega hasta disociar la función cerebral del simbolismo del pensar por el habla, o*—no nono no mierda ya está bien claro así como está y hay que dejarlo quieto, porque los médicos son los únicos pedantes elefantinos, los solos mamuts de la pedancia que quedan vivos una vez que se extinguieron en el MíoCideno Jaimes Joiyce y Eesra Pounk y Adolfo Solazar. Esos son los pretextos hipócritas, el diagnóstico

nightshift, which B., more economically or with less ceremony, called my shight sometimes and at other times my nift. But yesterday on Tuesday morning Silvestre calls me and tells me straight out that Bustrófedon had just died and I felt that the phone was telling something that meant the same whichever way round you put it, like one of those games he invented, and I saw that death was a far-out joke: an unknown combination: a palindrome that spilled out of the viscious holes of the eternally in mourning phone stopbathing my soul with a shower of muriatic acid: the ultimate spoilsport.

And it was at the phone, by a casual or causal chance of life, that Bustrophoneme, Bustromorphosis, Bustromorphema began really to change the names of things, really and truly, for he was already sick, not like in the beginning when he mixed everything up and we couldn't tell when it was a joke and when it was a yoke. But now though we didn't know if it was meant to be funny or phony we suspected it was serious, grave, gravely ill. Because it wasn't only the *feca con chele* for *café con leche* he'd taken from the Argentinian lunfard-language in New York (where he'd met Arsenio Cué off course: he was the first to see, the first to hear him, his disc-overer), as from gotan, which isn't Gotham but the reverse of tango, he derived the barum which is the opposite of the rumba to be danced in reversed gear, with the head on the floor and moving the knees instead of the hips. Or his recitation of his Numbers (more, later) which are: Amerigoes Prepucci and Hareun al-Hashish and Nevertitty, and Antigreppine the mother of Nehro and Dungs Scrotum and el con de Orgasm and Sheets and Kelly and Fuckner and Scotch Fizzgerald and Somersault Mom and Julius Seizure and Bertolt Bitch and Alexander the Hungrate and Charles le Magnate and Depussy and Mayor Wagner who wrote the Lord of the Rings and that cockieyed musical compositor Igor Strabismus and Prickasso and the philosopher avec le savoir-faire De Sartre (also called Le Divan Maquis) and Georges BricaBraque and Elder de Broiler and Gerónimo Ambusch and Versneer and Vincent Bongoh (to bug Silvio Sergio Ribot, better known as Eribó, thanks to B period) and wanting to write a roman a Klee, about a painter that lost its tale, and things-stings like forming an airway company to rivald Aer Lingus and with cunning call it Cunny Lingus, and likeness like calling

encubridor del crimen perfecto, el alibí hipocrático, la coartada médica, pero lo que en realidad quería era ver en qué rincón del cráneo de Bustrófedon, del Búcraneo como lo llamó tan bien Silvestre el Discípulo, en qué sitio, conocer el asiento particular de aquellas transformaciones maravillosas de la bobería y el lugar común y las palabras de todos los días en los dichos mágicos y nocturnos del Bustro, que ni siquiera se pueden conservar en un envase con formol nostálgico porque yo que soy quien más anda, andaba con él, soy un malo conservador de las palabras cuando no tienen directamente que ver con la foto que aparece arriba y aun entonces es un cojo pie de grabado que siempre me corrigen—como esto. Pero si los juegos se perdieron, los dicharachos como decía la madre de Cassalis y yo no sé repetirlos, no quiero olvidar (tanto que las conservo: no en la memoria memoranda de Silvestre ni en el rencor neurálgico de Arsenio Cué ni en el homenaje crítico de Rine ni en la exacta reproducción fotográfica que nunca pude hacer, sino en mi gaveta, únicas entre los negativos de una negra memorable, la foto, el affidavit desnudo de sus carnes blancas al trasluz, rubensianas como diría Juan Blanco y una o dos cartas que no tienen otra importancia que la que tuvieron entonces y el telegrama del estribo de Amapola del Campo, Dios mío qué seudónimo, el telegrama un día azul y ahora amarillo que todavía dice en un español aprendido por radio: el tiempo y la distancia me hacen comprender que te he perdido: escribir eso, señores del jurado, y dárselo al hombre del telégrafo en Bayamo ¿no demuestra que las mujeres o están todas locas o tienen más cojones que Maceo y su caballo heroico?) sus parodias, aquellas que grabamos en casa de Cué, que grabó Arsenio mejor dicho y luego yo copié y nunca quise devolver a Bustrófedon, menos después de la discusión con Arsenio Cué y la decisión violenta de los dos de borrar lo grabado—cada uno con razones diferentes y opuestas. Por eso guardaba eso que Silvestre quiso llamar memorabilia, que ahora devuelvo a su dueño, el folklore. (Linda frase ¿verdad? Lástima que no sea mía.)

Atanasia by the name Euthanasia (she was the cook at the Cassalis', so she only cooked Cassalores) or his cuntpetitions with Rine Leal, whom he once beat by a short head (Rine was lowering his I-brows at the time) saying that the Ukrainians had U-shaped heads and that their real name was Ucraniums, or just Craniums, if they happened to be non-U) or his put-ons like turning up saying he'd come implacably dressed when he meant dressed to kill or cuempeting with Silvestre to hear who could make the greatest number of variations on the name of Cué, on cue, or for X sample pseudonaming me Códac (it was a second baptism for me, a baptism of fireworks because the first initialtory write had washed off after the immersion, so the logo of Kodak, once revealed, blew up and superimposed on my prosaic habanero name the uninversal and graphic mark of my trade) saying, Come forth, Lazarus Ludwig the Second, knowing, as he knew, everything there is to be known about Ido and Volapuk and Dr. Esperanto and the Neo and Novial and after Idiom Neutral the beautiful front of Novesperanto with its Saussuges plus playing his Peano's and using & abusing the Basest English (for Forforeigners) and easing out the easiest and most perfect language, Malayalam, and expounding his theory that contrary to what happened in the Muddle Edges, when seven (7) languages all different came out of a single language like Latin or German or even Slav, in the tense future these twenty-one (he stared at Cué as he said it) languages would turn into one single long language based on or sticking to or on a guided turn with English, and man (and/or woman) would speak at least in this partition of the world and till eternity do us part an enormous lingua frangla, a sensible, possible, stable Babel. But at the same time and in the same breath this man B. was a termite attacking the scaffolding of the tower before they'd even thought of building it because every day he laid the Spanish language waste saying in imitation of Vitor Perla (whom he called Von Zeppelin because of the shape of his helium-filled head), saying sotisphicated and etoxic and decilious or boasting he had asex to the innard depths of a subject or complaining that they didn't understand his mal-or-odous humor in Cuba but taking a comforter in the thought that he'd be praised overseas or in that abroad of time which is the future. Because, he Mused, no man is a mofette in his own country.

When I'd finished listening to Silvestre, without saying anything, before hanging up, hanging up the suddenly black terrorphone, in morning that mourning, I said to myself, Fuck and shit, the whole world dies! Meaning the happy and the sad, geniuses and morons, the open and the inhibited and the cheerful and the gloomy and the ugly and the beautiful and damned and the bearded and the shaven and those with five-o'clock shadows and the tall and the short and the vicious and the innocent and the strong and the weak and the meek inheritors and the immortal and all the bald people too: everybody and even people like Bustrófedon who could make out of a couple of words and four letters a hymn and a joke and a song, these people, they also die and their memory dies too and even their songs die too, a little bit later perhaps but they die and ideas also die, so I said, Fuck! And nothing more—and right after that I said shit.

It was later, today, right now that I learned that in the autopsy before the funeral, which I refused to go to because Bustrófedon stuffed away in there, in that coffin, wasn't Bustrófedon but something else, just a thing, a useless bit of trash preserved down there in a strong box out of custom, when they'd finished trepanning Bustrófedon's skull in the form of a question mark for science and they pulled his brains out of their natural resting place and the psychopathologist had taken it in his hands and played with it and scratched its surface and patted its top as much as he felt like and had discovered finally that he had a lesion (he, poor guy, would have called it a lesson) since he was a kid, or earlier, from birth, or before he was even formed and that a bone (what do you think, Silvestre and Cué: an aneurysm, an embolism or a bubble in the humorous vein?), a knot in the spinal column, something like that, which pressed on his brain and made him say all those marvelous things and play with words so he ended his life as a new Adam, giving everything a name as though he really was inventing language (him talking to Dragon Lady, to Death: Madam I'm Adam) and Death proved him right, not *him* but that doctor who killed him, who didn't murder him, no, please don't get me wrong, he didn't even want to kill him, he wanted to *save* him, in his fashion, a scientific fashion, a medical fashion, because he was a philanthropist, a humanitarian, a Doctor Sch (you know who) whose Lambsarena was the orthopedic hospital where there were

so many deformed children and paralytic women and invalids in his care, who opened the skull shaped like B. to get rid of once and for always (terrifying word, that: *always*, eternity, the fucker) the repetitions and changes and alliteration or alterations in spoken reality, what the doctor called, to please Silvestre where it pleasured him most, bang in the middle of his hypocondria, tickling his scientific ribs, almost imitating Bustrófedon himself, but of courses with his medical qualifications, his diploma for genescide, the Dr and period among all the ornamental lettering and little drawings and signatures guaranteeing the impossible, using longer technical and medical words which all went to prove that all experts are liars but as people always believe in them they are always the greatest liars, saying Aesculapius' jargon, with Galen's stone (a philosopher's stone, or a touchstone or, more simply, a gallstone or a Keystone, or a tombstone, Arizona?), saying "aphasia," "disphasia," "ecolalia," things like that, explaining, very pretendentiously. So Silvestre said, that it was *Strictly speaking, a loss of the power of speech: of oral discrimination or if you prefer me to be more specific, a defect not of phonation, but derived from a dysfunction, possibly a decomposition, an anomaly produced by a specific pathology, which in its last stages dissociated the cerebral function from the symbolism of thinking by means of speech, or*—no no no for chrissakes! it's perfectly clear just as it is and you should leave him in peaces, can't you see doctors are the last elephantine pedants left, the only mammoths of palaeolitery pedantry still alive now that the megaesoteric J'aime Joys and Earza Pounk and Teas Eliot are gone—with the possumble exception of the foulaired George Ludwig Borgid? These are the hypocritical pretexts, the diagnosis to camouflage the perfect murder, the Hyppocratic alibi, the medical excuses, but what he actually wanted was to see in what corner of Bustrófedon's skull (his Bucranium as Silvestre the disciple called it zoo aptly), to find the particular habitation and place where ordinary clumsy language and commonplace logic and everyday words (our daily breath) were so marvelously changed into Bustro's magic nightwords, which you couldn't even preserve in that formol of memory called nostolgia because I, who am, was, the one who saw most of him, wasam very bad at keeping words when they don't have anything to do with the photo (above right) and even then it's a wreckedched caption I write with caution and I

【 ❧◉◟◉◞◉◞◉◠ 】

always have to have it corrected by somebody—like this one. But if the games, the dursty yokes as Cassalis' mother used to say, are all lost and so I can't repeat them, I don't want to forget (so far as I preserve them: not in the memoria memoranda of Silvestre—his formol logic—nor in Arsenio Cué's feedback in anger nor in Rine's criptical mass, nor in the exact photocopy I've never been able to make, but in my tallboy drawer, alone among the negatives of a memorable half-Indian half-Negro woman, mon violon d'Indegro, the picture, the naked affiche-davit of her white flesh against black light, her Rubensian flash as Juan Blanco would say and one or two letters that have and have not any importance other than what they had when written and the telegram from Poppy Fields, my god, what kind of a pseudo-pseudonym's that, the telegram that was once blue and is now yellow and which still says in a Spanish learnt on the radio: TIME AND DISTANCE MAKE ME UNDERSTAND I LOST YOU STOP: write this, gentlemen of the jury, and give it to the telegraph officer at Santiago—doesn't this show that women are either right out of their heads or that they have more *cojones* than Maceo e-ponymust and his heroic horse's balls as well?) his parodies, those we taped at Cué's place, which Arsenio taped rather and which I then copied and which I never wanted to return to Bustrófedon, still less after his discussion with Arsenio Cué and the radical decision they both made to wipe the tapes clean—each with a different and opposite motive. That's why I kept this thing that Silvestre wanted to call memorabilia, and which I now return to its rightful owner, folklore. (A nice sentence, ain't it? Too bad it's not mine.)

fertile Misremembrance: Translating Levertov's Neruda

AN ESSAY BY John Felstiner

"Celebration of Celery" by Pablo Neruda
TRANSLATED BY John Felstiner

A half-century after the war years in London, a poem by Pablo Neruda that Denise Levertov had come across during the war became the germ of a longish poem for her, entitled "Feet" (1997). Here is the first of six sections:

> In the forties, wartime London, I read
> an ode by Neruda I've never found again,
> about celery—celery the peasant, trudging
> stony Andean ridges to market on poor
> frayed feet.
>
>   I could search out the *Obras Completas*
> I know…But even if I never find it again,
> those green fibrous feet, upholding
> the tall stooped form with its flimsy cockscomb
> of yellowing leaves, plodded
> through me as if through the thin
> mountain air, maintaining
> their steady, painful, necessitous trudge, and left
> their prints in my dust.

This compassion-laden poem moves through Hans Christian Andersen's mermaid walking on knife blades, the poet's mother's poor circulation and narrow shoes struggling uphill in a Mexican town, a hungry homeless man with feet wrapped in green plastic, the aging Muriel Rukeyser embarrassed that a North Vietnamese nurse who otherwise ministered to mutilated victims was cutting Rukeyser's painful toenails, and prophetic consolation—"Blessèd are the feet of him who brings good tidings"—for the unwashed swollen feet of the poor, "the endless foot-after-foot journey of peasant celery."

Since she knew that my wife Mary suffered from rheumatoid arthritis, Denise in May 1997 gave her a handsome chapbook of "Feet," published in 170 copies by Tangram Press in Berkeley. Naturally, having myself been immersed in Neruda for years, especially in his 1943 Andean journey that yielded *Alturas de Machu Picchu* (and my book *Translating Neruda: The Way to Machu Picchu*)—naturally and instantly I went to the *Obras completas* to find Denise's source. I didn't think it was an ode, but anyway checked his several gatherings, alphabetical *odas elementales* from *alcachofa*/artichoke through *zanahoria*/carrot. What she'd been holding in mind all those decades, though, was not an ode but one of Neruda's *Tres cantos materiales* (1935), three "material songs" or "songs of matter" heartfully, hopefully composed in Madrid during Spain's short-lived republic: "Apogeo del apio" (Apogee of Celery), "Estatuto del vino" (Ordinance of Wine), and "Entrada a la madera" (Entrance into Wood).

While there are no "stony Andean ridges" in Neruda's poem, it does have "celery feet enter the market / one bruised morning" and "doors slam shut as they pass by," these "cut feet." As with "Entrance into Wood," Neruda wants to draw the celery's firm veins and wounded voice, its "Fibrous darkness and weeping light," deep down into his own "heart's mouth" and song. Maybe his lines also lie beneath "The Jacob's Ladder," where Denise's poet-pilgrim climbs up toward a Mexican church and "the cut stone / consoles his groping feet."

In May 1997, having lived across a green field from Denise during her winters at Stanford and absorbed so much from this "poet in the world," there was no way I would not translate Neruda's poem for her, in thankful return for her presence. And so I began.

It was clear that his title phrase, *Apogeo del apio*, asked for some equivalent playfulness in English, such as "Celebration of Celery." Also, for the fun of it, I took advantage of a toolbar's "Center" button to twirl my version around an upright central stalk. And astonishingly, it seemed possible to let some words migrate from Denise's poem "Feet"—no matter that she misremembered Neruda—to infuse my own lexicon. In translating Neruda, I adopted her "stooped" for *cae* (instead of "falls"), "trudge" for *van* ("go"), "frayed" for *herido* ("wounded"), "flimsy" for *quebradizo* ("fragile"), "fibrous" for *fibras* ("fibers").

Apogeo del apio

Del centro puro que los ruidos nunca
atravesaron, de la intacta cera,
salen claros relámpagos lineales,
palomas con destino de volutas,
hacia tardías calles con olor
a sombra y a pescado.
Son las venas del apio! Son la espuma, la risa,
los sombreros del apio!

Son los signos del apio, su sabor
de luciérnaga, sus mapas
de color inundado,
y cae su cabeza ángel verde,
y sus delgados rizos se acongojan,
y entran los pies del apio en los mercados
de la mañana herida, entre sollozos,
y se cierran las puertas a su paso,
y los dulces caballos se arrodillan.

Sus pies cortados van, sus ojos verdes
van derramados, para siempre hundidos
en ellos los secretos y las gotas:
los túneles del mar de donde emergen,
las escaleras que el apio aconseja,
las desdichadas sombras sumergidas,
las determinaciones en el centro del aire,
los besos en el fondo de las piedras.

A medianoche, con manos mojadas,
alguien golpea mi puerta en la niebla,

Celebration of Celery

From the pure core unsplit
by noise, from the firm wax
come clear lines of lightning,
doves marked for spiraling,
toward late-blooming streets that smell
of fish and shadow.
It's the celery veins! It's foam, laughter,
the celery's sombreros!

Celery signs, the taste
of glowworm, maps
steeped in color,
a stooped green angelhead,
slender curls grieve,
celery feet enter the market
one bruised morning and there's sobbing,
doors slam shut as they pass by,
and gentle horses kneel.

Their cut feet trudge on, their spilt green eyes
where secrets and raindrops
plunge for all time:
sea tunnels they emerge from,
stairways the celery counsels,
submerged disconsolate shadows,
decisions at the heart of the air,
kisses at the base of the rock.

Midnight, someone's soaking
hands bang on my door in the mist

y oigo la voz del apio, voz profunda,
áspera voz de viento encarcelado,
se queja herido de aguas y raíces,
hunde en mi cama sus amargos rayos,
y sus desordenadas tijeras me pegan en el pecho
buscándome la boca del corazón ahogado.

Qué quieres, huésped de corsé quebradizo,
en mis habitaciones funerales?
Qué ámbito destrozado te rodea?

Fibras de oscuridad y luz llorando,
ribetes ciegos, energías crespas,
río de vida y hebras esenciales,
verdes ramas de sol acariciado,
aquí estoy, en la noche, escuchando secretos,
desvelos, soledades,
y entráis, en medio de la niebla hundida,
hasta crecer en mí, hasta comunicarme
la luz oscura y la rosa de la tierra.

and I hear the celery's deep harsh
voice of an imprisoned wind,
frayed by roots and water it complains
and sinks its bitter rays into my bed,
its haywire scissors stick my chest
and seek my drowned heart's mouth.

Guest in your flimsy girdle, what do you want
in my funeral dwelling?
What ruined circle holds you round?

Fibrous darkness and weeping light,
blind ribbons, crisped energy,
river of life and filament essence,
green branches of precious sun,
here I am, hearing secrets by night,
vigils, solitudes,
and you enter amid sunken mist
till you grow within me, telling me
dark light and the rose of earth.

I sent this to Denise, and on June 30, 1997, she replied from Seattle: "Thanks *very* much for the translation (& detective work!). I had looked for an *Ode* which is no doubt why I didn't find it. I'm glad I didn't do so before writing *Feet*, because I'd never have been able to do so once I'd seen the actual poem, which is *so different* from my memory of it. The memory, not the poem itself, was the starter for me. I similarly misremembered a certain Corot painting which got into another poem of mine. Perhaps one's misremembrances are always more fertile than accurate recollections.... Anyway—I'm delighted to have the original and your custom-made version."

If only in having elicited such sentences, my translation earns its raison d'être. Fertile misremembrance: perhaps this can speak, in a way, for translation too. I cherish the chance to have revived a phantom beneath Denise Levertov's poem. She says Neruda's celery feet "left / their prints in my dust," so it seems only fitting to retrace those prints in "Celebration of Celery."

Denise Levertov
5535 Seward Park Avenue South
Seattle. WA 98118

June 30th 97

Dear John
         Thanks very much for the
translation (+ detective work (!)) I had
looked for an Ode which is no doubt
why I didn't find it. I'm glad I
didn't do so before writing Feet, because
             I'd never have been able to
do so once I'd seen the actual poem, which
is so different from my memory of
it. The memory, not the poem itself,
was the starter for me. I similarly
misremembered a certain Corot painting
which got into another poem of mine.
Perhaps ones misremembrances are
always more fertile that accurate
recollections... Any way — I'm delighted to
         have the original and your custom-
                    made version, +

Acknowledgments

Thanks first to the translators—both the exceptional group included here and all the others who have enriched our world: just imagine what it would be like without them. And special thanks to one of the most notable among them, Gregory Rabassa, for his kindness in offering a foreword to this anthology.

Olivia Sears, president of the Center for the Art of Translation, first asked me to participate in this project, at that time envisioned as simply a selection from the pages of *TWO LINES*. Olivia has performed heroic work on behalf of translation for many years, and I found it impossible to turn her down. Initially, the project was to be co-edited with Barbara Paschke, but Barbara was forced to drop out to address other compelling concerns. In the time we worked together, she shared some of her deep understanding of translation, and I was sorry indeed to see her go.

Zack Rogow, with whom I had worked on his translation of George Sand's novel *Horace* (published by Mercury House, where I was the director) joined *TWO LINES* as its artistic director after this project was already in progress. Zack felt that juxtaposing materials from other sources with those drawn from *TWO LINES* would make a stronger anthology, and the present shape of the book reflects that vision.

Sonia Valdez and Annie Janusch of the Center for the Art of Translation worked tirelessly to locate translators and materials, arrange permissions, proofread copy, and keep track of the schedule and the many details involved in book production. Perceptive, creative, and efficient, they played a key role in shepherding this book into print. Maria Gould and Anita Sagástegui, also of the Center, were careful and thorough in providing additional support.

Thanks also to Adriana Pérez, whose design ensures that the book's presentation is both functional and attractive, and to Peter Dreyer, for his thoughtful copy edit.

T.C.

contributors

Translators

ELIZABETH BELL is a San Francisco writer and translator. Her translations from Spanish have appeared in various periodicals and in *Light from a Nearby Window: Contemporary Mexican Poetry* (City Lights). She has also translated numerous French *bandes dessinées*, including Max Cabane's award-winning *Colin-Maillard* (*Heartthrobs*). In 1997, she and co-translator Moazzam Sheikh received India's Katha Prize for their translation of "Sheesha Ghat," written in Urdu by Naiyer Masud.

BRUCE BERGER has written various books on the intersection of nature and culture in desert settings, including *The Telling Distance* (University of Arizona Press), winner of the 1990 Western States Book Award. Two of his books focus on Baja California: *Almost an Island* (University of Arizona Press) and *Sierra, Sea and Desert: The Vizcaino* (Sierra Madre), available in English and Spanish editions in Mexico.

PAUL BLACKBURN (1926–1971) produced sixteen collections of poetry in his lifetime and is widely credited for helping shape the course of American poetry after World War II. His first book of translations, *Proensa*, and his first book of poems, *The Dissolving Fabric*, were published by Robert Creeley's Divers Press. In an interview with the *New York Quarterly*, Blackburn is quoted as saying that a translator must "be willing to let another man's life enter his own deeply enough to become some permanent part of his original author." In the course of his career he translated many writers, including Julio Cortázar and Federico García Lorca.

PETER BUSH has translated the works of Pedro Almodóvar, Nuria Amat, Juan Carlos Onetti, Leonardo Padura and Senel Paz, among others. His translation of Luis Sepúlveda's *The Old Man Who Read Love Stories* (Harvest Books) won the National Translation Award from the American Literary Translators Association in 1995. For his translation of Juan Goytisolo's *The Marx Family Saga* (City Lights), he was awarded the Ramón Valle-Incan Prize in 1998. He has held positions as a professor of literary translation at the Universities of Middlesex and East Anglia, where he was Director of the British Centre for Literary Translation.

THOMAS CHRISTENSEN's translations include works by Alejo Carpentier, Louis-Ferdinand Céline, Julio Cortázar, Carlos Fuentes, and Laura Esquivel; he often translates in collaboration with his wife, Carol Christensen. His translation of Louis-Ferdinand Céline's *Ballets without Music, without Dancers, without Anything* (Green Integer) was a finalist for a PEN translation award, and he received a special award for dedication to translation from the American Literary Translators Association. This is his seventeenth book as author, credited editor, or translator. Formerly the director of Mercury House, an independent trade book publishing company, he is now director of publications at the Asian Art Museum in San Francisco. He can be reached through his website, www.rightreading.com.

JOHN FELSTINER is a professor of literature at Stanford University. His book *Translating Neruda: The Way to Machu Picchu* (Stanford University Press) won the Commonwealth Club Gold Medal for Non-Fiction. *Paul Celan: Poet, Survivor, Jew* (Yale University Press) was named a finalist for the National Book Critics Circle award and the MLA's James Russell Lowell prize, and won the 1997 Truman Capote Award for Literary Criticism. Felstiner's *Selected Poems and Prose of Paul Celan* (W.W. Norton & Co.) won the Modern Language Association, American Translators Association, and PEN West translation prizes, and was finalist for the American PEN and the Helen and Kurt Wolff prizes. In 2005 he was made a member of the American Academy of Arts and Sciences.

FORREST GANDER's most recent books are *Eye Against Eye* (New Directions) and *A Faithful Existence* (Shoemaker & Hoard). His translations include *No Shelter: Selected Poems of Pura López-Colomé* (Graywolf) and, with Kent Johnson, *The Night: A Poem by Jaime Saenz* (Princeton University Press). Gander is a professor at Brown University.

London-born **DONALD GARDNER** has lived in Holland since 1979 and earns his living as a translator, most notably of Octavio Paz and Ernesto Cardenal's work. Gardner's own books of poetry include *Peace Feelers* (Cafe Books), *For the Flames* (Fulcrum Press), and *How to get the most out of your Jet Lag* (Ye Olde Font Shoppe Press), as well as three chapbooks under his own imprint, Forget-me-not Press.

EDITH GROSSMAN is an award-winning translator of many Spanish-language writers, including Mario Vargas Llosa, Mayra Montero, Alvaro Mutis, and Julián Ríos. She has also translated all of Gabriel García Márquez's works since *Love in the Time of Cholera* and, most recently, produced a much-praised translation of Miguel de Cervantes' *Don Quixote* (Ecco).

SEAN HIGGINS is a public high school teacher in Santa Clara, California. He received his BA in Latin American Studies from UC Santa Cruz and an MFA in Writing from the University of San Francisco. His previous translations of Peri Rossi's work have appeared in *City Lights Review* and *Translation Review*. Higgins co-translated the novel *Rattlesnake* by Arturo Arias (Curbstone Press) and has also translated a book of children's stories, *When I Was a Boy, Neruda Called Me Policarpo* (Groundwood Books), by Chilean author Poli Delano.

MICHAEL KOCH, a painter, poet, and translator, works as a mental health counselor. His translations have appeared in *Light from a Nearby Window: Contemporary Mexican Poetry* (City Lights), *Soup, Durak, Compages, TWO LINES,* and other publications. His visual art can be viewed on his website, www.miguelin.org.

HELEN LANE (1921–2004) translated from French, Spanish, Portuguese, and Italian literature—ranging from the popular to the political. She translated works by Mario Vargas Llosa, Juan Goytisolo, Augusto Roa Bastos, Elena Poniatowska and Octavio Paz. She received PEN translation prizes for her renderings of Mario Vargas Llosa's *The War of the End of the World* (Farrar, Straus & Giroux) and Juan Goytisolo's *Count Julian* (Viking Press).

SUZANNE JILL LEVINE's published translations include the works of Guillermo Cabrera Infante, Manuel Puig, Severo Sarduy, and Adolfo Bioy Casares. A professor at the University of California in Santa Barbara, Levine is the author of the literary biography *Manuel Puig and the Spider Woman: His Life and Fictions* (Farrar, Straus & Giroux). Her honors include a Guggenheim Fellowship and the PEN Award for Career Achievement in Hispanic Studies.

C.M. MAYO is the author of *Miraculous Air: Journey of a Thousand Miles through Baja California, the Other Mexico* (University of Utah Press), and *Sky Over El Nido* (University of Georgia Press), which won the Flannery O'Connor Award for Short Fiction. An avid translator of Mexican literature, Mayo is the founding editor of *Tameme*, a bilingual literary journal now operating as a chapbook publisher. She is also the editor of *Mexico: A Traveler's Literary Companion* (Whereabouts Press). She divides her time between Mexico City and Washington, DC. Her website is www.cmmayo.com.

SUSAN OURIOU is a literary translator and interpreter of Spanish and French as well as a fiction writer. Her translation of José Luis Olaizola's novel *The Thirteenth Summer* (Red Deer Press) was runner-up for Canada's John Glassco Translation Prize. Her translations from French of Michèle Marineau's *The Road to Chlifa* (Red Deer Press) and of Guillaume Vigneault's *Necessary Betrayals* (Douglas &

McIntyre) were short-listed for the Governor General's Award for Translation. She is also the author of the novel *Damselfish* (XYZ Publishing).

BARBARA PASCHKE is a freelance translator who lives in San Francisco. She has published translations of Daisy Zamora's poetry, *Riverbed of Memory* (City Lights), and Alberto Blanco's children's book *The Desert Mermaid* (Children's Book Press). Paschke co-edited Roque Dalton's *Clandestine Poems* (Curbstone Press); *Volcán* (City Lights), a book of Central American poetry; and *Clamor of Innocence* (City Lights), a book of Central American short stories.

ELISABETH PLAISTER is a British translator of contemporary Spanish-language literature. She has translated Fernando del Paso's *Palinuro of Mexico* and several works by Catelonian author Manuel Vázquez Montalbán, including his novel *The Pianist* (Quartet Books), which was adapted to film in 1998. Of her translation of *Palinuro of Mexico* del Paso remarked, "in English many things sounded far better, more original than the Spanish original."

GREGORY RABASSA is among the foremost translators of Latin American literature, having brought into English the works of Jorge Amado, Mario Vargas Llosa, Julio Cortázar, Octavio Paz, and Gabriel García Márquez, among others. He has translated more than thirty works of contemporary Latin American literature, from both Spanish and Portuguese. Rabassa is the recipient of numerous prizes and awards, including a National Book Award in Translation for Julio Cortázar's *Rayuela* (*Hopscotch*) and a PEN American Center Gregory Kolovakos Award for career achievement. He is a Distinguished Professor of Languages and Literatures at Queens College and the Graduate School and University Center, CUNY.

MARK SCHAFER is a literary translator and visual artist from Cambridge, Massachusetts. His translations from Spanish include works by authors such as Alberto Ruy Sánchez, Virgilo Piñera, Jesús Gardea, Eduardo Galeano, and Antonio José Ponte. In 2004, Junction Books published *Migrations/Migraciones,* a bilingual edition of his translations of Mexican author Gloria Gervitz's epic poem. In 2005, Schafer received an NEA Literature Fellowship in Translation for his work with Mexican poet David Huerta.

JOHN OLIVER SIMON is Artistic Director of Poetry Inside Out, a project of the Center for the Art of Translation. He has traveled extensively in Latin America, translating the poets he has met, and was awarded a 2001 NEA Literature Fellowship in Translation for his work with the Chilean poet Gonzalo Rojas. Simon's most recent book of poems is *Caminante* (Creative Arts).

JASON WEISS is the author of *Writing at Risk: Interviews in Paris with Uncommon Writers* (University of Iowa Press), *The Lights of Home: A Century of Latin American Writers in Paris* (Routledge), and the novel *Faces by the Wayside* (Six Gallery Press). He edited the anthology *Back in No Time: The Brion Gysin Reader* (Wesleyan University Press), as well as *Steve Lacy: Conversations* (Duke University Press). He has also translated Marcel Cohen's stories, *Mirrors* (Green Integer), and the selected poems of Argentine writer Silvina Ocampo, forthcoming.

DONALD A. YATES is professor emeritus of Spanish American literature at Michigan State University. He is the translator of novels and short stories by many Spanish American authors, including *Labyrinths: Selected Writings of Jorge Luis Borges* (New Directions), edited and translated with James Irby of Princeton University, and the celebrated novel of Adolfo Bioy Casares, *Diary of the War of the Pig* (McGraw-Hill). The 1962 Borges translation was the first collection of the late Argentine author's work to appear in English. Yates received an NEA Literature Fellowship in Translation to bring into English the novels and short stories of Argentine writer Edgar Brau.

Authors

SIGFREDO ARIEL was born in 1962 in Santa Clara, Cuba. He lives in La Habana Vieja, where he is a writer and director for radio and television. Ariel also records and produces traditional and popular Cuban music.

RENÉ ARIZA (1940–1994) was one of the most celebrated figures in Cuban theater during the first decade after the Revolution, winning national awards as a playwright and acclaim as an actor both on television and the stage. In 1971 he was expelled from theater by the government and was later sentenced to eight years in prison for "ideological deviation," a charge linked to his homosexuality. Upon his release from prison, Ariza went into exile in the U.S.

MANLIO ARGUETA was born in San Miguel, El Salvador in 1935. A poet, novelist, and political activist, he is best known for his book *One Day of Life* (Vintage), which was banned in El Salvador due to its critical portrayal of the government. After living in exile for more than twenty years in Costa Rica, Argueta returned to El Salvador in the 1990s, where he is currently the Director of the National Public Library.

EDGAR BRAU was born in Resistencia, Argentina in 1953. He worked in theater and the fine arts before publishing his first collection of short stories in 1992. Also a poet, novelist, and playwright, Brau was writer-in-residence at the University of Nevada in 2002. His most recent book is *Casablanca and Other Stories* (Michigan State University Press).

GUILLERMO CABRERA INFANTE (1929–2005) was a Cuban novelist, essayist, translator, and critic. A one-time supporter of the Castro regime, Cabrera Infante went into exile in London in 1965. He is best known for the novel *Tres tristes tigres*, a portion of which appears in this book. In 1997 he received the Premio Cervantes, the Spanish-speaking world's highest literary prize.

JULIO CORTÁZAR (1914–1984) was born to Argentine parents in Brussels. His family returned to Buenos Aires after World War II, where Cortázar worked as a literary translator, bringing the works of authors such as Daniel Defoe and Edgar Allan Poe into Spanish. Although he moved to France in 1951, he remained active in Latin American politics, donating his 1973 Prix Médicis prize money, won for his book *Libro de Manuel*, to the United Chilean Front. His 1963 novel *Rayuela* (*Hopscotch*) earned Cortázar an international following.

ESTELA DAVIS was born in 1935 in Loreto on the Gulf of California. Davis worked most of her life as a journalist and columnist. It wasn't until she was sixty, a seasoned writer but new to fiction, that she began to record the tales she remembered from childhood in the short story collection *La perla del mojón*.

FERNANDO DEL PASO was born in Mexico City, Mexico in 1935. A novelist, essayist and poet, he lived in London for fourteen years, where he worked for the BBC, and in France, where he worked for Radio France Internationale and served briefly as consul general of Mexico. He has won several international awards, including the Rómulo Gallegos Prize, the Xavier Villarutia Award, and the Premio Novela México.

LUISA FUTORANSKY was born in Buenos Aires, Argentina in 1939 and has lived in Paris since 1981 after spending more than a decade in Rome, Israel, Tokyo, and Beijing. She has written three novels, three book-length essays, and a dozen books of poetry, including *The Duration of the Voyage: Selected Poems* (Junction Press). She is the recipient of a Guggenheim Foundation fellowship and was made a Chevalier de l'Ordre des Arts et Lettres by the French government.

GABRIEL GARCÍA MÁRQUEZ was born in Aracataca, Colombia in 1928. He was the recipient of the Nobel Prize in Literature in 1982. His works include *Autumn*

of the Patriarch, *Love in the Time of Cholera*, and *Strange Pilgrims*. His novel *One Hundred Years of Solitude* has sold more than ten million copies worldwide. In 1999 Márquez was diagnosed with lymphatic cancer and shortly thereafter began writing the first volume of his memoirs, *Living to Tell the Tale*. His most recent novella, *Memories of My Melancholy Whores*, was published in 2004 by Vintage.

FRANCISCO HERNÁNDEZ was born in Veracruz, Mexico in 1946. He has written several books of poems, including *Moneda de tres caras* and *Mar de fondo,* for which he was awarded the Aguascalientes National Poetry Prize in 1982.

DAVID HUERTA, born in Mexico City, Mexico in 1949, is an acclaimed poet, journalist, critic, and translator. He was awarded the Diana Moreno Toscano Prize in 1972, a Guggenheim Fellowship in 1978, and the Premio Xavier Villaurrutia, Mexico's most prestigious literary prize, in 2006.

BÁRBARA JACOBS was born in Mexico City, Mexico in 1947. She has written novels, short stories, and essays and is a regular contributor to a Mexican daily newspaper. Her novel *The Dead Leaves* (Curbstone Press) was awarded the Premio Xavier Villaurrutia in 1987.

MIRKO LAUER was born in 1947 in what was then Czechoslovakia and moved to Peru as a child. He has been active for many years in the Peruvian human rights movement and is a director of the literary magazine *Hueso húmero*, which can be found on the web at www.huesohumero.com.pe. Lauer also writes detective novels and is a political commentator for the Peruvian newspaper *La Republica*. His short novel *Orbitas. Tertulias* won the Juan Rulfo prize in 2005.

MÓNICA LAVÍN was born in Mexico City, Mexico in 1955. She is the author of several award-winning short story collections, including *Uno no sabe*, which was a finalist for the Antonin Artaud literary prize, and *Ruby Tuesday no ha muerto*, for which she was awarded the Gilberto Owen Literary National Prize in 1996. Her novel *Café cortado* won the Colima Narrative Prize for best published work in 2001 and is soon to be published by the University of Wisconsin Press in the collection *The Americas*.

DENISE LEVERTOV (1923-1997) was born in England and came to the United States in 1947. A longtime teacher in Stanford's creative writing program, Levertov published many prized collections of poetry, including *With Eyes at the Back of Our Heads*, *Jacob's Ladder*, and *Relearning the Alphabet*.

PURA LÓPEZ-COLOMÉ was born in Mexico City, Mexico in 1952 and studied literature at the Universidad Nacional Autónoma de México. She has published literary criticism, poems, and translations in a regular column for the newspaper *Unomásuno* and is the author of several books, including *No Shelter* (Graywolf) and the forthcoming *Aurora* (Shearsman Books). She is also one of the leading translators of English literature into Spanish and has translated such authors as Samuel Beckett, Seamus Heaney, and Virginia Woolf.

PABLO NERUDA was born in Parral, Chile in 1904, and died during the 1973 military seizure of his country. Lauded as "the greatest poet of the twentieth century in any language" by Colombian author Gabriel García Márquez, Neruda was awarded the Nobel Prize in Literature in 1971. Among his extensive published works are *Twenty Love Poems and a Song of Despair* and *Canto general*.

SENEL PAZ was born in Las Villas, Cuba in 1950. His novella *The Wolf, the Forest, and the New Man* won Radio France Internationale's Juan Rulfo Prize in 1990 and has appeared as a stage production several times. In 1993 the story was adapted to film as the Academy Award-nominated movie *Strawberry and Chocolate*, directed by the late Tomas Gutiérrez Alea. Paz currently resides in Havana.

CRISTINA PERI ROSSI was born in Montevideo, Uruguay in 1941 and began her literary career in 1963 with the collection of short stories *Viviendo*. She emigrated to Spain in 1972, where she continues to live, teach, and publish. An essayist, novelist, journalist, and poet, Peri Rossi has published such works as *Ship of Fools* (Allison & Busby), *The Museum of Useless Efforts* (Bison Books), and *Panic Signs* (Wilfred Laurier).

LUISA VALENZUELA was born in Buenos Aires, Argentina in 1938. A novelist, journalist, and essayist, she is one of the most widely translated female writers in Latin America. She has been described by Carlos Fuentes as "the heiress of Latin American fiction," and her novels, which include *The Lizard's Tail* (Farrar, Straus & Giroux) and *Black Novel with Argentines* (Simon & Schuster), have achieved wide recognition in the United States, where she spent much of the eighties teaching at Columbia and New York Universities.

JORGE VOLPI was born in Mexico City, Mexico in 1968. He is an author, scholar, and diplomat, who has written nine books of fiction. Volpi's novel *En busca de Klingsor (In Search of Klingsor)* won the Biblioteca Breve Prize in 1999. His other books include *A pesar del oscuro silencio* and *El fin de la locura (The End of Madness)*. He is the director of the Mexican Cultural Center in Paris.

permissions

Thank you to the authors, translators, and publishers who generously granted permission to use the following materials:

Manlio Argueta: "Ganar la calle" by Manlio Argueta. Copyright ©1988 by Manlio Argueta. Reprinted by permission of the author.

Manlio Argueta: "Taking Over the Street" by Manlio Argueta, translated by Barbara Paschke. Copyright ©1988 by Barbara Paschke. Reprinted by permission of the translator.

Sigfredo Ariel: "La luz, bróder, la luz" by Sigfredo Ariel. Copyright © 1998 by Sigfredo Ariel. Reprinted by permission of the author.

Sigfredo Ariel: "The Light, Hermano, the Light" by Sigfredo Ariel, translated by John Oliver Simon. Copyright © 1998 by John Oliver Simon. Reprinted by permission of the translator.

René Ariza: "El fantasma del puerco" by René Ariza. Copyright © 1994 by René Ariza. Reprinted by permission of Aida Ariza and Gloria Ariza.

René Ariza: "The Ghost of the Pig" by René Ariza, translated by Michael Koch. Copyright © 2000 by Michael Koch. Reprinted by permission of the translator.

Edgar Brau: "El viaje" by Edgar Brau. Copyright © 1998 by Metzengerstein Ediciones. Reprinted by permission of the author.

Edgar Brau: "The Journey" by Edgar Brau, translated by Donald Yates. Copyright © 2003 by Donald Yates. Reprinted by permission of Michigan State University Press. Published in

Casablanca and Other Stories, Michigan State University Press, 2006.

Guillermo Cabrera Infante: Excerpt from the work *Tres tristes tigres* by Guillermo Cabrera Infante. Copyright © 1967 by Guillermo Cabrera Infante. Reprinted by permission of Miriam Cabrera Infante.

Guillermo Cabrera Infante: Excerpt from the work *Three Trapped Tigers* by Guillermo Cabrera Infante, translated by Donald Gardner and Suzanne Jill Levine. Copyright © 1967 Guillermo Cabrera Infante.

Julio Cortázar: "Continuidad de los parques" from the work *Final del juego* by Julio Cortázar. Copyright © 1956 by Herederos de Julio Cortázar.

Julio Cortázar: "Continuity of Parks" from the work *End of the Game and Other Stories* by Julio Cortázar, translated by Paul Blackburn. Copyright © 1963, 1967 by Random House, Inc. Used by permission of Pantheon Books, a division of Random House, Inc.

Julio Cortázar: Excerpt from the work *Rayuela* by Julio Cortázar. Copyright © 1956 by Herederos de Julio Cortázar.

Julio Cortázar: Excerpt from the work *Hopscotch* by Julio Cortázar, translated by Gregory Rabassa. Copyright © 1996 by Random House, Inc. Used by permission of Pantheon Books, a division of Random House, Inc.

Julio Cortázar: "Vestir una sombra" from the work *Último round* by Julio Cortázar. Copyright © 1969 by Herederos de Julio Cortázar.

projects of the center for the art of Translation

For fifteen years, *TWO LINES* has published translations of poetry and fiction from more than fifty languages and fifty countries—from Arabic to Zulu, and from Austria to Vietnam. Every edition features the best in international writing, showcasing diverse new writing alongside the world's most celebrated literature and presenting exclusive insight from translators into the creative art of translation. Through the annual volume of *TWO LINES: World Writing in Translation*, the World Library, and a series of engaging public readings, *TWO LINES* opens the borders of world literature to give readers access to the most vibrant writing from around the world.

Since 2000, Poetry Inside Out, the first imaginative writing and translation program offered in public schools, has been teaching bilingual students the life-changing power of great literature. Working with their teachers and Poetry Inside Out's professional poet-translators, students study poems in their original language; translate those works into English; write their own poems and translate the poems of their peers; and read their work in class, in the community, and at literary festivals. The remarkable *Best of Poetry Inside Out* anthology series features the finest student writing from the year.

Read more of the world in *TWO LINES* and the Poetry Inside Out anthologies. Order copies of *TWO LINES: World Writing in Translation* or the *Best of Poetry Inside Out* online at www.catranslation.org.